CELIA'S HOUSE

CELIA'S HOUSE

D. E. STEVENSON

First published in Great Britain 1943 by Ferrar & Rinehart

Published in Large Print 2001 by ISIS Publishing Ltd.
7 Centremead, Osney Mead, Oxford OX2 0ES
by arrangement with the author's estate, c/o Penny Kent

British Library Cataloguing in Publication Data
Stevenson, D. E. (Dorothy Emily), 1892–1973
Celia's house. – Large print ed.
1. Love stories
2. Large type books
I. Title
823.9′12 [F]

ISBN 0–7531–6565–1 (hb)
ISBN 0–7531–6566–X (pb)

Printed and bound by Antony Rowe, Chippenham and Reading

Author's Note

The characters in this book are imaginary and have no relation whatsoever to any persons who may happen by accident to bear the same name. The places mentioned do not exist in fact, but are intended to present a composite picture of the Scottish Border Country and to reproduce the atmosphere with artistic rather than literal truth.

D. E. STEVENSON

PART 1

Old People in the House

CHAPTER
ONE

June, 1905

Some people call the Rydd Water a good sized stream, others call it a small river; it starts away up in the hills of the Scottish Border as a score of tumultuous burns which come leaping down the steep slopes between rocks and heather, and creeping through pockets of bog; leaping, creeping, tumbling hastily down the hills to meet in the valley below. The valley of the Rydd is wide and open, a shallow bowl, tilted a little towards the south; there are farms in the valley and quiet villages, and big houses with fine gardens; there are stretches of meadow land and woods with tall trees — chestnut, oak and beech. When it reaches the valley the Rydd seems to lose its youthful impatience and begins to dawdle peacefully, wandering first this way and then that, as if it were loath to leave so pleasant a place . . . and one of its silver loops brings it within earshot of Dunnian House, brings it sweeping through the belt of woodland beyond the lawn. Sometimes the voice of the Rydd is loud, and fills the whole house with a rushing sound, sometimes it is so soft that one has to listen to hear it . . . but it is always there, roaring, rippling or whispering through the lovely old rooms: it is as much a part of the place as the solid grey stones of which Dunnian is built.

Generations of Dunnes, born and bred at Dunnian and afterwards scattered to the four corners of the earth, are sometimes awakened at night by the rustle of trees or the roar of tropical rain and are transported home to Dunnian and childhood.

It was a lovely afternoon and Dunnian House slept peacefully in the sunshine; two or three of the tall chimneys were smoking idly, the smoke rising straight and hanging in little clouds in the still air. The main rooms in the house faced south-west with french windows opening on to a sheltered terrace with a stone balustrade . . . and here in the sunshine sat Miss Dunne, wrapped in rugs and shawls, her feet on a footstool and a cushion behind her head. The sun was warm but old blood runs slowly and Miss Dunne was very old indeed.

For reading Miss Dunne required strong spectacles, but she needed no spectacles to see the hills . . . how green they were after yesterday's warm soft rain! Her bright brown eyes moved from one well-known landmark to another, she knew every stone and every tree. She saw Rydd Hill with its girdle of dark green conifers and, to left and right, Carlesknowe and Timperton Law . . . and, beyond these rounded hills, peeping over Souden Gap, the sterner darker face of Winters Gill. The hills were always the same and yet they always looked different, for sometimes they seemed quite near and sometimes far away; sometimes they gathered clouds of mist about them and hid their faces;

sometimes they smiled and sometimes they frowned. To-day they were smiling — and no wonder — for the sun lit them so that they glowed like jewels, and the cloud shadows moved over them slowly, caressing them.

How lovely they were, thought Miss Dunne, looking at them with deep affection, looking at them with her farsighted eyes. Here and there she saw a gleam of silver. The burns were up, yesterday's rain had filled them and they were filling the river, for she could hear the river's voice speaking to her from the dell. Closing her eyes for a moment Miss Dunne looked at the river with her "inward eye" — it was the easiest thing imaginable — and saw the bright water sliding past the roots of the trees, dimpling and sparkling in the sunshine; she saw the stepping-stones, fringed with lacy foam, and the deep peaty-brown pools with movement stirring in their depths. She looked beyond the river to the woods, green and freshly washed, carpeted with hyacinths, lit by an occasional bush of blazing rhododendrons . . . yes, the rhodies would be out now, past their best, of course, but still full of fire and colour.

At this moment there was a heavy step on the gravel path and Miss Dunne's reverie came to an end abruptly. She sat up and her small face assumed a look of alertness, of interest and animation, for although she loved the hills she was fond of people too.

"Johnson!" cried Miss Dunne. "Johnson, I want to speak to you."

The man came forward and leaned his arms upon the balustrade and smiled at her. "Well now, it's real nice to see you, Miss Dunne. You're better, then?"

5

"Much better," she replied, nodding at him. "Becky thought it wouldn't do me any harm to sit in the sun."

"It's a nice day for you, that's certain."

"A beautiful day. Perfectly beautiful. I feel much better already."

They were silent for a few moments — it was a friendly silence — for they knew each other so well that there was no need to speak unless they felt inclined. Johnston was almost as much a part of Dunnian as Miss Dunne herself. He had been born there, in the gardener's cottage, and had lived here all his life. Like her, he would die here — but not so soon ... these thoughts passed through Miss Dunne's mind as she looked at him.

"I've peas, to-day," said Johnson, lifting a trug of vegetables and showing it to her.

"So you have," she said. "Peas and radishes and a lovely crisp lettuce —"

"And new potatoes and green gooseberries," added Johnson.

"They're lovely," she told him, feasting her eyes upon the basket. "I think vegetables are as pretty as flowers in their own way — look at the colours in them."

"They're not bad," he agreed, looking at them.

She stretched out a tiny, fragile hand and took one of the peapods from the basket; it was a beautiful bright green and smooth and cool and shiny ("like jade," said Miss Dunne softly). Inside was a little row of bright green beads.

"They're very wee," said Johnson.

"That's how I like them."

"I know that fine, but Mrs. Drummond will be saying they're too small."

"You'll have an answer for her, no doubt," replied Miss Dunne dryly.

Johnson chuckled. He watched her eat the peas one by one — it reminded him of a bird. He thought, not for the first time, that Miss Dunne was very like a bird, like the robins that came and sat on the handle of his barrow and watched him digging . . .

"The sweet peas are coming on nice," said Johnson, "and the herbaceous border near the potting shed that I sorted last year. I'd like fine if you could see it, Miss Dunne."

It was a temptation, and she hesitated for a moment before she refused: "Another day," she said, with a little sigh of regret. "Another day, Johnson, you shall give me your arm and I'll walk down to the garden, but not to-day — I mustn't tire myself to-day."

He nodded understandingly. "They were telling me," he said, with a jerk of his head towards the kitchen premises. "They were saying that Mr. Humphrey is expected."

"Yes, he'll be here quite soon. He'll enjoy your peas, Johnson."

"It will be nice seeing him again. He's not been here for a long time."

"He's been abroad."

"Aye, he'll be glad to be back, no doubt."

"He's a lieutenant-commander now," continued Miss Dunne. "He's thirty-five, you know." She made this statement with an air of surprise, for it seemed very odd that Humphrey should be thirty-five. He was the grandson of Miss Dunne's youngest brother and she had always thought of him as "quite a boy," but she had looked up the date of his birth and there was no doubt about it . . .

"Aye, he'll be about that," Johnson agreed. "He's ten years younger than me and I'll be forty-five come September. The years slip past . . . they're saying he's married, too."

Miss Dunne had long since ceased to marvel at the fact that her servants knew almost as much as she did about the affairs of her family. "Yes," she replied. "He's been married for six years and he's got three children — one son and two daughters."

"Is that so?" said Johnson politely, but she was aware from his manner that it was no news to him (he probably knows their names, she thought with a little smile).

"His ship was stationed at Hong Kong," she continued. "It was there that he met his wife. Two of the children were born there."

"It's a far cry from Hong Kong to Dunnian," said Johnson thoughtfully.

This statement seemed to mark the end of the conversation and after a moment's silence Johnson lifted his trug. "I'll be going along now," he said.

"Perhaps you'd better," agreed Miss Dunne. "I'll come and see the garden soon — in a day or two."

"When you're stronger-like," he nodded, touching his cap and turning away.

He was smiling as he went down the path, for there was nothing he liked better than "a wee crack" with

Miss Dunne. It put a different complexion on the day. "They" had been saying that Miss Dunne was failing; and Johnson, when he heard it, had felt a queer stirring of his heart for he could not imagine Dunnian without Miss Dunne. She had always been here . . . she was part of the place. Johnson had felt sad and he had also felt apprehensive for he did not like Mr. Maurice Dunne at all, and Mr. Maurice was Miss Dunne's nephew and her heir. He did not like Mrs. Maurice, either — stuck up, that's what *she* was — she thought she knew everything and had a long Latin name for every flower. Johnson didn't know the Latin names (cat-mint and wallflower and love-in-a-mist were good enough for him) but he knew how to grow the flowers and the vegetables, too. Mrs. Maurice couldn't teach *him* anything about his job . . . but she would try. Oh yes, she would try. There would be changes at Dunnian when the Maurice Dunnes came and Johnson was quite sure the changes would not be for the better. He had considered it carefully and had come to the conclusion that it might be a good plan to look about for another place. It would be a sad wrench to leave Dunnian but maybe it would be worse to stay and see everything altered . . .

But there was no need to worry, thought Johnson. Miss Dunne wasn't failing — it wasn't true what they were saying — her eyes were as bright as ever and her brain as clear. She had been ill, of course, but now she was better and soon she would be on her legs again, pottering about the garden in her old black hat, chatting to him, picking the flowers. *She* wasn't failing — not her — she was good for another ten years — well, five years, anyway — "they" talked too much and wildly at that. Johnson whistled cheerfully as he walked across the yard to the kitchen door.

"You're spry to-day," Mrs. Drummond suggested as she took the basket from his hand.

"Aye, I'm feeling fine."

"That's nice for *you*," declared Mrs. Drummond with sarcasm.

"It's grand for me," agreed Johnson innocently.

"Maybe you wouldn't be so spry if you had my wurrk to do. D'you call those peas?"

"Peas!" echoed Johnson. "These are pet-its poise."

"What's that?" inquired Mrs. Drummond, raising her eyebrows.

"They're French and quite the latest thing."

"They look to me like half-grown peas."

"I'm surprised you don't know pet-its poise when you see them, Mrs. Drummond. Maybe you'd like me to show you the way to cook them."

"You can come and shell them for me, Mr. Johnson."

"Can the kitchenmaid not manage it?" inquired Johnson with an air of surprise. "You should train her to prepare the vegetables, Mrs. Drummond."

This battle of wits was one of many, in fact such encounters were of almost daily occurrence. They were always conducted with complete gravity and an outward show of politeness. Usually Mrs. Drumomnd was the victor for she had a quicker brain than Johnson and a caustic tongue, but to-day Johnson felt that the honours lay with him.

CHAPTER
TWO

Humphrey

Miss Dunne slept for a little while after Johnson had gone and presently, when she opened her eyes, she saw that her guest had arrived. He was at the other end of the terrace leaning on the balustrade, gazing at the hills. He looked older than Miss Dunne had expected, he looked grave and responsible — almost careworn — and his blue lounge suit was a trifle shabby though neatly pressed. Miss Dunne had time to have a good look at her great-nephew before he turned and saw that she was awake.

"This is a fine way to welcome you, Humphrey," she said, holding out her hand to him as he advanced. "The silly creatures should have wakened me — what were they thinking of?"

He took her hand and replied, "I wouldn't let them waken you, Aunt Celia. You looked so comfortable and there was no hurry." He was smiling at her now and the smile lit his face so that he seemed much younger.

"You haven't changed really," she told him.

"I've changed more than you — and Dunnian hasn't changed at all," replied Humphrey sitting down beside

11

her in a basket chair. "Dunnian is exactly as I remember it — just as peaceful and beautiful as ever."

Miss Dunne nodded. "Dunnian was built to last. It was built by my grandfather — your great-great-grandfather — Humphrey Dunne. The stone came from the quarry on Timperton Law."

"They don't build so solidly now."

"No indeed. Old Humphrey was thinking of the future when he built Dunnian, he was thinking of his children's children and their children's children . . . but here am I running on and I haven't asked for your news. When are you going to bring your wife to see me?"

"Alice would have liked to come but she couldn't leave the children," replied Humphrey politely.

"They're at Portsmouth," she prompted.

"Yes, we took a small house there and then my ship was sent to the Clyde. We were disappointed because we had hoped to have a little time together — but it's all in the day's work."

"Does she like Portsmouth?"

"Not very much, I'm afraid. It's a noisy crowded place and it doesn't seem to suit the children."

"You should move," said Miss Dunne firmly.

Humphrey did not reply. It was easy for Aunt Celia to say they should move but moving ran away with money and they were already in debt (not badly sunk, thank heaven, but still it was worrying for there seemed no possibility of saving money and paying off arrears); he wondered if he could "touch" Aunt Celia. She would not miss a few hundred pounds and it would make all the difference to him and Alice — but no, he was too proud. I shan't even hint at it, he thought.

"What is she like?" inquired Miss Dunne.

"Who? Oh, Alice —" He took a little case out of his pocket and opened it. Inside it was a coloured photograph of a fair-haired girl with blue eyes.

Miss Dunne examined it carefully. "Very pretty," she said.

"It doesn't do her justice," declared her husband earnestly. "It doesn't show her expression. She's so sweet and good, Aunt Celia. She's such a splendid mother. I wish you could see her."

"I wish I could," replied Miss Dunne, handing back the case, "but apparently I shall have to do without seeing her. If she suits you that's the main thing."

"We suit each other," Humphrey said, blushing under his tan. "She's quite perfect. I knew the moment I saw her — I knew she was — was just what a woman ought to be. If only we could be together — I mean we're quite happy — but of course I'm away so much —"

He stopped suddenly and looked up. Aunt Celia was smiling but she was smiling quite kindly. "Lucky man!" she said.

Now that he had time to look at Aunt Celia more carefully Humphrey saw that she had changed more than he had thought. She had always been thin and light and very small but now she looked frail as well — a fragile, dainty old lady in a pale grey dress with a cross-over fichu of fine net — her cheeks were flushed with the excitement of talking and her brown eyes were very bright.

"I'm ninety," said Miss Dunne, meeting his glance.

"You don't *seem* ninety, Aunt Celia. You're so alive."

"My brain is as good as ever," she returned, smiling a little. "It's my legs that are old. I still want to do things and then I find I can't, but I'm not complaining, Humphrey. I'm quite happy."

"You look happy."

"I have my books," she said. "I have my hills to look at, and I still have a few friends who come and see me now and then. There's Mrs. Raeworth, for instance. She's a young creature — just about your age — but we have a good deal in common. I'd like you to meet Evelyn Raeworth some time."

"Yes," said Humphrey politely. He was not much interested in Aunt Celia's neighbours, for what was the use of being interested in people one would never see again?

"And then there's Selma Skene," continued Miss Dunne, smiling. "Perhaps you remember Lady Skene. They're our nearest neighbours. Selma amuses me a good deal — she runs the county. Their boy is a major now, he's married and has two children who are dumped at Ryddelton House when their parents want to get rid of them."

"I used to go fishing with Jack Skene," said Humphrey thoughtfully.

Miss Dunne nodded. "He's a major, now," she repeated.

It was quiet, leisurely talk, the sort of talk which suited the warm afternoon. Humphrey felt peaceful and relaxed. Every now and then there was a little silence and then the talk went on again. Two neat maids brought the tea equipage and laid it on a table beside Miss Dunne (a lacy cloth, white as snow, a heavy silver tray with tea-pot, cream jug and sugar basin to match, cups and saucers of fine transparent china and plates of scones and cakes).

"Ninety years is a long time," said Miss Dunne suddenly. "I was born the day after Waterloo. My mother wanted a son — she would have called him Arthur, of course. I believe I just escaped being Arethusa!"

"Celia is a good deal better," said Humphrey, smiling.

"It's a good name," agreed its owner. "I've worn it a long time. Very few people call me Celia now — that's the worst of outliving contemporaries. You know, Humphrey, it's a great blessing to have a good memory; I'm very grateful for mine; it's my picture book and I can turn over the leaves when I like. So many of my memories are centred here in Dunnian, so many people have lived in the old house. There were seven of us and they're all dead except me, but I can see them if I shut my eyes. Their youth is here — still here in Dunnian."

"I think I understand," Humphrey murmured. It was odd to imagine the old quiet house full of young voices and light footsteps — that was how Aunt Celia saw it.

"They're not ghosts, you know," declared Miss Dunne. "There's nothing alarming about them. No, they're just memories — Willie and Mary and John and Ellen and Harry and Isabel — I can see them all clearly but Isabel most clearly of all. She was so gay and pretty — the baby of the family. I can remember other things too — things that I saw and did when I was young. I

15

remember going to London by stage coach and my father took me to see King William driving in the park. I've never forgotten that."

"It's — it's astounding," declared Humphrey, looking at the small, dainty old lady in amazement.

"Yes, I've seen a good many changes but you'll see more. These motor-cars — noisy smelly things — they've come to stay, I'm afraid."

"They'll improve," said Humphrey thoughtfully.

"There's much need of improvement," declared Miss Dunne with spirit. "Maurice has bought one. You never saw such a hideous contraption in your life. It seems to me that all the new inventions are ugly and noisy . . ."

Humphrey took a scone and buttered it — what lovely butter it was, rich and yellow and creamy!

"The hills don't change, thank God," continued Miss Dunne. "There's Timperton Law — it looks the same to-day as it did before I was born and it won't look different when your children's children are dead and buried. You shot your first grouse on Timperton Law, Humphrey."

"Fancy you remembering that!" he exclaimed in surprise. He was rather touched that she should remember his first grouse. The day came back to him very clearly: it was in early September and the heather was a blaze of purple and humming with wild bees. Maurice had been staying at Dunnian and the two of them had driven over to Timperton in the dog-cart — they had taken Johnson to carry the bags. Maurice had been very decent to Humphrey, showing him how to swing his gun, giving him the best chance. Maurice had been a good-natured sort of fellow — what was he like now, Humphrey wondered. Some day Dunnian would belong to Maurice . . .

"Have you met Maurice's wife?" Aunt Celia was asking.

Humphrey shook his head. "I've been abroad so much. One's friends are apt to drift away — it's natural, I suppose. Have they any children, Aunt Celia?"

"She prefers dogs," said Aunt Celia shortly.

Humphrey chuckled. "They're less trouble," he said.

"Nina's dogs are more trouble than children," replied Aunt Celia. "She's quite crazy about them. I like dogs myself but not silly little toy dogs that yap all day. Do you remember old Boris?"

"Yes, of course."

"Johnson still has a grand-daughter of old Boris. He wanted to give me one of her puppies but I can't walk far enough to exercise a spaniel — my dog days are over." She sighed and added in a different tone. "It was good of you to come and see me, Humphrey. I wanted to talk to you and there isn't much time."

"I've got three days' leave —"

"I dare say, but how much leave have I got?" she asked, looking at him with a mischievous twinkle in her bright eyes.

"You mean —"

"You know what I mean, Humphrey. The doctors have a lot of long words for it but it's quite simple really. My poor old heart is worn out. Ninety years is a long time for a heart to go on beating."

"I don't like to hear you say that!" he exclaimed.

She smiled and said, "Some people think I've been here too long."

"Aunt Celia!"

"It's true. Maurice and that expensive wife of his are getting quite impatient. She's made all her plans, of course. She's decided to cut down part of the wood and open up a 'vista.' The lawn is to be cut up into round beds for bedding out — so I'm informed — and there's to be a rock garden with alpine plants."

Humphrey gazed at her, wide-eyed, but when he saw that she was smiling his face relaxed into a grin. "How do you know all that?" he asked.

"My dear boy, everybody knows everything here — it goes round and round and comes back to me in the end. Sometimes I would rather not hear but you can't close your ears. Pour me out another cup of tea."

He rose and poured it out for her and was glad of the occupation, for it was extremely difficult to know what to say.

"What do you think of the idea?" she asked as she took the cup. "How do you think the lawn would look cut up into round beds full of geraniums and lobelias?"

He looked out over the lawn; it was green and smooth as velvet, sloping gently down to the line of tall stately trees. Beneath the trees was a carpet of wild hyacinths, blue as the sea on a summer's day. "I think it would be horrible," he said gravely.

"Horrible," she agreed, nodding vehemently. "It would change the character of the place. The sweep of grass leads the eye to the trees and the hills beyond. Fussy beds of flowers would spoil the whole effect . . .

and that's one of the reasons," she continued, smiling at him. "That's one of the reasons — but only one of the reasons — why I've decided not to leave Dunnian to Maurice. I shall leave it to you, instead."

There was complete silence. Humphrey was so amazed, so taken aback, so flabbergasted, that he could find nothing to say. He sat down heavily and stared at Miss Dunne with his mouth half open.

She laughed and exclaimed, "If only you could see your face!"

"To *me*" he asked, finding his voice with difficulty.

"You're fond of Dunnian, aren't you?"

"It's the most beautiful place in the world," declared Humphrey with pardonable exaggeration.

"Well, then, that's settled."

"Aunt Celia, you don't really mean it?"

"This isn't the first of April, Humphrey."

"I thought," he began. "I thought Maurice was your —"

"Listen to me," said Miss Dunne, holding up her hand to stop him. "Listen to me, Humphrey. Everyone has always taken it for granted that Maurice would have Dunnian when I was dead; it's true that he's Willie's son and Willie was my eldest brother, but that doesn't seem much of a reason to me. Dunnian isn't entailed — I shouldn't be here now if it had been entailed."

"No, I suppose not," said Humphrey with a bewildered air.

"Dunnian belongs to me and I can do exactly what I like with it; I could leave it to a Cats' Home if I wanted. The money will go with the place, of course. You'll need

19

it to keep Dunnian as it should be kept. Your pay wouldn't go very far."

"No," said Humphrey in a dazed voice.

"There's no need for you to retire," she continued. "In fact I think it would be a mistake. You can settle your family here and make it your home. I shall want your assurance that you will make it your home, Humphrey. Dunnian must not be shut up or let to strangers."

He was beginning to realise that she really meant it. She had thought it all out — "Aunt Celia, I can't believe it," he said in a low voice.

"You'll get used to the idea," she told him. "Oh yes, you will. You can walk about and accustom yourself to the idea . . . but be careful what you say in front of the servants; I don't want it to leak out. Maurice will hear about it soon enough when I'm in my grave." She hesitated and then continued, "It isn't a sudden decision, Humphrey. I've thought about it a great deal. Dunnian means a lot to me — it's my best friend. I've outlived all my human friends. I want someone who loves the place to have it when I'm gone."

"I shall love it," he said gravely.

"I know," she nodded. "I know you will — and your children will grow up here. For years and years there have been old people in the house and it's high time there were children. There should be children here, young things growing up in the house, running about the grounds, playing by the river. Dunnian needs youth," said Miss Dunne dreamily.

Humphrey could not speak.

"You've got three children," said Miss Dunne after a little silence. "Perhaps you'll have more."

Humphrey was still feeling bewildered. "I hope so," he murmured. "If we were settled ... Alice likes children ... so do I ... it's difficult when you're moving about ..."

"You will be settled. You should certainly have more children — not that I like children very much (I find them tiresome) but they grow up into people if you give them time. In my young days parents were not afraid to admit that they found their children tiresome. Now it is considered unnatural and yet people have fewer. That always strikes me as strange."

"They didn't have to bother with their children," Humphrey pointed out. "They just handed them over to a competent nurse, and —"

"That's exactly what I mean," said Miss Dunne. "They didn't pretend they liked them. Now they pretend they like them and don't have them."

"I like mine," Humphrey said.

"How often do you see them?" she asked with a mischievous glance. "Well, never mind, Humphrey, I won't tease you. We'll say your children are never tiresome, never noisy or sticky or greedy or quarrelsome."

He smiled at her. Although he did not agree with all she said he did not feel inclined to argue with her.

"That brings me to another point," she said. "Perhaps I should have explained this at the beginning. My intention is that you shall be life-rented in the place.

After your death I want Dunnian to go to your daughter Celia."

"You mean Edith, of course —" began Humphrey in some surprise.

"I mean exactly what I say," retorted Miss Dunne. "Dunnian is to go to your daughter, Celia. She will be born in the house — perhaps she will live in it for ninety years."

Humphrey drew a long breath. He was beginning to see the idea. It was a most extraordinary idea, but still —

"I suppose you think I'm mad," said Miss Dunne, glancing at him sideways. "My lawyer, Mr. Wanlock, as good as told me to my face that I was raving, but that didn't upset me at all. I told him that if he couldn't draw up my will as I wanted it I should send for somebody else. That brought him to his senses. He's gone back to Edinburgh to put the whole thing into legal jargon and a fine thing he'll make of it I don't doubt. He's to come back to-morrow with it all cut and dried and if you've no objections I shall sign it."

"Objection!" Humphrey exclaimed.

Miss Dunne smiled. She said, "What about your wife? Perhaps you'd rather wait and consult her about it. Would she be happy here? It's quiet, you know. There are nice neighbours, but if she has been used to town —"

"Alice would love it," declared Humphrey. "Aunt Celia, you've no idea what this means . . ."

His voice died away and there was a little silence. Humphrey saw that she was tired and he felt guilty for he had been warned not to tire her. He was just wondering whether he should leave her to rest for a little when he saw Becky come out of the drawing-room window. Becky had been with Miss Dunne for years — she was an old friend — and Humphrey rose and shook hands with her.

"Well, I never!" Becky said. "You're older than I expected, Mr. Humphrey."

"You're younger than I expected," replied Humphrey, laughing. "People who live here never grow older."

"You were always one for a joke," Becky replied. "I'm getting older like everybody else. Look at my grey hair!"

"It's very becoming," he retorted. She was a good-looking woman, tall and slim in her neat black dress. Her complexion was clear as a girl's and her grey eyes full of humour.

"Get on with you, Mr. Humphrey," she said. "I'm too old for your cozening. You'd better take a walk round the garden and let Miss Dunne have a wee rest before dinner."

"I hope I haven't tired her," Humphrey said.

"I've tired myself," declared Miss Dunne. "I've talked too much but I'll be all right if I have a rest. Here's my shawl, Becky."

CHAPTER
THREE

The Red Rose

Humphrey was shaving. His hair was very dark and if he wanted to look well he was obliged to shave twice a day. To-night he felt that he must look his best — it was the least he could do for Aunt Celia — besides she might expect him to kiss her when he said good-night. Humphrey was not particularly fond of kissing but he felt he would like to kiss Aunt Celia. Quite gravely (for he had a grave nature and not much sense of humour) Humphrey considered the question — to kiss or not to kiss. Would she like it or would she think it silly? Better to be prepared, any way, thought Humphrey as he lathered his chin industriously. He had spent the hour before dinner wandering about the grounds, wandering along the banks of the stream, the Rydd Water, which ran through the property, curving past the trees beyond the lawn. He remembered it all very well but he had looked at it with new eyes for some day it would be his.

There were trout in the Rydd, quite good ones. He had seen one lying in the shadow of a rock. Mark would catch that trout some day — he and Mark together — what an exciting, what an amazing thought! Having settled the fate of the trout Humphrey wandered on to the lawn and examined it carefully. It had looked smooth and velvety from a distance and it was no less smooth and velvety at close quarters — it would be desecration to cut it up into beds — no wonder Aunt Celia had been angry. Used as he was to wide stretches of sea and far horizons Humphrey took immense pleasure in the smooth, green sweep of grass. It was dignified and gracious, it gave one a feeling of space.

He walked down to the kitchen garden and found Johnson in the potting shed and renewed his acquaintance. Johnson was friendly and Humphrey felt friendly too, but he was very careful with Johnson, for the news must not leak out through anything he said or did or looked. Humphrey was aware that a look might give away the whole show — a possessive sort of look. He admired Johnson's peas — which were admirable — and evinced his pleasure when he learnt that peas were on the menu for dinner — peas and green gooseberries. He walked down the garden with Johnson and saw how beautifully it was kept. It was on the tip of his tongue to ask how many men were employed in the garden but on second thoughts he refrained from the inquiry.

"The old greenhouse needs doing up," said Johnson, pointing to it. "I was wondering if you would mention it to Miss Dunne."

"No," replied Humphrey. "No, I couldn't do that."

"It needs new glass and a wee lick of paint. I thought you might just say you had seen it —"

"No, I don't think so."

"Maybe I'd better wait till Mr. Maurice comes."

"Yes, I should," said Humphrey, turning away to hide an involuntary smile.

Johnson might have said more about the greenhouse but his companion changed the subject.

"What are those called?" he asked, pointing to a bed of deep red roses which grew in a sheltered corner near the wall.

"They're Duke of Richmond, Mr. Humphrey. Maybe you'd like a few, they've got a nice smell."

"I'll take one if I may," replied Humphrey, and he produced his knife and cut a newly opened bud, choosing it with care.

"That's right," said Johnson, nodding approval. "I don't like to see folk tearing at roses. You've chosen a good one, too."

Humphrey thought of all this as he shaved his left cheek. The rose was now on his dressing-table, standing in a tumbler of water. He thought it would be nice to give it to Aunt Celia — it was her own, of course, but women liked these small attentions. This thought led him to Alice (who set a good deal of value on small attentions). Poor Alice, thought Humphrey. Poor Alice, shut up in that poky house with the three children and only one inexperienced servant-girl to help her! How he wished he could have her brought to Dunnian on a magic carpet! He thought of Alice longingly, of her fair soft skin and gentle blue eyes. She was not very clever, perhaps, but who wanted a clever wife — not Humphrey. Humphrey was used to being with men, to hearing loud, virile voices and seeing strong, rugged faces . . . Alice was the most delightful change and rest.

She was a "womanly woman," soft and pretty and (to Humphrey) mysterious. He had always wanted to "give her things" but had never been able to afford anything worthwhile. Alice did not seem to mind, she had been most awfully good about it (thought Humphrey); she had accepted trivial gifts rapturously and done her best to economise. It was wonderful to think that the days of pinching and scraping, of cheap lodgings and hideous furnished houses were nearly over. Not that Humphrey was in a hurry for Aunt Celia to depart — no, quite honestly he was not — but obviously Aunt Celia could not live for ever.

Alice would love this place. The children would adore it. They would grow strong and fit in the lovely air with plenty of milk and cream and rich golden butter from the farm. They would be perfectly happy and he would be happy thinking of them . . . and he would come back here for his leave to a real home, to a safe harbour. This place would give him roots, and Humphrey wanted roots for himself and his family. He wanted roots all the more because his life was nomadic, because he had never known what it was to have a real settled home. He was so excited by these thoughts that he felt quite giddy and he was obliged to lay down his razor until he could command his emotions.

I must write to Alice, he thought. Nobody else must know but I must tell Alice. I'll write to-morrow when it's settled but I mustn't build on it too much until the will is signed . . . supposing Aunt Celia were to die in the night! Nonsense, of course, she won't. Why should she?

There was no reason why she should (unless, of course, from the joy of beholding her great-nephew) and Humphrey banished the thought; but he was immediately assailed by another which was almost as alarming. What would happen if another Celia failed to appear? What provision would be made for the contingency? Fortunately Alice liked babies and produced them without much trouble but you could not tell for certain. Humphrey considered the matter. He had two daughters already — it seemed a pity that neither of them would do.

Humphrey was tying his black tie by this time and he smiled at his reflection in the mirror; the whole thing was so absurd! He smiled and then he frowned. Mark ought to have Dunnian, of course. Mark was the right person to have it: his son, not a young daughter still unborn.

Already Humphrey was beginning to get used to the idea of possessing Dunnian and to cavil at the terms of possession.

CHAPTER
FOUR

Family Affairs

Humphrey went down to the drawing-room in good time and found his hostess sitting by the fire, rested and refreshed. She smiled at him and said, "I always have a fire in the evening."

"It looks nice," he remarked, coming forward and holding out his hands to the blaze. Aunt Celia looked nice, too, and Humphrey had a feeling that she was dressed for a "special occasion" just as he was. Her pale grey dress was of heavy silk which rustled when she moved and she wore cobweb-fine lace at her neck and wrists. A magnificent diamond brooch, pinned in the front of her bodice, twinkled and sparkled in the light of the fire. Humphrey offered her the rose and he saw that she was pleased — even though it was her own —

"You picked it in the bed beside the south wall," she told him as she took it and pushed its stalk through the brooch. "They're the best roses in the garden and the Duke is my favourite."

"I think he's my favourite, too."

"Did you speak to Johnson?"

"Yes, I asked his permission to cut it. He said I had chosen a good one."

"So you have," said Miss Dunne with the little sharp nod that was so characteristic. "It's a beautiful rose, Humphrey. I hope you were careful what you said to Johnson, he's very much all there."

Humphrey smiled and replied that he had been very careful indeed. He wondered whether he should tell her about the greenhouse — she would appreciate the joke — but before he could make up his mind the tablemaid appeared and announced that dinner was served. Miss Dunne rose at once and, Humphrey offering her his arm, they went into the dining-room together.

They chatted casually during the meal (Humphrey spoke of Hong Kong, of his children and of his ship); but when the port had been put on the table and the servants had gone they were free to speak of what was in their minds.

"There are several people to be helped and cared for," said Miss Dunne after a moment's pause. "You will do that for me, won't you? You'll be kind to Becky — she has been a true friend."

"Of course," said Humphrey quickly. "You must tell me all you want done. I'll do everything in my power." He hesitated and then went on: "I hardly know what to say, Aunt Celia. It seems absurd to say 'thank you,' doesn't it?"

"Quite absurd. I can't take Dunnian with me."

"But I mean — I feel —" he began.

"Don't worry. I know what you feel — I can see it in your face," replied Miss Dunne. "There's Becky to look after — and there's Joan. She's the grand-daughter of my youngest sister so she's your generation, Humphrey.

That branch of the family has been rather unfortunate and I've helped them a good deal. If you begin helping people you have to go on. I shall leave Joan some money, of course, but money isn't everything."

"I'll look after her," Humphrey said.

Miss Dunne took a sheet of paper from her grey silk bag and spread it out on the table. "There," she said. "I wrote it out for you because you'll be the head of the family — we can't expect Maurice to do much — so you ought to know who's who. The family tree is in the safe, you had better have a look at it sometime (it goes back to the reign of James IV) but this is all that concerns us at the moment."

Humphrey examined the paper with interest; the tree was incomplete, of course, but it gave him a very good idea of the ramifications of the family — which was all that was intended.

"This will be very useful to me," Humphrey said.

"There were seven of us," Miss Dunne told him, "but I've only put in five. Arthur was drowned at sea and Catherine died when she was seventeen. The diagram is just to give you a rough idea —"

"It's splendid," declared Humphrey. He added, "Maurice is a generation before me, of course."

"Yes," nodded Miss Dunne. "Yes, Maurice is my nephew, he must be about fifty — you see William married late in life and his wife was a good deal younger than himself. She's still alive — Ellen Dunne, I mean — a stupid woman (I never could get on with her) and she chose a stupid name for her son. The Dunnes have always been Williams or Henrys or Humphreys . . .

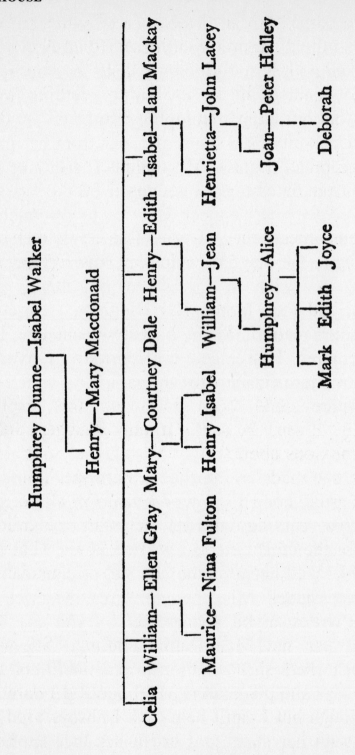

then we come to Mary," said Miss Dunne, putting her finger on the diagram. "Mary married an American and went back with him to Pittsburgh; she had two children. I've lost sight of them since Mary died so we don't know what has happened to that branch of the family."

"Rather a pity!"

"Deplorable," agreed Miss Dunne. "They must have moved from Pittsburgh, I suppose. I've written several times . . ."

"Then comes Henry, my grandfather," said Humphrey, returning to the diagram which lay between them on the table.

"Yes, and then Isabel. Her daughter, Henrietta, is a delightful creature. She's a widow and she lives at Bournemouth. I haven't seen Henrietta for years but I hear from her occasionally."

Humphrey had been following this explanation carefully. "I see," he said. "It's her daughter, Joan, that you're anxious about."

"Yes, she made an imprudent marriage. Young Halley was an artist, not a very good artist, I'm afraid. He died about two years ago and left her with one child. I felt sorry for the creature and I wanted to see what she was like so I asked her to come and stay at Dunnian — but she never came."

"She writes to you, I suppose."

"Oh, yes," said Miss Dunne, smiling. "She writes to me when she's short of money and that's not seldom. Becky says she plays on my feelings and I dare say it's true enough but I can't help that. I always used to help Isabel with her sums and brush her hair for her so it seems natural that I should look after her grand-daughter."

"Does she live with her mother at Bournemouth?"

"No, no, it would never work. Parents and children are better apart if they don't get on well together; besides Henrietta isn't well off herself . . . I'd like to see Henrietta again," added Miss Dunne thoughtfully.

There was a little silence after that; Humphrey broke it. "That's a portrait of old Henry Dunne, your father, above the mantelpiece, isn't it?" he inquired.

"No, that's my grandfather. That's Humphrey who built Dunnian House. I remember him quite well — just like that — it's an excellent portrait. He was always beautifully turned out, *point device*, and I remember," said Miss Dunne, smiling, "I remember he smelt of lavender water when I kissed him. He used to tell us stories, true stories about things he had seen when he was a boy, about Prince Charles riding into Edinburgh at the head of his troops and —"

"Do you mean he had seen Prince Charles?" asked Humphrey incredulously.

Miss Dunne nodded.

"Did he take part in the rising?"

"No, he was too young; but even if he had been old enough he wouldn't have gone out for he wasn't a believer in the Stuart cause. He used to say that the Stuarts made good stories but they didn't make good kings."

"I suppose that's true, really," said Humphrey thoughtfully.

They moved back to the drawing-room and settled down by the fire. The lamps had been lit but the french windows were wide open and although the sun had gone down behind the trees it was still light outside.

"I like the gloaming," said Miss Dunne. "Sometimes I sit here and watch for the first star . . . do you want to ask me anything, Humphrey?"

"Yes, Aunt Celia. I know you've thought a great deal about this arrangement so I suppose you've realised that there may not be another Celia."

"I think there will be."

"Even if there is another Celia," continued Humphrey, choosing his words with care. "You realise that she may marry, in which case —"

"Of course Celia will marry," interrupted Miss Dunne. "All the Dunne women marry — except me, of course — but you needn't think I couldn't have married if I'd wanted to."

"I never thought that."

"There were several young gentlemen," said Miss Dunne with a reminiscent smile, "but the only one I wanted was Courtney Dale and he preferred Mary."

"She must have been very attractive."

"That's rather nice of you, Humphrey," she said gravely. "The fact was we never met until he and Mary were engaged, so of course . . . but perhaps it was just as well in the long run for I might not have been happy so far away from Dunnian."

There was a little silence. Miss Dunne was thinking of Courtney Dale. There had never been a word of understanding between them — scarcely a glance — but they had both known that a wrong turning had been taken and that something beautiful had been missed. He and Mary had been married and had gone from Dunnian, never to return, and Celia had remained single.

After a little Humphrey returned to the subject which was occupying his mind. He said, "Aunt Celia, have you realised that if there is a Celia and she marries there won't be Dunnes at Dunnian any more?"

"Celia's husband will take the name," said Miss Dunne firmly. "I know all those arguments, Humphrey, and I know the answers. It has all been considered most carefully and every contingency allowed for. Mr. Wanlock will explain it to you to-morrow. He doesn't approve, of course; in fact he argued with me for hours. First of all he didn't want me to pass over Maurice, and then, when he found I was adamant on that point, he wanted me to entail the property so that it would go to your son."

"That is the usual thing —"

"Of course it's the usual thing but I prefer my own way. Celia's children will be Dunnes every bit as much as Mark's . . . and any way what on earth induced you to call the child 'Mark'? He should have been 'Henry.'"

"Alice's father was Mark," said Humphrey miserably.

"He should have been Henry," repeated Miss Dunne.

Humphrey said no more for he saw that it was useless, and a little silence ensued.

"You had better put in electric light," said Miss Dunne suddenly. "I believe it is quite satisfactory if you get a good man to do it and it will be safer with the children running about. You'll need another bathroom, of course.

I should put it on the nursery floor if I were you. The house is perfectly sound but it needs redecorating, I haven't bothered about paper and paint."

"I wish you wouldn't talk like that, Aunt Celia."

"Why not?" she asked. "I may as well face up to it. I confess that sometimes I feel a little frightened — but then I look at the hills. There they stand, always the same. It gives one courage to see them." She was silent for a moment and then she added dreamily, "The only thing that can beat Death is Life — new Life."

Humphrey did not speak.

"I shall be sorry to leave Dunnian," added Miss Dunne with a sigh.

"But you mean to come back," said Humphrey. He was surprised when he heard himself say the words but having said them he knew that they were true and that this was the solution of the mystery.

"I wonder," said Miss Dunne. "I wonder if I shall. We don't know much, do we? I wonder what sort of a place I'm going to. I've lived here so long — I haven't been away from Dunnian for years — so it's rather an adventure."

CHAPTER
FIVE

August, 1905

Mr. and Mrs. Maurice Dunne drove up to Dunnian House in their new motor car. They had had two punctures on their way from Edinburgh (which had annoyed them a good deal) and they both wished that they had come by train in the comfortable old-fashioned manner. They were both out of temper not only with the new car but also with the new chauffeur. Maurice had a feeling that the man was incompetent but he could not be sure for he, himself, knew nothing about motor cars. Nina was certain that the man was incompetent — he was impertinent as well — she had made up her mind that Maurice must give him a month's notice.

As the car drew up at the door Nina noticed that all the blinds in the house had been drawn down. She said in a low voice, "We're too late, Maurice."

"Too late for what?" asked her husband, adding almost at once, "Oh, I see what you mean."

There was an odd sort of stillness in the house. Nina noticed it the moment she crossed the threshold. Dunnian was always quiet but to-day it was quiet in a different way. She left Maurice to speak to the lawyer, who had met them in the hall, and followed the housemaid upstairs . . . she found herself trying to walk quietly but her high heels went click, click, click on the polished floor. The best spare bedroom, which had been prepared for Nina as usual, was full of sunshine, shining through the light yellow blinds. It was not so quiet here, for the birds were singing outside the window and Nina could hear the ripple of the Rydd Water in the distance.

"When did it happen?" asked Nina in a low voice.

"It was very sudden," replied the housemaid. "She was sitting on the terrace this morning —"

"Was she all alone," asked Nina in dismay.

"Oh no, ma'am. Becky was there, but she hadn't time to call anybody or get the doctor or anything. She was gone in a moment."

"The telegram said she was ill."

"Yes, ma'am. We didn't know what to say. It seemed we thought it was better to say she was ill —"

"I see," said Nina. She turned away to hide a smile — *breaking it gently*, she thought.

"It feels funny without her," continued the girl with a little tremor in her voice. "She was so quiet that you wouldn't think it would make much difference — her not being here — but the house feels funny without her."

"Yes, it's dreadully sad." Nina took off her hat as she spoke, it was draped with a voluminous motor veil which was white with dust from the road.

"She seemed better," continued the girl. "She seemed more like her old self the last few days. Yesterday she walked down to the garden — she hadn't been as far as the garden for weeks. Becky blames herself for letting Miss Dunne do it."

"Becky mustn't do that," said Nina with conviction.

"No, that's what I said to Becky. I said, "You mustn't blame yourself. Miss Dunne wanted to do it, I said."

"She was very strong-minded," said Nina. By this time Nina had recovered a little from the first shock and was looking round the room. The paper is frightful, she thought, but the room is a good shape. I believe I shall take this as my room — I should never feel comfortable in hers — pale green wall-paper and chintz — Liberty would be the best place for the chintz — my wardrobe would look well between the fireplace and the door —

"Mr. Wanlock, the lawyer, came at lunch-time," continued the housemaid. "He's busy arranging everything, and Mr. and Mrs. Humphrey are expected to-morrow night."

"Oh, they're coming, are they?" Nina exclaimed.

"Mr. Wanlock sent them a telegram," replied the girl. She was surprised and a trifle ashamed to find that she was enjoying herself; although she was sincerely grieved about the old lady it was exciting to talk to Mrs. Dunne and to be able to tell her all the news.

"I forget what your name is," said Nina, smiling at her.

"It's Lizzie, ma'am."

"Of course," agreed Nina. "Silly of me to forget. I think I'll have a bath before dinner. I suppose there's still only the one bathroom."

"I'll get it ready for you," Lizzie said eagerly.

There were all sorts of things that Nina wanted to ask but she decided that it would not do to appear inquisitive

— she must be careful. She smiled to herself as she thought how careful she had been in her conversation with Lizzie, she hadn't said *anything* . . .

Lizzie prepared the bath and put everything ready, then she ran downstairs. She was longing to find an audience and she was aware that the audience would be awaiting her, ready and willing to hear all she had to tell.

"She said," began Lizzie, as she burst in at the kitchen door, "She said, 'It's dreadfully sad' — but there wasn't much sadness about *her*."

"There wouldn't be," said Mrs. Drummond acidly.

"She was in a rare taking when she heard Mr. and Mrs. Humphrey were expected. 'What are *they* coming for, I should like to know,' she said."

"She didn't!"

"Well, that's what she meant. Then I told her about Becky blaming herself for letting Miss Dunne go down the garden and she said, 'Becky needn't *blame* herself,' she said. No, thinks I, you'll not blame Becky for *that!* Then she said, 'I think I'll have a bath before dinner. I suppose there's still only the one poky wee bathroom,' she said."

"You're making it up."

"No, it's maybe not the exact words but it's near enough. So I said, 'Yes, ma'am,' I said. It was a scream, I can tell you . . . and the way she was looking round all the time — like as if she was tearing the very paper off the walls! There'll be changes here before we're much older."

"There'll be a change in the kitchen any way," declared Mrs. Drummond as she opened the oven door and popped in her soufflé. "She'll not get me to stay, not if she was to go down on her bended knees."

CHAPTER
SIX

Alice

Humphrey and Alice arrived at Dunnian the following evening just in time for dinner. They had travelled all the way from Portsmouth and Alice was exceedingly tired; she was so tired that she found it difficult to "take in" Dunnian and her first impression of the place was confused and dreamlike. It seemed immense after the little house at Portsmouth.

Nina and Maurice received the travellers graciously. "Don't bother to change," said Nina. "Just come in as you are. Cook doesn't like us to be late for dinner; she's an absolute gorgon."

Nina was in black velvet and diamonds, her dark hair was piled upon her small head in rows of shining curls, she was the picture of elegance and assurance. If Alice had been permitted to bathe and change she might have felt better able to cope with Nina but, as it was, she could find nothing to say except "yes" and "no." She was tired and, although she had washed her face and hands, she still felt dirty and she was aware that her tweed coat and skirt were shabby and old-fashioned. Looking across the table at Humphrey, Alice realised that he ought to have shaved. She noticed that his suit was shiny and remembered that he had had it for three years. I ought to have sponged and pressed it, she thought, miserably. Humphrey was smiling at her but Alice found it difficult to smile back for suddenly she was quite certain in her own mind that there was some mistake; she was certain that Dunnian House was not coming to Humphrey. These people were successful and secure; they were the sort of people who "got things" and she and Humphrey were the sort of people who didn't. She and Humphrey were unlucky. If they happened to put five shillings on a horse it was sure to come in last. They had invested a little money in an orange grove in Africa — it had sounded marvellous — but there was a drought or something and the orange trees had died. Nothing good ever came to her — or Humphrey — they were always in trouble of some kind . . . "to those that hath shall be given" thought Alice vaguely. It seemed unfair, of course, but there it was: Maurice and Nina had everything and they would have Dunnian too. Alice was very near tears.

Alice looked round the table. Nina had given up trying to talk to her and was talking to Humphrey and Maurice; Mr. Wanlock was completely silent, drinking his soup. Mr. Wanlock was the only person who *knew*, thought Alice. He would know if Miss Dunne had changed her mind and made another will. He would know; but he wouldn't say — lawyers were so careful. She swallowed a lump in her throat but it was still there, choking her, so that the soup would not go down.

"You haven't been here before, have you?" asked Nina, making another effort to draw Alice into the conversation.

"No," said Alice, adding with some difficulty, "It's a lovely house."

"It needs a great deal doing to it," declared Nina, looking round the room. "The wall-paper is hideous — I can't think how any one can have chosen it — and the furniture is terribly old-fashioned."

"I think it suits the house," Alice said in a very small voice.

"Suits the house?"

"Yes, I like it." She put down her spoon as she spoke for it was impossible to swallow another drop.

Mr. Wanlock put down his spoon at the same moment — his plate was empty. "I hope the children are well," he said, addressing Alice.

This was the first remark he had made and Alice was taken aback. "Not very," she replied. "They've all had whooping-cough. Mark had it *very* badly."

"Perhaps they need a change of air," said Mr. Wanlock with immense gravity.

Alice looked at him quickly but he was gazing straight before him, gazing at the heavy silver epergne filled with roses. His mouth was pursed a little, drawn in at the corners. Had he meant anything or not, Alice wondered. She was not as a rule very perspicacious but her hopes and fears had made her more so than usual. Her heart lightened a little.

"Oh, yes," agreed Nina, smiling kindly. "Children should always have a change of air after whooping-cough. I believe Margate is supposed to be the best place. It's so bracing."

"Some doctors believe in hill air," said Mr. Wanlock thoughtfully.

"Have some more sherry, Humphrey," Maurice suggested. "Aunt Celia's sherry is excellent; I'm afraid I can't say the same of her port."

"I had some the last time I was here. It was quite sound, I thought," replied Humphrey.

"You were here in June, weren't you?"

"Just for a few days. I'm glad I saw her again — I was very fond of Aunt Celia."

"She was a great lady," said Maurice gravely. "She was one of the old school. Her mind was perfectly clear up to the day of her death — you'll agree with me there, Mr. Wanlock."

"Perfectly clear," said Mr. Wanlock with the ghost of a smile.

"Most unusual," Maurice continued (and Humphrey had a feeling that this was Aunt Celia's funeral oration and that Maurice had prepared it carefully beforehand). "Most unusual for a woman of her age to retain her faculties as Aunt Celia retained hers, but she had a splendid brain and a tremendously strong personality. It was impossible to persuade Aunt Celia to act contrary to her judgment."

"Very true," murmured Mr. Wanlock, sipping his sherry with every appearance of enjoyment.

Maurice talked on, extolling Aunt Celia, and Humphrey had an opportunity to glance round the table. Humphrey was thankful to see that Alice was feeling better and was eating her fish quite happily — a few minutes earlier he had looked at her and had received the impression that she was on the verge of tears — he had no idea what had upset Alice nor what had restored her; it was rather mysterious, really. Mr. Wanlock wore a prim expression, he was as close as an oyster; Nina looked like a cat with a bowl of cream in front of her, a very elegant well-bred pussy-cat, thought Humphrey, eyeing her with a good deal of admiration . . . and last but not least there was Maurice, his smooth round face shining with good-humour and complacency. (Humphrey wondered what Maurice's face would look like to-morrow when he heard . . . it was an uncomfortable thought). Maurice was good-looking, he was well set-up and impeccably dressed and Nina was his natural mate. They were a handsome pair — nobody could deny that, thought Humphrey. If Dunnian belonged to Maurice he would polish up the old house till it shone; he would entertain largely and magnificently; the old house would be filled with smooth, successful, well set-up men, like Maurice, and elegant women (like Nina) with high-heeled shoes and shining curls. But Dunnian would never belong to Maurice (thought Humphrey), Dunnian was coming to him and Alice — Aunt Celia had said so and he never doubted for a moment that she had kept her word. For a moment Humphrey felt quite alarmed. Would he and Alice be able to "live up to" the place? They were used to a different standard of life and to all sorts of makeshifts and expediencies; this would be quite a new experience with new responsibilities, and new problems to solve . . . and then he remembered the children and his heart was suddenly at peace, for the children would make the old house into a home and that was what it should be. Dunnian had been built by old Humphrey Dunne, not as a sort of glorified hotel in which to entertain strangers, but as a family house for his children and his children's children. Young Humphrey raised his eyes and saw old Humphrey looking down at him from the wall. It was a friendly look.

They had finished dinner, and Humphrey had risen to open the door for the ladies, when they were all considerably surprised to hear the sound of wheels on the drive.

"Who's that, I wonder!" exclaimed Maurice, getting up from his chair.

"Someone with flowers," suggested Nina, for flowers had been arriving all day, tributes to Miss Dunne from all over the county.

"Not flowers at this hour," Maurice said.

For some reason they were all interested, and they were all in the hall when the front door was opened. A small slight woman appeared out of the darkness and walked in. She was about sixty, Humphrey thought; she was dressed in a grey squirrel coat and was carrying a dressing-case in her hand. Her hair was white beneath her small red toque and her eyes were brown and very bright. She stood there looking at them and it was obvious that she was surprised to see them here — just as surprised as they were to see her. Humphrey was the first to find his tongue. He went forward and took the dressing-case from her hand. "I think you must be Cousin Henrietta," he declared, smiling down at her.

"Yes," she said, looking at him uncertainly.

"Aunt Celia told me about you."

"Is she — is she ill?"

"Didn't you get the telegram?"

"No, I left home two days ago — I stayed in London. Oh, dear, don't say she's very ill. I had a letter from her, you know. She said she wanted to see me, and somehow or other I felt — I had a feeling — so I just packed up and came." She looked round the little group and added, "Oh, dear, you don't mean —"

"She was very old, you know," Humphrey said. The control of the situation seemed to have passed into his hands — he did not know how or why.

"I know," agreed Mrs. Lacey. "I know she was old. Oh, dear, why didn't I come before?" She sat down suddenly on the big sofa which stood at the bottom of the stairs and took out her handkerchief. "Oh, dear," she said again. "I was looking forward to seeing her — it's been such a long journey —"

"You must be tired," said Humphrey. "We'll have a room prepared —" he looked at Nina as he spoke.

"Of course," said Nina, coming forward.

When Mrs. Lacey had tidied herself and had been fed on what remained of the dinner she rejoined the rest of the party in the drawing-room and Humphrey, for one, was exceedingly glad to see her. He was feeling the strain by this time, the strain of talking to Maurice and avoiding difficult ground. They had discussed the latest play in London — *The Little Michus* — and the latest star which had just arisen in the theatrical firmament — her name was Lily Elsie — and they had both agreed that her song, "Nobody from Nowhere," was the high light in the play. But even that subject was not inexhaustible, and when it was exhausted neither of them could find another. Maurice was just as embarrassed as Humphrey; he found himself playing the part of a genial host and pulled himself up with a jerk for, although he was in reality Humphrey's host, it would not look well to assume the part until the matter was officially confirmed.

Humphrey, on the other hand, wished to appear non-committal — neutral as it were — it would be hypocritical to acknowledge Maurice as his host, it was exceedingly difficult not to. There was the little incident of the "drinks" for instance. Humphrey wanted a drink. It would help a good deal to have a drink at his elbow, Humphrey felt. Should he rise and ring the bell and ask for it? No, that would be a bit too free and easy. Should he ask Maurice for a drink? No, he didn't feel he could do that, either. He thought about it for a little and at last he hit on a middle course. "What about drinks, Maurice?" he suggested.

"Of course," cried Maurice. "How stupid of me! Why didn't you say so before . . . I mean," he added in a different tone. "I mean of course we must just ask for — for anything we want, mustn't we?"

"Yes," said Humphrey firmly.

"Yes. So if you ring the bell I'll — er — order the drinks," said Maurice.

But even with a whisky and soda on the table beside him Humphrey still felt uncomfortable. He felt a blank. They were incomplete. Aunt Celia ought to be here, sitting in her own straight-backed chair. The chair was empty and once or twice Humphrey found himself glancing towards it as if he half-expected to see the small, dainty figure sitting there . . . her grey silk dress spread out all round her and a red rose pinned to her bodice with a diamond brooch.

So it was that when Mrs. Lacey appeared, looking somewhat restored, Humphrey welcomed her with open arms.

"Here you are!" he exclaimed, rising to give her his seat. "Come and sit near the fire, Cousin Henrietta."

"Thank you, Maurice," she replied.

"I'm Humphrey," said Humphrey hastily. "That's Maurice and that's Nina and this is Alice, my wife."

"Uncle Harry's son," she said, looking at Humphrey with interest. "No, Uncle Harry's grandson, of course. I remember him quite well. You're rather like him you know, you're a real Dunne. Maurice takes after his mother's side of the family."

"Some people think I'm like my grandfather," Maurice declared.

"No," said Mrs. Lacey, looking at him critically. "No, I can see no resemblance whatever. Grandpapa was an extremely handsome man."

Neither Maurice nor Nina was pleased at this statement and Humphrey thought it time to change the subject. He saw that Cousin Henrietta did not think it necessary to be tactful but preferred to speak exactly what was in her mind. She was like Aunt Celia in this as well as in other ways. All the same he was very grateful for her presence; perhaps to-morrow when the awful moment arrived he might be able to shelter behind her petticoats.

CHAPTER
SEVEN

Becky

The following morning was fine and dry. Humphrey retired to the library to write some necessary letters and while he was there Becky came in and asked if she might speak to him.

"Of course," said Humphrey at once. He drew up a chair and made her sit down . . . how tired and haggard she looked! Her plain black dress was as neat as ever and she was perfectly composed, but her eyes were red-rimmed with tears. Humphrey did not know what to say to Becky but he need not have worried for Becky had come to talk — not to listen.

"I'm glad you're to be here, sir," she said. "Oh, yes, I know all about it. Miss Dunne talked to me about it many a time. She knew I was safe to talk to. There's some people will get a shock this afternoon when the will's read, and serve them right. They never came here except to suck up — but Miss Dunne could see as far through a brick wall as most people. I was with her thirty years, Mr. Humphrey."

"I know," he replied. "She spoke to me about you. She said you were a true friend."

"Did she say that?" asked Becky with a little tremor in her carefully controlled voice. "It was nice. I won't forget it — and it was good of you to tell me. She was a great lady. There was so much in her; so much interest. She was old but she was never dull, not dull in herself nor dull to other people. You couldn't be dull when you were with her for she was so unexpected. You would think she was cross and all at once she would be laughing! Oh, she was a bit impatient sometimes, but never for long — and she was always just. Her heart was gold. The one thing that she couldn't stand was sham and affectation. She liked everything above board; she liked people to look her in the face and say what they were thinking. That was why she couldn't abide Mrs. Maurice with her soft, smarmy ways."

Humphrey glanced at the door.

"It's all right," Becky assured him. "They've gone down the garden to decide where the new greenhouse is to be put."

Humphrey could not help smiling and he saw that there was the ghost of a smile lingering round Becky's mouth. He said, "Everything will be kept the same."

"She didn't mean that," said Becky thoughtfully. "She knew there would have to be changes. She wouldn't want you to feel tied, Mr. Humphrey. She said to me, just that very morning before she died, she said to me, 'Changes are coming, Becky. They have to come but I'm too old to like them.' I'm glad I was with her at the last."

"So am I."

"Yes, she thought she'd be frightened but she wasn't frightened at all. I was pouring out her tea for her — she

54

liked a cup of tea at eleven in the morning — and suddenly she said quite naturally, 'I'm going now, Becky.' She said it so natural that at first I didn't know what she meant — I thought she meant she was going down the garden and I didn't want her to — and then I looked at her and saw she was very white and I thought I would give her the medicine . . . but there wasn't time. There wasn't time for anything. She just looked up and smiled and she was gone. She wasn't frightened."

"I'm glad," said Humphrey uncertainly. There was a lump in his throat.

"It was a good way to go," said Becky, nodding. "I've been blaming myself for letting her do too much the day before but maybe it was all for the best. She wanted to see the garden and she saw it. I'm not grieving for her — it's for myself I'm grieving. She was a part of me — the best part. She's spoilt me for other people, that's the truth of it. Maybe I shan't be long after her."

"You're quite young, Becky," Humphrey said.

"I'm fifty-one," said Becky. "It's not old — but I feel like a hundred."

"I know you're bound to feel like that, but perhaps —"

"I've nothing to *do*," she broke in desperately. "I've looked after her all these years and now there's nothing to do for her any more."

Humphrey was silent for a few moments and then he said, "I should be very grateful if you'll stay on here and look after things."

"I'll see," said Becky. "I didn't think you'd be wanting me. I don't quite know. Dunnian isn't the same without her, but maybe another place would be worse. I'll stay on a wee while and see how I feel — that is if you're sure Mrs. Humphrey will want me."

"Of course we shall want you."

She smiled. "Oh, well, I'll stay till you get settled in. Maybe it will be difficult for Mrs. Humphrey at first; moving and getting settled in a strange place."

Humphrey was obliged to hide a smile. He thought of all the strange places to which Alice had moved, bag and baggage, with nobody at all to help her; and of all the arrivals (sometimes late at night) with the babies tired and cross after the journey. Alice had had to contend with unsympathetic landladies, she had been obliged to improvise and make things do. Nobody would think, to look at Alice, that she was a capable woman, but somehow or other she had "managed" and even in the most unlikely places she had created an atmosphere of home. Alice could move to Dunnian and settle in as easily as a bird settling on to its nest . . . but all the same it would be quite a good thing if Becky would stay and help her.

"I've plenty to live on," Becky was saying. "There's no need for you to worry about me. Miss Dunne took out an annuity for me and I get it paid every month. It was her own idea: she wanted me to be independent, so she said. I could take a wee house in Ryddelton and be quite comfortable, too."

"You must do exactly as you like," Humphrey told her. He wondered if he ought to thank her for all she had done, for looking after Aunt Celia so well, but somehow he felt it would be an impertinence. Aunt Celia had meant so much more to Becky than to himself. Becky was the only person on earth who was really deeply grieved at Aunt Celia's death, it was a personal loss to Becky as it could not be to him. He sighed and added, "I wish I had known her better."

"I wish you had," nodded Becky. "She was well worth knowing — but it couldn't be helped. Sailors have to go where they're sent. She often spoke of you, Mr. Humphrey, and she always had the little photograph of the children on the table beside her bed. She used to look at the picture and say, 'The boy is a Dunne. I like the look of him, Becky.' It's a pity she couldn't have seen the children, isn't it?"

"She didn't like children, Becky."

"She'd have liked to *see* them," Becky declared. "Especially Master Mark."

CHAPTER
EIGHT

Aftermath

Alice was lying on her bed with a hot water-bottle at her feet and a handkerchief, soaked in eau de cologne, on her forehead. The blinds were drawn down and the window was open at the bottom. It was very peaceful; she could hear the whisper of the river in the distance, and the blind was making a little tapping noise against the window, but apart from these gentle noises there was no sound at all; she felt relaxed and the pain in her head began to subside. It was nice to be taken care of like this, thought Alice. Becky was really kind. Somehow or other Alice was aware that Becky had enjoyed taking care of her . . .

The door opened very quietly and Alice knew, by the sounds of movement in the room, that Becky — or somebody — had come in. She hoped it was Becky, for even Humphrey would be less welcome at the moment.

"Is that you, Becky?" she asked.

"Yes, I've brought you a wee cup of tea," replied Becky in a low voice. "D'you think you could take a wee cup of tea, Mrs. Dunne?"

Alice thought she could. She raised herself a little and Becky slipped another pillow behind her head and settled the tray. "There," said Becky cheerfully. "There we are. You're looking a wee bit better already. A cup of tea will be just the thing. I'll pour it out for you, shall I?"

"You might lock the door, Becky," said Alice, looking towards it apprehensively.

"Lock the door?"

"I've just thought . . . perhaps she might come up . . ."

"They've gone," said Becky, nodding significantly.

"Gone away!"

"Yes, just this minute. I was watching from the stair window. They couldn't get the motor car to start and then suddenly it started and away they went. I wouldn't trust myself to one of those machines for a good deal."

"Oh, dear, it was awful," said Alice with a groan.

"Don't think about it," advised Becky. "Drink up your tea and don't think about it any more. It's over now. We won't see them again in a hurry."

"You don't think they'll come back?"

"No, I don't."

"He said he was going to see his lawyer. He said he would bring his lawyer here —"

"His lawyer couldn't do a thing. What could he do? You may be sure Mr. Wanlock has made everything water-tight. That's what Miss Dunne used to say, 'I've told him to make it water-tight,' she said. No, no, there's little need to worry. Mr. Maurice said a good deal but it was just talk."

"*Talk!*" exclaimed Alice, moving her head on the pillow. It seemed a colourless word to describe the terrific row which had taken place. She shuddered as she thought of it — the scene rose before her eyes and made her feel quite sick. Loud voices and angry words were bad enough at any time and in any place, but here and now, in the cloistered peace of Dunnian library with the mistress of Dunnian only just that moment in her grave, they had seemed like desecration. Alice had known that Maurice and Nina would be angry and disappointed but she had never imagined that they would behave "like that." It was like a scene in the nursery; only of course a thousand times worse, for these were not children. Oddly enough it was Mr. Wanlock who had come in for most of the abuse.

"You influenced her," Maurice had roared. "She was in her dotage and you persuaded her to alter her will."

Mr. Wanlock might have replied that Miss Dunne was not a person who could be influenced but he had said nothing. He sat quite still in his chair with his mouth buttoned up.

"You knew all the time — all of you," Nina had stormed. "You were laughing at us, I suppose, thinking you had made fools of us, but it isn't settled yet. We'll see who are the fools — we'll see —"

"Really, Nina!" Mrs. Lacey had exclaimed, her soft voice breaking in upon Nina's ravings. "Really, Nina, one would think ... we all know this is a disappointment to you, but surely there's no need to shout like that ... the servants, Nina ..."

But Nina was past caring what the servants thought. "You knew, too," she declared, turning upon Cousin Henrietta like a fury. "You took good care that your bequest wasn't cut out of the new will ..."

"I knew nothing," replied Cousin Henrietta with spirit. "I shan't say I'm not glad of the money, because it will make a lot of difference, but —"

"You knew she intended to humiliate Maurice and me."

"I knew nothing," repeated Cousin Henrietta. "I knew nothing at all about it but I think Aunt Celia was very wise to leave the place to Humphrey."

"It was just like her," cried Nina. "Horrible deceitful old woman! When I think of all I've done for her — and all the times I've stayed in this nasty shabby old house —"

"Really, Nina —"

"It's Humphrey's fault," she declared. "Yes, I can see the whole thing. That's why he came here in June, to wheedle the old lady, to flatter her and insinuate himself into her good graces . . ."

She had raged on but Humphrey had not replied. His face had gone hard, hard like a stone, only his eyes had blazed.

When Nina had finished, Maurice began again, "I shall see my lawyer," he declared, spluttering with rage.

"You had better see your doctor as well," put in Cousin Henrietta, raising her voice above the din. "You are not at all a good colour, Maurice, I should be afraid of apoplexy if I were you."

It was at this point that Alice had left the room (she had got up and gone and nobody had noticed her departure). She had been obliged to leave the room because she was almost certain that she was going to faint . . .

"It was awful," said Alice again.

"It sounded awful," said Becky, nodding. "I could hear the noise from the top landing."

"She said Humphrey was a snake in the grass."

"Did she?" said Becky, soothingly. "Well, who cares what *she* says. Mr. Humphrey is a very nice gentleman indeed."

"She was the worst," declared Alice.

"She would be," agreed Becky, "but never mind. They've gone away. You have another cup of tea and forget about it."

"I can't," Alice said. "I shall never forget it, Becky, never so long as I live. The house didn't like it."

"The house?"

"No," said Alice, shaking her head. "It was wrong anywhere, but worse here. Dunnian didn't like it."

Becky looked at her in some alarm. "You shouldn't have gone down," she declared. "You shouldn't have been there —"

"I know, but I wanted to be there, in case — but I wasn't any use at all. Mrs. Lacey was far more use than I was."

"She's a warrior," said Becky smiling. "She's a wee bit like Miss Dunne — knows her mind and isn't afraid to speak it."

There was a little silence and then Alice said, "What are they doing now?"

"They're having tea on the terrace — the three of them — you can hear them talking if you listen."

Alice listened, she heard the sound of voices and the chink of tea-cups ... and suddenly she heard

Humphrey's laugh. It was a deep-throated laugh,
whole-hearted and infectious, and the sound of it
comforted Alice considerable. If Humphrey could laugh
like that . . .

"You see — they're laughing," said Becky as she took
away the tray.

Alice felt so much better that she was able to come
down to dinner, and what a different meal it was from
last night! They were all cheerful, almost gay, it was as if
a cloud had vanished from the sky. Even Mr. Wanlock
came out of his shell and became quite human and
jovial. He told funny stories — quite proper ones, of
course — and made them all laugh heartily. During the
fish course when Humphrey and his cousin were talking
of something else, Mr. Wanlock leaned forward and said
to Alice, "Are you thinking of sending the children to
Margate, Mrs. Dunne?" and Alice saw the joke at once
and replied, "Some doctors believe in hill air, Mr.
Wanlock."

"What's the joke?" inquired Humphrey when he saw
them laughing, but Mr. Wanlock would not tell him.
"It's a private joke," he said. "A private joke between
Mrs. Dunne and me, you wouldn't understand it."

Alice had impressed Mr. Wanlock very favourably;
she was exactly the sort of woman he admired and he
was of the opinion that Humphrey had been extremely
fortunate. Some naval men married impossible women.
If Mr. Wanlock had known Alice before, he would not
have tried to persuade old Miss Dunne to leave the
property to Maurice — no indeed — he would have

concentrated all his efforts on the other point and tried to persuade her to entail Dunnian instead of leaving it to an unborn child . . . and who can say that I might not have succeeded, Mr. Wanlock thought. By the time Mr. Wanlock had argued the first point and been defeated he had used up all his ammunition (so to speak) and had had his failure to hamper him and to destroy his morale. It really was most unfortunate; however . . .

"There are several little details to be settled," said Mr. Wanlock, smiling at Alice in a friendly way. "Perhaps you would rather leave it for a day or two. I must return to Edinburgh to-morrow, I'm afraid, but I could come back on Monday."

"I'm going south to-morrow," Alice said.

"But Alice!" exclaimed her husband. "There are all sorts of things to be settled —"

"I can be back by the middle of next week."

"But why —"

"I'm going south to fetch the children."

"To bring them here?"

"Yes, of course. It will take me three days to pack. I can be back here on Wednesday."

"You can't," Humphrey declared. "There are all sorts of things to be done. The place isn't ready for them."

"It looks quite ready to me."

"You mean you're going to settle in without doing anything."

Alice nodded.

"We're going to put in electric light," said Humphrey patiently. "We're going to put in another bathroom; Mr. Wanlock is going to see a builder about it."

"It will make a considerable mess," Mr. Wanlock explained.

"But Humphrey —"

"Aunt Celia told me that she wanted me to do it, Alice."

"Yes, and we will," said Alice. "We'll do it all. We'll put in two more bathrooms and a new kitchen range, and we'll make another window in the servants' hall. The pantry must have a new sink and — oh, there are several other things that want doing."

"Well, then," said Humphrey, somewhat surprised at having the wind taken out of his sails in this fashion. "Well, then, Alice —"

"But we aren't going to do it *now*," said Alice firmly. "There isn't time. We'll move in at once and leave all the alterations until next year."

"She's right, you know," said Cousin Henrietta. "Alice is absolutely right. You should move into the house, bag and baggage."

"You mean in case Maurice —"

"Yes, possession is nine points of the law — and, besides, when you've lived here for a bit you'll know exactly what you want to do."

"I know I'm right," Alice declared. "Portsmouth has never suited the children. They need a change and I'm going to bring them here."

"I'll come south and help you, of course," said Humphrey.

PART 2

Children in the House

CHAPTER
NINE

Mark

It seemed to Mark that they had been in the train for days and days. At first he had asked continually, "Are we nearly there?" but after a bit he had given up asking — he had given up hope of ever reaching Dunnian — and then, quite suddenly, Daddy had got up and begun to take the things down from the rack, and Mummy collected her belongings and stowed them into her bag. Edith was asleep, she was cross when they wakened her, and Baby was asleep too, but she woke up by herself and stared round with big blue eyes.

"Hurry, Mark," said Daddy. "Put on your coat. Come on, old fellow."

"Is this Dunnian?"

"No, it's Ryddelton. The train doesn't go to Dunnian. We've got some way to drive."

"Don't cry, Edith," said Mummy. "Hold up your chin while I tie your bonnet."

The train stopped with a jerk and they all bundled out. It was quite dark, of course, and the platform was dimly lit but several people emerged from the shadows and seized the rugs and bags and baskets. Mark saw a tall lady in a black coat, and a short red-faced man in a green coat with silver buttons. Mark clung to Daddy's hand for he was a little shy with strangers. The train did not stop very long, it steamed away out of the station and left them standing on the platform surrounded by luggage — prams and cots and baskets and trunks, most of which were extremely shabby, having accompanied the family half-way round the world.

"Say, how do you do to Becky," said Daddy, pushing Mark's hand foward.

He said "How do you do," obediently and shook hands with the tall lady — and then held out his hand to the red-faced man.

"How do you do, Master Mark," said the man, seizing his hand and shaking it cordially.

Everybody seemed to be shaking hands and talking — there was excitement in the air.

"We mustn't stand here, it's cold," said Daddy.

"I'll take Baby," said Becky, seizing the bundle of shawls from Mummy's arms. "Downie can take Miss Edith. Pick her up, Downie, she's half asleep, poor wee lamb."

They talked in a funny way, Mark noticed. Their voices went up and down — as if they were singing — but he liked it.

"What about the luggage?" Mummy asked.

"Wilson will bring it up in the cart."

They moved out of the station into the yard. It was quite dark here, and there was a sort of nip in the air. Mark felt it catch his throat but he managed to choke back his cough. There was a carriage waiting for them, it had two horses and two little lamps on the sides and it was very shiny — not like a cab.

"That's our crest," said Mark, pointing to the little picture on the door.

"Of course it is," agreed Downie. "You're a Dunne, Master Mark."

Clip clop, clippety cloppety clop went the horses' feet on the road. The carriage was rolling along smoothly and the hedges slipped past the window . . . Mark saw dark hedges and tall dark trees outlined against the sky. The grown-up conversation slid in at one ear and out of the other.

"I found a nurse," Becky was saying. "It was lucky, really. She had *very* good references so I just engaged her as you said. I hope you'll like her, Mrs. Dunne, if not —"

"I'm sure I shall like her," said Mummy.

"Cook decided to stay on after all. She's a little difficult sometimes but she's very reliable and trustworthy."

"Mrs. Lacey —"

"She's still here," said Becky. "She thought she might be able to help you; there's letters and papers to be looked through."

"We must get on to that job," Daddy said.

It was dull talk, thought Mark, gazing out of the window. His heart was beating rather fast for they were getting near Dunnian now. "Dunnian" was a sort of magic word to Mark, it had been on everybody's lips for days . . . "When we get to Dunnian —" "You can have that when we get to Dunnian." "It will be all right when we get to Dunnian." "Never mind, darling, just wait till we get to Dunnian." And now they were nearly there.

The carriage swung round and Mark saw that they were passing between stone pillars. The horses' feet made a different sound now, a crunching sound, and the hedges had come closer. Mark would have liked to ask, "Are we nearly there?" but the grown-ups were talking and he did not like to interrupt. The horses were going slower now for it was up-hill, and the hedges had vanished. There was grass at either side and tall trees . . . and then suddenly Mark saw a big house with lighted windows and he knew that they had arrived.

The front door stood wide open and a shaft of light streamed out into the night. Mark was dazed by the sudden glare in the hall. There were more people here, a little old lady in a black dress, who kissed him and said he was like his great-grandfather, and maids with white aprons and smiling faces; and then, somehow or other, Mark found himself walking up the broad shallow staircase and discovered that his legs were very tired.

"This way, I'll show you," said Becky, taking his hand.

"Mummy," he said, "You come too, Mummy —" but Mummy didn't hear.

There was a fire blazing in the nursery grate and the table was covered with a white cloth, and there were spoons and mugs and blue bowls laid out on it, and there was a small fat person with a starched apron bustling about and talking all the time.

"Yes," she was saying. "Yes, it's all ready. I'll just put Baby into my own bed until the cot comes. Yes, I'll manage fine. Take off your coat, Mark, there's a good boy."

"Mummy —" began Mark uncertainly.

"Mummy will be up presently when you've had your supper. You like bread and milk, don't you? That's the boy! We'll wash your hands first — my word, they're dirty, aren't they?"

"I want Mummy," said Mark.

"Yes, she'll come soon. She's going to have her dinner. You're a big boy, aren't you? I should think you were six."

"I'm five and a half."

"Well, I never! You *are* big. The little boy I was with before was six and a half and he wasn't as big as you."

This was very gratifying, and Mark began to feel better. "What's your name?" he asked as he held his hands over the basin and had them thoroughly scrubbed.

"Nannie," she replied, smiling down at him.

"We had an amah in China," Mark said.

"My word! Fancy you having been to China. You'll tell me all about it, won't you?"

Suddenly Mark felt that horrible tickle at the back of his throat. He swallowed hard but it was no use. He began to cough and he went on coughing and whooping — then he was sick. As a rule Mark hated being sick when any one was there — even when the person was Mummy — but somehow or other it didn't seem to matter with "Nannie." She took it as a matter of course. She didn't mind a bit. She wasn't sorry for him.

"I'm not really 'fectious," said Mark hoarsely.

"No, of course not," she agreed. "What a good thing you were sick now instead of waiting until after supper! It was clever of you, wasn't it?"

"Yes," said Mark, smiling a trifle wanly.

"We'll get a bottle of emulsion. I know all about whooping-cough. We want to get rid of it before the winter sets in — once you get clementised," said Nannie cheerfully. "Once you get clementised your cough will go like winking."

"Clementised," repeated Mark, nodding. He thought it was a nice new word — as indeed it was.

"Used to the new kind of air," Nannie explained.

"Yes, of course," said Mark.

He had felt a little shy of Nannie but now they were friends and they ate their supper together in complete accord. You couldn't go on feeling shy with a person who was so understanding, so small and busy and talkative, so interested in all you told her. He quite forgot that he had felt "funny" and wanted Mummy to come, and he was quite surprised when the door opened and Mummy appeared.

"Is everything all right?" asked Mummy.

"Yes, ma'am," replied Nannie, rising from her chair. "The little girls are both asleep and Mark's nearly finished his supper. We won't bother with a bath tonight, he'll just go straight off, I expect. We're getting on *very* nice. Yes, ma'am, everything's quite all right."

Mummy sat down for a minute and Nannie, who had finished her supper, bustled about, putting everything to rights. "It's a lovely nursery," she declared. "Such nice cupboards and cork carpet on the floor and nice light washable blinds. I had wooden blinds in my last nursery, nasty heavy things that were always going wrong — venereal blinds they were called."

Mummy laughed and choked. Her voice was quite trembly as she said, "I'm glad you like the nursery, Nannie."

"I'd be hard to please if I didn't," said Nannie emphatically.

The next morning was fine and sunny. Nannie took out her sewing and settled herself on the seat beneath the old beech-tree at the end of the lawn. Baby was asleep in the pram and Edith was sitting on a rug looking at a picture book. Mark stood and stared about him. It was all so strange. It was all so different — even the air had a different kind of smell.

"You needn't stay here," said Nannie, smiling at him. "Go and explore, Mark."

It was a new word. "Explore?" he asked.

"Go and look round," explained Nannie. "Go wherever you like. I'll call you when it's time for your milk."

He walked away across the grass. It was funny to walk on grass instead of on pavements; it was funny to be told you could go wherever you liked. Once or twice he stopped and looked back at the little group beneath the tree. Nannie waved to him, and he waved back. He felt big and grown up. He was going to explore.

There was a path leading down between the trees and bushes. Mark walked along solemnly. He heard the birds singing and a rushing sound in the distance; that was the sea, of course. It was funny to walk along all by yourself with nobody in sight. It was rather nice, but — but supposing you got lost? Supposing you couldn't find your way back? He hesitated and looked up the path — there was nothing to be seen but trees and bushes. He began to go back and then he stopped again. He was going to explore. He hadn't explored anything yet. Nannie would think he was silly. Mark turned again. He put his hands in his pockets and marched on, head in air. Presently he came to a big high wall with a door in it. The door was open and Mark stood in the entrance and looked in. There was a garden inside the door, a huge big garden with all sorts of things growing in it and there was a man with a rake, raking one of the beds. Mark watched the man for a little. The man couldn't object to Mark looking in at the door and watching him.

When he had finished raking the bed the man looked up and saw Mark and said, "Good-morning."

"Good-morning," said Mark politely.

"It's a fine day," said the man.

"This is a very nice garden," said Mark.

"It's not bad. Are you coming in, Master Mark?"

"May I?" asked Mark eagerly.

The man laughed. He said, "Well, I don't know who's got a better right. Come away in and we'll find an apple."

Mark came in and looked round. He followed the man along the path and soon they came to a part of the wall where there were trees growing, little trees with apples on them.

"I'll need to find you a ripe one," said the man. "They ripen early on this wall. It faces south."

Mark watched him looking for a ripe apple. He said, "I live at Dunnian, now."

"So do I," replied the man. "I was born here. My name's Johnson."

"It's a very nice name," said Mark politely.

Johnson picked an apple off a tree and offered it to Mark.

"Thank you," said Mark taking it and looking at it. The apple was small but it was very pretty — yellow and brown and red.

"Are you not going to eat it?" Johnson inquired.

"Mummy peels them," explained Mark.

"You don't want it peeled. Bite it. That's what your teeth are for."

Mark bit a small piece off the apple. It was sweet and juicy. "It's very nice," he said. "Mummy will pay you for it."

"That's good!" declared Johnson, laughing heartily. "That's the best thing I've heard for a long time." He took out a huge red handkerchief and blew his nose violently.

"Don't you want to be paid?" asked Mark uncertainly.

"It's your own apple," replied Johnson.

"My apple?"

"Well, your father's apple, then. This is your father's garden, Master Mark."

"All of it?" asked Mark, looking round in amazement.

"Every bit."

Mark said nothing. He could find nothing to say.

"Have you been down to the river?" Johnson asked.

"Is it near here?"

"Can you not hear it?"

"I thought that was the sea," explained Mark. "I'm more used to the sea . . ."

"Come and I'll show you the river," said Johnson.

Mark took Johnson's hand — it was terrifically hard and horny, but there was a nice friendly feeling in it all the same — and they went across the garden and out of another door in the wall. The noise of the rushing water was much louder here, it grew and grew, and a moment later they were standing on a bank with rocks all round and looking down at a little waterfall.

"What do you think of that?" Johnson inquired.

Mark did not know what to think of it. He had never seen anything like it before. The noise of the falling water was so loud and the sun shining on the spray was so dazzling that Mark felt glad he had hold of Johnson's hand.

"There's nothing to be frightened of," Johnson said.

"No," agreed Mark in a doubtful tone.

They stood and watched it for a few moments.

"Is that where the fish lives?" asked Mark after a little, raising his voice to be heard above the roar.

"What fish?"

"The fish that Daddy and I are going to catch — is that where it lives?"

"I shouldn't wonder," said Johnson.

Mark was in bed (he was very tired after his first day at Dunnian, there had been so much to do and see). He had said his prayers and Nannie was just going to turn out the lamp when Daddy looked in.

"Here's Daddy!" Nannie exclaimed. "Now you'll be a happy boy!"

Mark was quite happy already but he was delighted to see Daddy. He put his arms round Daddy's neck and kissed him.

"Had a good day?" asked Daddy.

Mark nodded. Of course he had — this was Dunnian.

"You've made a lot of new friends," said Daddy.

Mark nodded again. "Who is the lady?" he asked.

"What lady? Do you mean Cousin Henrietta?"

"No."

"Becky, then?"

"No," said Mark, shaking his head vigorously.

"Who do you mean?"

"She's nice," said Mark. "She's old but she's very nice."

"Did she speak to you?"

"No," said Mark.

"I don't know who it could be," said Daddy, wrinkling his forehead.

"He's been talking about her all the time he was having his supper," Nannie declared. "He said he met her on the stairs —"

"A lady," repeated Mark nodding.

"What was she like?"

Mark could not answer this. He knew what she was like, of course, but he did not know how to describe her.

"Did she know you?" Daddy asked.

"Yes," said Mark. "Yes, of *course*. She knew I was Mark. She was pleased to see me."

"But she didn't speak to you?"

"No."

"She's a mystery," said Daddy, laughing.

"Is that her name?"

"What?"

"Miss Terry," said Mark.

"I think it must be," Daddy said.

CHAPTER
TEN

Settling In

The parish church in Ryddelton was always very well attended but for a long time now the Dunnian pew had stood empty save for the slim figure of Becky in her neat black coat and hat. On the Sunday morning, following the arrival of the Humphrey Dunnes, Becky was early on the scene and instead of sitting in her usual place she moved up the pew to the far end, leaving vacant a large expanse of red-cushioned seat. This unusual circumstance was noticed by a good many people with a good deal of interest.

After a bit there was a rustle of silk and Mrs. Humphrey Dunne swept up the aisle. She was followed by a little lady in black and, behind the little lady, came a tall man with a clean-shaven face and a very small boy in a sailor suit.

A little stir, like wind in a field of corn, passed through the church. Heads were turned and necks were craned eagerly. Some of the Ryddelton people knew the Maurice Dunnes and thought they had been badly treated, others held the opinion that Miss Dunne was entitled to do as she pleased with her own property, but one and all were anxious to see the newcomers for, in a small community such as Ryddelton, it mattered a good deal what sort of people one had as neighbours. The Dunnes appeared unconscious of the interest they had aroused. They filed into the Dunnian pew and sat down.

On the other side of the aisle was the Raeworths' pew. Mr. Raeworth was tall and grey-haired, Mrs. Raeworth was small and plump. They sat one at each end of the seat and between them sat two of their children, Andrew and Angela. Andrew had heard about the "Dunne boy" and was so anxious to see what he looked like that he stood on a hassock and leaned right over the book-rest . . . he was pulled back to his proper place by his mother. Mrs. Raeworth had not turned her head but somehow or other she had accomplished the seemingly impossible and had caught a glimpse of "the new Mrs. Dunne." Grey silk and black furs and a large black hat — all very nice and proper.

I shall call, thought Mrs. Raeworth as she rose for the first psalm, I shall call at once. Dear old Miss Dunne would like me to call . . . it will be nice to have neighbours with children.

Lady Skene was even less conveniently placed for seeing her new neighbours, for the Skenes always sat in the front pew. She heard the stir and was aware what had occasioned it, but she would have to wait until after the service to make up her mind about the newcomers (Lady Skene's daughter-in-law was a friend of Nina Dunne and had written to Lady Skene saying that the Humphreys were quite impossible . . . but Lady Skene was not prepared to accept this statement as gospel truth. She would judge for herself). Unfortunately she was delayed after the service and reached the church door just as the Dunnian carriage was driving away. She stood there, peering after it with her short-sighted eyes, but it was nothing but a blur.

"*Quite* nice," said Evelyn Raeworth's voice at her elbow. "Grey silk and black furs — just right, don't you think?"

"You mean black might have been just a little —"

"Yes, I think so," said Mrs. Raeworth nodding.

"I shall call, anyway," said Lady Skene. "I mean there are so few people now, and Celia would have liked me to call."

"I'm sure you're right."

The Skene carriage had driven up to the door but Lady Skene hesitated. She said in a low voice, "Did Celia ever give you a hint —"

"Never," replied Mrs. Raeworth.

They looked at each other and smiled. "Just like her," said Lady Skene with a deep chuckle.

The county called in state. Broughams with sleek horses drove up to the door of Dunnian House and deposited ladies in furs with card-cases clasped in their hands on the Dunnian doorstep . . . and Alice received them with smiles and polite conversation and regaled them with tea and cakes. It was a new experience for Alice and at first she was somewhat alarmed but she soon discovered that there was nothing to be afraid of — everyone was very friendly. Humphrey had gone by this time, he had rejoined his ship, and Cousin Henrietta had returned to Bournemouth so Alice was alone in her drawing-room.

"My dear," said Lady Skene as she settled herself in the most comfortable chair she could see. "My dear, you must take your proper place in the country. A few little dinners perhaps —"

"Not until Humphrey comes back!" cried Alice in dismay.

"No, perhaps not, but we must see what we can do. Dear old Celia was one of my best friends. She was a personality — one of the old guard. She will be greatly missed."

"Oh, I know," agreed Alice. "I'm afraid I could never —"

"You'll find everyone quite ready to be friendly — too ready perhaps. You must pick and choose, Mrs. Dunne. Some *very* queer people have come into the neighbourhood. They'll probably call. You must return the call, of course, but be sure to go on a fine afternoon when they will be out — and then make an end."

"Yes," said Alice meekly.

"I shall look after you, of course," declared Lady Skene. "I shall give a little luncheon to introduce you to the county — just a few of the right people."

"It's very kind of you, Lady Skene."

"Not at all. We're very glad you've come," said Lady Skene with a royal air. "We did not care for Nina. In any case they would have spent at least half their time in town. It's much more satisfactory to have settled neighbours. Personally I think Celia has been well advised to leave the place to Humphrey and I shall say so to all my friends."

"I'm glad," said Alice, smiling happily. "I was afraid, perhaps —"

"Dear me, no," interrupted Lady Skene. "Everyone knows that Celia always did exactly as she pleased. Nobody on earth could have wheedled Celia into doing anything that she didn't want to do. Of course the Maurices are furious."

"Yes, I'm afraid so."

"I had a letter from my daughter-in-law — my son is stationed in Edinburgh at the moment — and she tells me that Nina is positively ill with rage. I must say I should have liked to see her face when she heard that all her trouble had been wasted."

"I don't think you would have liked it," said Alice with more spirit than she had shown.

"Oh, it was as bad as that, was it!" exclaimed Lady Skene with her characteristic chuckle.

Fortunately the tea equipage appeared at that moment and the conversation turned into safer channels. Lady Skene was expecting her grandchildren to stay. Oliver was older than Mark, and Tessa was almost exactly the same age as Edith.

"I shall give a children's party," Lady Skene declared. She was extremely well pleased with Alice. Alice was a neighbour after her own heart. Alice was pretty and nicely dressed and would do exactly as she was told.

Mrs. Raeworth was the next caller at Dunnian House. She and Alice walked round the garden together admiring Johnson's dahlias which were particularly fine that year.

"You're lucky to have Johnson," Mrs. Raeworth said. "He's the best gardener in the neighbourhood. He knows his job from A to Z."

"Yes, it's lucky," Alice agreed. "I know nothing about gardens. We've never had a garden before."

"You'll soon learn," said Mrs. Raeworth comfortingly.

Alice was not so sure. She had conducted Mrs. Allworthy round the garden and had discovered that every plant had a long and almost unpronounceable Latin name. It was somewhat humiliating to be brow-beaten by a stranger in one's own garden — so Alice found — and she had done her best to be upsides with Mrs. Allworthy. She had pointed out the snapdragons, there was a huge bed of them near the toolshed, and had commented on their lovely colours. "Ah, yes, antirrhinum," Mrs. Allworthy had said. After this set-back Alice had given up trying and had tagged along after her erudite visitor saying "yes" and "no" and letting the stream of Latin names flow in at one ear and out of the other. Mrs. Raeworth was quite different, of course. She did not air her knowledge but she gave Alice one or two useful hints.

"Make Johnson put the things in clumps," said Mrs. Raeworth, pointing to the herbaceous border. "Gardeners always like to put plants in rows but they don't look nearly so effective."

"Yes, I will," said Alice, nodding.

It did not take long for Mrs. Raeworth to make up her mind that Mrs. Dunne was a very desirable neighbour. She was pleasant and friendly and there was no nonsense about her — how different from Nina!

"You must come over to tea and bring the children," said Mrs. Raeworth cordially. "The children must be friends —"

"It will be lovely for them," Alice agreed.

This was the beginning of a firm friendship between the two families. Hastley Dean was only two miles from Dunnian by the path across the moor and, as Evelyn Raeworth was a good walker and enjoyed exercising her dogs, it became a recognised custom for her to walk in the Dunnian direction and drop in for a chat. Alice was not so fond of walking but she could have the carriage when she liked and she often visited Hastley Dean.

The first visit to Hastley Dean was a great success. Alice took Mark and Edith to tea, dressed in their best and suitably warned to be on their best behaviour. The Raeworth children were friendly and cheerful and eager to make their guests feel at home. They chattered happily while their mothers gossiped and grew to like each other better. By this time Alice had discovered that her new friend was fond of painting and spent a good deal of her time pursuing the art.

"Do you paint landscapes?" Alice inquired.

"Sometimes," said Evelyn Raeworth, smiling. "But I like portraits best. I should like to show you a portrait I did last year. I'm rather proud of it, to tell you the truth."

The portrait was produced without further comment and Alice looked at it with interest and admiration. It was the portrait of an old lady in a grey silk dress. She was sitting in a high-backed chair, leaning forward a little as if she were just going to speak. Her eyes were brown and bright and her face was full of animation.

"Oh, Mrs. Raeworth!" exclaimed Alice impetuously. "I had no idea you were a real artist!"

Evelyn Raeworth laughed, for the naïve compliment pleased her. She was aware that none of her friends and neighbours gave her the credit she deserved.

"It's lovely," continued Alice. "It's perfectly beautiful. What an expressive face she has!"

"It's Miss Terry!" cried Mark in surprise. "That's who it is. It's Miss Terry."

"I'm afraid you're wrong, Mark," replied Evelyn Raeworth, smiling down at the eager little face. "That's a picture of old Miss Dunne — your great-great-aunt Celia —"

"Daddy said her name was Miss Terry," said Mark, nodding his head emphatically. "Daddy said —"

"Hush, Mark," said Alice gently.

"She was a wonderful subject," said Mrs. Raeworth, looking at the portrait affectionately. "I loved doing her. You never saw her, did you?"

"No, I wish I had," Alice replied.

The friendship with the Raeworths solved the problem of Mark's education, a problem which had begun to cause his parents some anxiety. The Raeworth children had a governess and she was willing to take Mark into the schoolroom and teach him with the others. It was arranged that he should be driven over to Hastley Dean every morning in the pony-cart and brought back to Dunnian in time for his midday meal.

The days passed, the family shook itself out, settled down and formed new habits. Alice began to feel she had lived here all her life. It had been a little difficult at first but Becky was a great help to her, and guided her past a good many pitfalls with unfailing tact and sense. There was no talk of Becky leaving Dunnian now, for Alice needed her and all that Becky asked of life was to be needed and liked. Becky knew everybody and could tell Alice all sorts of interesting and amusing details about the people in the neighbourhood.

"That's Mrs. Browne-Pilkington," she said, when Alice described a woman she had met at a luncheon party. "Yes, that's who it is. Sticking out teeth and bright red hair?"

"Yes," said Alice, nodding.

"*She* won't be much use to you," declared Becky scornfully. "All gush — that's what Miss Dunne used to say about her. She takes up with anybody new and then drops them like a hot potato. Don't you bother with *her*."

"No," said Alice meekly. "I didn't think she was quite my sort of person, Becky."

"I could tell you one or two things about Mrs. Browne-Pilkington," declared Becky with a chuckle . . . and after a very little persuasion Becky did.

"Now, the Miss Farquhars," said Becky. "They're quite different. You'd like the Miss Farquhars. They won't be calling because they haven't got a carriage. Miss Dunne used to go over and see them and take them a few flowers."

"Do you think I should go?"

"Why not?" asked Becky. "They're right out in the country, over Timperton direction, they'd like to see you."

Becky was a help in other ways as well. She knew exactly how a large house should be run; which duties belonged by right to the head housemaid and which should be assigned to her inferiors. "Don't you stand for any nonsense," Becky advised. "If you give them an inch they'll take an ell — that's what Miss Dunne used to say. They'll respect you and like you all the better if you show them you know what's what."

Alice did not know what was what but she was learning rapidly.

"And don't let Mrs. Drummond come over you," Becky continued earnestly. "That piece of cod last night — she'd no business to serve it up without a sauce. She'd never have dared to when Miss Dunne was here."

"I don't mind very much about food when I'm all by myself."

"That's neither here nor there. She's got to be kept up to the mark and you've got to do it.

Mark was settling down too, and finding his new life easy and pleasant. He liked driving over to Hastley Dean for his lessons, it gave him a feeling of pride and importance to come out of the front door every morning and find Downie waiting for him in the pony cart. He liked his lessons and he liked the Raeworth children. Andrew was a little older than Mark but Angela was exactly the same age, they battled through the multiplication tables together and became fast friends. Lessons were interesting but Dunnian was even more enthralling, he was allowed to go out by himself and "explore." Soon he began to know the place pretty thoroughly, every stone and tree became familiar to him.

He gave his own names to the various localities, names which he made up out of his head or which grew naturally from some incident associated with them. There was, for instance, "Hornie Path," where Mark had encountered a very alarming cow with horns upon its head . . . and had turned and fled for dear life; and there was "Sunny Patch," a little glade in the woods where a tree had been felled and left an open space.

The woods were Mark's chief playground; they were full of rabbits, and sometimes, if you sat very still for a long time, you saw a squirrel peeping at you from a tree. There were pigeons, too, and in spring they filled the woods with peaceful cooing sounds which blended with the rustling of the leaves. At first Mark was interested only in the geography of the place, the stones, the rocks, the hills and the winding paths, but after a little he wanted to know more about Dunnian, about things that had happened there long ago.

Mark found that Becky could help him here, for Becky knew all sorts of interesting things about Dunnian. She told him about the building of the house, how the stones for it were brought in carts from the quarry at Timperton Law, so that really and truly Dunnian was a part of Timperton Law — that was interesting. She told him about the ruined cottage which Mark had found in the wood, and about the old mill on the Rydd Water which was hundreds of years old but was still working, sawing up timber; but, best of all, Mark liked the stories about Great-great-aunt Celia when she was a little girl.

"You must be *very* old, Becky," said Mark one day, looking at her with large, innocent eyes.

Becky laughed. "Oh, I'm not as old as all that," she replied. "I wasn't born then, it's just what I've learned from other people, and I've heard a good deal. My mother was maid to Miss Dunne before she was married — and that's not yesterday — and there's an old, old woman in Ryddelton who remembers when the Miss Dunnes were all young and could tell you all about the balls and junketings and about Miss Isabel's wedding."

"I'd like to see her," Mark said.

"So you shall," promised Becky. "I'll take you to see her one fine day — she'll be as pleased as a dog with two tails."

These talks with Becky gave Mark a feeling for history, they made the dry bones of history come alive. Mark found he could remember the date of Waterloo because Aunt Celia had been born the day after the battle . . . and Aunt Celia's grandfather (whose picture hung over the mantelpiece in the dining-room) had seen Prince Charlie with his own eyes which made Prince Charlie real. Dunnian itself was all mixed up with history, for, although the house was not really old, there had been a fort at Dunnian for unknown ages. This fort — or peel — was ruined now and its only inhabitants were owls and jackdaws, but long ago people had lived there — and the people were called Dunne

Mark loved to hear stories about these ancestors of his, stories about battles against the English, stories about forays and cattle raids when the Dunnes armed themselves and rode over the Border to "get their beef."

"Tell me more, Becky," he would say when Becky paused for a moment to collect her thoughts. "Tell me about Sir Humphrey Dunne being knighted by Robert the Bruce."

"You've heard it before."

"I know, but I like hearing it. Tell me again."

"Once upon a time," began Becky, taking up a stocking and beginning to knit industriously. "Once upon a time, long, long ago, the Borders were very unsettled and the Border Barons were powerful and bold. Some of these Barons were more powerful than the Dunnes and had more men under them but none of them had stronger men nor better equipped than Humphrey Dunne. Thirty-six men at arms, he had, all picked for boldness and strength and cunning and all well mounted too. It was in the time of Robert the Bruce, he went to Ireland for a bit and while he was away there was talk of an English invasion so Sir James Douglas built a strong encampment near Ferniehurst and you can see the remains of it to this very day. Things were quiet enough for a wee while and then Sir James got word that the English were coming — ten thousand men, there were, with axes, and they were going to cut down the forest of Jed which was one of the places where the Scots had ambushed the English before. The Forest of Jed was one of the best defences Scotland had, for it lay directly in the path of an advancing army and the Douglas was not going to stand by and see it levelled to the ground — not he. The Border Barons were summoned, but time was short and the distances were long and the English were coming down from the passes before the Barons had assembled. The Douglas only had a very small force of men-at-arms and some crossbow-men but he had a head on him and he knew just what to do. Well, what he did was to make a trap for the English, he wove a lot of branches together and made a sort of maze and then he hid his men and waited until the English came. As soon as he saw that they were into his trap he gave the order to start and his men rose up from their hiding-places shouting: 'A Douglas, a Douglas!' and fell upon the English and fought them tooth and nail. It was in the middle of the battle that Humphrey Dunne arrived on the scene, he had ridden thirty miles at break-neck speed and he did not hesitate now — into the battle he plunged shouting: 'The Dunnes are here!' and his thirty-six men were not far behind him. That turned the tide and the English broke and fled for their lives the way they had come and the Dunnes and the Douglases after them. It was for arriving so soon and helping in the battle that Humphrey Dunne got knighted by Robert the Bruce."

"And that's our motto now," said Mark, looking at Becky with shining eyes. "That's what's written on our crest, isn't it? 'The Dunnes are here!'"

CHAPTER
ELEVEN

June, 1910

As the train steamed slowly into Ryddelton Station, Commander Humphrey Dunne put his head out of the window and saw the little group which stood near the bookstall awaiting his arrival. Nannie was fatter than ever, her round rosy face was creased with anxiety as she scanned the windows of the train. She had a little girl on each side of her and was holding their hands tightly, while, beside her, capered Mark, half-crazy with excitement. It was usually Alice who brought the children to meet Humphrey but a new baby was due to arrive shortly so Humphrey had not expected Alice to come to the station to-day. He was glad to see that the children looked well — they had grown considerably since last September.

"There he is!" cried Mark. "There's Daddy!" and he started to run after the train, followed more slowly by the rest of the party.

"All well, Nannie?" asked Humphrey as he hugged and kissed the children.

"All well, sir," replied Nannie, nodding significantly over their heads.

They went out of the station into the yard where the new motor car was waiting; it was an open car, very large and green, and it stood high off the ground. Its brass fittings winked and gleamed like gold in the bright afternoon sunshine.

Humphrey looked at it with pride. "Well, Downie, how is she going?" he inquired.

"Grand, sir," replied Downie. "It took me a wee while to get used to, but I wouldn't go back to horses — not now I wouldn't. Takes ten minutes to get to the station instead of half an hour."

"Unless you have a puncture, of course," said Mark gravely.

They got in and drove off.

"I want a pony, Daddy," Edith began.

"Now then," said Nannie. "Now then, what did I tell you? I told you not to start asking your Daddy for things the very first moment."

"This isn't the very first moment," said Edith sulkily.

"Billy has got a new tooth," said Joyce.

"He's got all his teeth now," declared Nannie proudly.

"But he was too small to come and meet Daddy," Joyce pointed out. "I'm six now," she added.

"Of course you are," agreed Humphrey. He always felt shy with his children just at first. It was difficult to know how to talk to them for they grew up so quickly that he could not keep pace. He went away leaving a lisping baby and returned to find it articulate. He was sorry that Joyce was six. At five she had been attractively babyish, she had sat on his knee and listened with bated breath to the story of Red Riding Hood —

now she was a person, self-possessed and incredibly mature ... but she was still very pretty, thought her father, glancing at the round, rosy face and fair hair.

"Everything is coming on very nicely after the rain," said Nannie, making polite conversation.

"Yes, it's looking beautiful," Humphrey agreed. "You've had a lot of rain have you?"

"The weather has been very invidious," she replied.

She smiled complacently, as she always did when she produced her grand words, and Humphrey smiled too; for some reason he was reminded of a monkey-jacket which had been put on hastily and the buttons inserted into the wrong buttonholes — and that was exactly what happened, Humphrey thought. Nannie's words were all right but she put them into the wrong places, and the effect was quite as absurd as the effect produced by the wrongly-buttoned garment.

"We had peas for dinner," Joyce informed him.

"You're having some to-night," added Mark. "I saw Johnson bringing them into the kitchen."

"What were you doing in the kitchen, Mark?" Nannie inquired.

"Talking to Mrs. Drummond," mumbled Mark, getting rather red in the face.

"You know you've no call to go into the kitchen and bother Mrs. Drummond!"

"I wasn't bothering — she likes me."

"H'm," snorted Nannie. "I know Mrs. Drummond. She likes you one day and the next day she's complaining about you. Now listen to me —"

"Honestly, Nannie! Mrs. Drummond *said* —"

"No, Mark. Just listen to me. You know perfectly well . . ."

Humphrey said nothing. He felt as if he were dreaming. He always had this feeling of unreality when he moved suddenly from one kind of life to the other. This life of the country, of home and trivialities and children's chatter was superimposed, as it were, upon the austere life of a naval commander. He seemed to see one through the other and neither of them clearly. In a day or two he managed to adjust himself, of course; it was only just at first that he felt so strange.

Alice was overjoyed to see Humphrey — she always was — and the two of them had tea together on the terrace. It was exactly five years since Humphrey had taken tea on the terrace with Aunt Celia and, to-day, he was reminded very forcibly of that occasion. Alice was not like Aunt Celia, of course (in fact one could scarcely imagine any one more unlike) but everything else was the same; the smooth, green lawn, the stately trees, the golden light on the far-off hills . . . even the tea-service, the scones and cakes and the creamy butter in the crystal dish . . .

"Where did you find that stool?" asked Humphrey, pointing to the carpet-covered hassock under Alice's feet.

"Becky found it," she replied. "Becky said Aunt Celia always used it when she sat out on the terrace."

"I know she did," said Humphrey.

"Becky is a great comfort," Alice continued. "Really I don't know what I should have done without Becky. I haven't felt quite so well this time and it has been terribly dull for me."

"This must be the last," said Humphrey firmly.

"Yes, if it's a girl," nodded Alice; "and I think it will be, somehow. I'm sure this will be Celia."

Humphrey did not remind her that she had said exactly the same two years ago before Billy's arrival upon the scene. Billy had been a disappointment — though not a very severe one, for, in her heart of hearts, Alice had wanted another son and there was plenty of time —

"How does Nannie like the idea of another baby?" Humphrey inquired as he helped himself to a scone and buttered it lavishly.

"She's delighted; Nannie would like a new baby every year."

"Good Lord!"

"But five in the nursery is quite enough," added Alice firmly.

Humphrey did not answer that. He looked slightly uncomfortable and after a short hesitation he said, "Alice, you know Aunt Celia asked me to look after Joan."

"Yes, and *have* looked after her. You've done all you could, haven't you? Nobody could have done more."

"I've just got a letter from Joan," said Humphrey, and he took it out of his pocket and began to unfold it.

"Oh, goodness!" exclaimed Alice in great vexation. "Oh, goodness, I know what *that* means! You've never had a single letter from Joan which didn't cause some sort of trouble. She's in a fix, I suppose, and you've got to go south and see her. It's always the way when you come home on leave, *always*."

"She isn't exactly in a fix this time," said Humphrey, smiling. "The fact is she's going to be married."

"Married!"

"Yes, to an Indian Army officer."

"What a mercy," said Alice. "We'll send her a really fine wedding present and that will be the end of it."

"Well, not quite, I'm afraid. You see she can't very well take Debbie to India with her —"

"Humphrey, you don't mean . . ."

"Yes, I'm afraid so. You see I feel responsible, really. If we don't offer to have Debbie she would just be sent to Cousin Henrietta which wouldn't be at all suitable."

"She's the child's grandmother."

"But she's getting old. It would be much better for the child to come here."

"If Debbie is like her mother —" began Alice in horrified tones.

"She isn't," said Humphrey quickly. "She isn't the least like Joan. She's a funny, mousey little creature, very small and quiet. Oh, I know it's a nuisance, Alice, and I'm awfully sorry to have to worry you just now, but I don't see what else can be done."

"But, Humphrey —"

"Would one more child in the nursery make much difference?" said Humphrey in a persuasive tone.

Alice sighed. Men were so awfully queer; they didn't understand. A strange child — probably very badly brought up — was to be dumped into her own

100

well-ordered nursery and Humphrey thought it would not make much difference!

"Nannie would soon get her into shape," said Humphrey, who was less blind than his wife imagined.

Alice sighed again. She saw it was no use saying anything more. If Humphrey thought it was their duty to have the child they must have her and make the best of it.

"The children have grown," said Humphrey after a little silence. "They're all very nice-looking, but Joyce is the beauty of the family."

"Edith is pretty too," said Alice quickly. "Edith is really the prettiest. She has such a lovely complexion and her hair is beautifully curly. You can't judge Edith properly at the moment because of her teeth — no child can look her best without any front teeth, you know."

"Of course not," agreed Humphrey. He was still feeling "wandered." It seemed so odd to be sitting here on the terrace, with Alice, discussing children's teeth and hair. At the same hour yesterday Humphrey had been standing on the bridge of his destroyer conning her into port. He remembered that someone had brought him a cup of tea — a large thick cup full of bright brown tea — and he had drunk it as he stood there, and been very glad of it. Of course teeth and hair were very important, especially girls' teeth and hair (thought Humphrey vaguely) because, later on, good teeth and hair would help them to obtain good husbands.

"What are you thinking about?" Alice inquired.

"I can't provide for the girls," said Humphrey — for this was the point to which his thought had brought him.

"They will marry, of course," said Alice comfortably.

CHAPTER
TWELVE

Celia

Of all the hours in the day the one that Humphrey most enjoyed was when Alice had gone up to bed and he was left alone to sit quietly by the drawing-room fire with his pipe and his book. It was then that he had time to appreciate the peace that enveloped Dunnian, it was then that he could look round the beautifully proportioned room and take pleasure in the fact that it was his. When he was at sea, when he was watch-keeping, this was the hour that he remembered and for which he was "homesick." He was very fond of Alice and the children, and enjoyed their company, but his greatest happiness, and peace of the soul, came to him when he was alone.

On this, his first night of leave, he felt the perfection of the hour more keenly than ever (some day he would retire and come to live at Dunnian, and there would be no more comings and goings, but, although he envisaged that time with a good deal of pleasure, he was aware that something would be lost. He would not appreciate Dunnian so much if he lived here all the while. It was the comings and goings that heightened his perception, it was the odd juxtaposition of the two different lives which made Dunnian seem so wonderful).

The windows stood wide open and it was almost dark outside — as dark as it ever is in June — a fire had been lit and a log of wood flamed fitfully on its bed of red ashes. It was all perfect. Humphrey raised his eyes and saw a star, faintly twinkling, and he remembered that Aunt Celia had sat here night after night watching for the first star.

Ten minutes more — just one last cigarette — and then he must go upstairs to bed, thought Humphrey. Ten minutes more . . .

He was just lighting the cigarette when he heard Alice calling him and there was such urgency in her voice that he flung the cigarette into the fire and ran for his life . . . he took the stairs three steps at a time and found Alice standing on the landing in her nightdress.

Humphrey had expected to find her in bed . . . he had thought of all sorts of contingencies during his mad rush upstairs . . . but Alice seemed all right, neither frightened nor very much perturbed.

"Somebody came in," said Alice with a puzzled air.

"Came into your room?"

"Yes. I thought at first it was Nannie, but it wasn't Nannie . . . it wasn't Becky, either."

"You were dreaming, darling," said Humphrey, putting his arm round her shoulders and leading her back to bed.

"But I wasn't asleep, Humphrey," she replied. "How could I have been dreaming when I wasn't asleep. I had only just got into bed and lain down. I was going to read for a little while . . . and then, all at once, I had a feeling that someone had come into the room . . . and when I looked up I saw her."

"Who was it?"

"I don't know, darling. It was nobody I had ever seen before."

She was speaking so calmly and naturally that only an anxious husband could have felt any apprehension, but Humphrey was an anxious husband. He was all the more apprehensive because it was so unlike Alice to "imagine things."

"It's all right, dearest," he soothed as she got into bed. "Lie down and go to sleep. It's very late, you know."

"Who was she, I wonder," said Alice as she lay down obediently.

"You mustn't alarm yourself, Alice."

"I'm not *alarmed*. There was nothing alarming about her. She was — she was *friendly*, you know. It wasn't until she had gone that I began to feel a little frightened and to wonder who she was . . . so I called you."

"Yes, of course — but I'm sure you were dreaming —"

"No, Humphrey, she was quite real," replied Alice, as she laid her head on the pillow. "She came and stood by my bed and smiled at me . . . an old lady with very bright eyes . . . and a beautiful diamond brooch."

"You were dreaming," said Humphrey for the third time but with much less conviction.

"Grey silk," continued Alice in a sleepy voice. "Grey silk . . . it rustled when she moved . . . and lovely old Mechlin lace . . . and she was so tiny, no bigger than Edith . . ."

"She's gone, darling —"

". . . and a scent of roses," murmured Alice as she closed her eyes. "A scent . . . of red . . . roses . . ."

Was it imagination or did a faint scent of red roses linger in the air? Humphrey could not be sure.

Celia Dunne was born very early the next morning with the least possible fuss. She was small and neatly made and from the very beginning of her life she was nice to look at, not red or wrinkled as the other babies had been. Her eyes were blue at first but very soon they began to turn brown, and Humphrey, as he looked at her lying contentedly in her beribboned bassinette, could have sworn that there was recognition in them and something approaching a twinkle. He did not like it at all for he hated anything "queer" (and anything "queer" in his own family was profoundly to be deprecated).

Humphrey was so upset about it that he was very short indeed with Alice's nurse when she remarked that Celia "wasn't like a baby, somehow." (They were having lunch together in the morning-room and Celia was barely three weeks old.)

"What do you mean?" demanded Humphrey. "She looks to me just like any other baby."

"Oh, I didn't mean anything like *that*," declared Nurse Walker hastily — and somewhat enigmatically — "I just mean she has such a strong personality. I just mean she's so very noticing for her age. You should have seen the way she looked about her when I carried her downstairs this morning — so pleased she seemed — as if the whole place belonged to her, dear wee lamb!"

"Nonsense!" exclaimed Humphrey angrily.

Nurse Walker was surprised. The Commander was usually very pleasant and genial. She wondered what could have provoked him and made him so cross.

"I hope you haven't said anything like that to Mrs. Dunne," continued Humphrey after a short silence. "She's apt to be — er — rather fanciful and we don't want to worry her."

Nurse Walker was even more surprised at this, for it had seemed to her a very innocent remark. Of course she had told Mrs. Dunne; mothers liked to hear things like that about their babies and Mrs. Dunne was no exception to the rule. Mrs. Dunne had not been "worried," in fact she had been very much amused and had laughed so heartily that she almost cried. It was this success that had encouraged Nurse to repeat her little joke to the Commander.

"No, of course we mustn't worry her," agreed Nurse in her most professional manner.

CHAPTER
THIRTEEN

Debbie

Humphrey found that Alice had forgotten all about her "dream." She was calm and happy, pleased with Celia and even more pleased with herself for her cleverness in producing Celia to order. Humphrey did not remind Alice of her dream, he was thankful she had forgotten it and only wished that he could forget about it himself. In spite of his slight feelings of discomfort which were connected with the new baby Humphrey managed to enjoy his leave and he did not miss Alice's companionship as much as he expected because he found a companion in his elder son. Mark was now ten years old; he was still doing lessons with the Raeworth children but during Humphrey's leave he was released from his studies. Lessons were important, of course, but Humphrey considered it even more important that he and his son should become friends. Next term Mark was to go to a preparatory school called Welland House and unless Humphrey could manage to wangle his leave in the official school holidays he would never see Mark at all. The girls did not matter so much (Humphrey thought) so they continued to drive over to Hastley Dean every morning as usual. There was a certain amount of unpleasantness over this arrangement but it did not reach Humphrey's ears.

Humphrey had always envisaged Mark in the Navy but now, as he became better acquainted with his son, he began to wonder whether the Navy was "the right thing" for Mark; he sounded Mark carefully and found that Mark shared this doubt — Mark was not particularly keen to be a sailor though he found his reasons difficult to explain.

The two companions went for long walks together over the moors and through the woods. Mark knew far more than Humphrey about Dunnian, more about its geography and more about its history, and he was only too pleased to share his knowledge with his father. They did nor confine their expeditions to Dunnian itself but took sandwiches and roved far afield and found all sorts of interesting things to see. Sometimes they took rods and went up the Rydd, returning at night tired and hungry with a basketful of small but tasty trout. Humphrey was learning to drive the car and, as he had a flair for machinery, it did not take him long to become proficient — much more proficient than Downie if the truth were told. One day he and Mark drove over to Timperton and leaving the car at the Inn they set out to climb Timperton Law. It was a breezy day with clouds racing in from the west, great white clouds chasing each other across the blue sky. There were sheep on the hill, nibbling the sweet grass, and the larks were singing above their heads. When they had reached the top and had added their stones to the cairn upon the summit they found a place in the shelter of a rock and sat down to eat their lunch.

"I think it's because I like the land so much," said Mark after a little silence, and he waved his hand towards the glorious spread of country which lay before their eyes.

Humphrey understood at once, for he and Mark were in such complete accord that explanations were not necessary between them. He understood all the better because he, too, liked the land. Sometimes after long days at sea he would feel a positive hunger for the land, for green fields and trees and the smell of good brown earth.

"It's no good going into the Service if you feel like that," Humphrey replied.

"I think I'd like to be a farmer . . . it would be so — so *useful*."

"I know what you mean. It would be a fine life, but I'm afraid you can't be a farmer, old boy. I haven't enough money to buy you a farm. You'll have to think of something else."

Mark nodded. He did not mind very much for there were plenty of other things to do. He was glad that Daddy understood why he did not want to go into the Navy.

This was the last expedition together before Humphrey went south to Joan's wedding. He did not want to go for he was enjoying himself at Dunnian, but that could not be helped, and, as Humphrey was used to the discipline of putting duty before pleasure, he would not only go to the wedding but would behave as if he liked it.

"I needn't stay long," declared Humphrey as he said good-bye. "I'll be back on Thursday night — with Debbie, of course."

"Yes, of course," said Alice in a resigned voice.

Alice was resting in bed when Humphrey returned. He brought his small charge into the room and presented her to her "aunt."

"Here she is!" said Humphrey cheerfully. "This is Debbie."

Alice looked up and saw the child hanging back in the doorway, she was a small wispy looking creature with a tiny, sallow face and large frightened grey eyes. Her clothes were very peculiar, she seemed lost in them; they made her look like a little old woman cut short, and this odd resemblance was further heightened by the fact that she was clasping in her arms a large doll, dressed like a baby, which Humphrey had bought her in London.

Alice called her over to the bed and kissed her and asked her how she was.

"Answer Aunt Alice," said Humphrey, who was anxious that his protégée should make a good impression.

"Quite well, thank you," said Debbie in an almost inaudible voice.

"She's shy," explained Humphrey. "She's tired after the journey. She'll feel much better to-morrow, won't you, Debbie."

Most unattractive, thought Alice, looking at Debbie with a feeling akin to dismay. She had been prepared to cherish Debbie and make the best of her, but she saw it was going to be difficult to make the best of Debbie. She was so plain, so sallow, so small and delicate.

"I thought she was older," said Alice, looking at her again. "If I had known she was so young I would have sent Becky with you to look after her in the train."

"She's seven," said Humphrey. "And as a matter of fact she was no trouble at all. I'm sure Nannie won't find her any trouble."

The subject of these remarks listened to them in silence. She looked dazed, she looked as if she scarcely understood what was being said.

"She's very small for seven," said Alice with a sigh. "We must feed her up. I must speak to Nannie about it . . . codliver oil and malt, perhaps."

Nannie and Alice had a good many talks on the subject of how to fatten Debbie and of how to improve her appearance. "It's her hair," Nannie would say. "That queer streaky brown colour and as straight as a pound of candles. I've tried curl-rags but it's as straight as ever in half an hour. It's so soft you can't do nothing with it."

"Do you think if we cut it quite short with a fringe —"

"Maybe," said Nannie doubtfully. "It couldn't be worse than it is, whatever we did to it."

"And her skin —" Alice exclaimed. "Her skin is so sallow. The other children have such beautiful skins."

"And her legs are like sticks," added Nannie hopelessly.

Oddly enough neither Nannie nor Alice noticed that Debbie had good points as well as bad ones. Her neat features, her small red mouth and her large, dewy eyes were unremarked and unsung.

"She isn't naughty, is she?" Alice inquired, for it was her fear that Debbie might have a bad influence upon the other children. Debbie was Joan's daughter and Alice did not approve of Joan at all.

"Naughty!" exclaimed Nannie. "No, indeed. Sometimes I wish she was. I'd know how to deal with a naughty child . . . in fact I rather like them naughty," admitted Nannie with a reminiscent smile. "I rather like spunk — I've got an infinity with naughty children, if you know what I mean."

"Yes," said Alice, but she said it doubtfully.

"Now Debbie is different," continued Nannie. "Debbie doesn't take any interest. She doesn't eat as much as would nourish a fly and she doesn't play with the other children. I can't even get her to talk."

"Can't you, Nannie?"

"She's so quiet you can scarcely see her," declared Nannie, shaking her head.

"You don't think she's unhappy, do you?"

"Unhappy!" exclaimed Nannie in surprise. "Why should she be? Everybody's kind to her. She's got good food to eat and all those nice new clothes and the lovely doll the Commander bought her in London. Why should she be unhappy, I'd like to know?"

It was true that Debbie was kindly treated, well fed and comfortably housed, but in spite of this she was very unhappy indeed. Everything here was so different from what she had known: the place, the people, the mode of living. She was used to a very irregular sort of life with meals at any time and cups of tea in between. She was used to staying up late at night and lying in bed late in the morning. She was used to sharing the worries and responsibilities of life, of doing the shopping and helping to make ends meet. It was therefore extremely difficult for her to settle down in the Dunnian nursery where everything went like clockwork; where there were no responsibilities at all, and nothing to do except play. "Go and play," Nannie would tell her, but Debbie did not know how to play. Debbie could dust a room, she could make a bed as well as any housemaid, she could even do a little simple cooking but none of these accomplishments was required of her at Dunnian — "Go and play," said Nannie.

In addition to this Debbie often wondered how Mummy was getting on. Who would look after Mummy when she had a headache? Who would bring her a cup of tea in the morning before she got up? Who would see that Mummy didn't spend all her money at once, leaving nothing to tide her over to the end of the month? She often wondered why Mummy had sent her here — for this had never been properly explained to her — didn't Mummy love her any more? Didn't Mummy want her? Debbie's heart was very sore when she thought of her mother, for, although Joan was anything but a good parent, and was always selfish and often cross, she was the only companion that Debbie had ever known. They had shared things.

Debbie was so quiet you could scarcely see her — it was Nannie's phrase and although it was a bit muddled it was essentially true. People did not realise she was there and said things about her without thinking. Thus she came to know that she was not really wanted at Dunnian, that it was "kind" of her relations to give her house-room. "It's a pity she isn't like the others," said Nannie one day. How Debbie wished she were "like the others!" The Dunne children were large and robust; Debbie was small and delicate. She was often tired; they ran about the garden all day long and never seemed tired at all. She admired their looks enormously, their pink and white complexions and fair curly hair. She felt herself an inferior being, and Edith and Joyce, quite naturally, took her at her own valuation. They were not actually unkind to her, but they had nothing in common. *That* was the whole trouble, of course, though nobody (Debbie least of all) recognised the fact: Debbie had nothing in common with her new house-fellows. She had no niche at Dunnian, no point of contact with any one. The grown-up people treated her as a very small child, the children knew she was not like themselves, she was serious and apprehensive and unchildlike. (Joan had treated her as a contemporary and burdened her with cares but at least she had been a "person" in Joan's eyes, at least she had filled a niche.)

The only bright spot for Debbie in this strange new world was the baby. At first Nannie would not let her come near the baby and would tell her to leave Celia alone and go and play, but gradually it became evident that Debbie was "good with the baby," she was gentle and quiet and careful, and, seeing that this was the case, Nannie allowed her to do little things for the baby now and then. She was allowed to put out the soap and towels and wait on Nannie while Nannie gave Celia her bath. Sometimes she was allowed to hold Celia in her arms while Nannie prepared the bottle; this was the brightest moment of the day.

Quite often Alice came upstairs when Celia was being bathed for it pleased her to see the deft way in which Nannie performed this office, and it amused her to hear Nannie talk.

"My word!" Nannie would say, addressing the small naked Celia, lying in her lap. "My word, we'll have to mind our P's and Q's — we've got an ordinance to-night, Celia."

And Celia would smile quite happily as if she understood that she must be on her best behaviour.

Debbie had been at Dunnian for six months before she began to feel less strange and miserable, before (as Nannie put it) she began to get clementised to the place. It was Mark who helped Debbie to make friends with Dunnian. Mark came back from school in the Christmas holidays and his first thought was to make a tour of the place and revisit his old haunts.

"Take Debbie with you," said Nannie. "Put on your things, Debbie, and go out with Mark. A walk will do you good."

Debbie would much rather have stayed at home but she did as she was told and presently she was walking along beside Mark, reserved and silent as usual. The other children were confined to the house with colds, but Debbie, in spite of her delicate appearance, scarcely ever had a cold.

"I'm sorry," said Debbie after a long silence. "I know you didn't want me but I couldn't help it. Nannie didn't understand."

"Understand what?" asked Mark in some surprise.

"You wanted to go alone."

It was true that Mark had wanted to go alone, but he was a kind-hearted boy. He looked down at her and smiled. "I don't mind *you*," he said good-naturedly. "You don't chatter all the time like Edith and Joyce."

"No," agreed Debbie. She was a little puzzled because this was the first time she had been praised for silence.

"Edith and Joyce are funny," continued Mark. "They're always quarrelling, but they like each other just the same. If I like people I don't quarrel with them."

"No," said Debbie.

"They squabble and fight — but then, if any one else comes into it, they suddenly band themselves together."

"Yes," said Debbie, she had noticed this strange phenomenon herself.

They walked on in silence for a little and then Mark began to talk again. "Do you like the woods?" he inquired.

"Not awfully," said Debbie in a low voice. "You see, I'm not used to being where there aren't any people. It's so very quiet in the woods. No people anywhere," said Debbie, trying to explain. "Just trees and trees and trees."

"There used to be people here."

"Do you mean savages?" she asked, looking round apprehensively.

"No, people like us; people who lived in houses and slept in beds and cooked their food in saucepans. Look at that heap of stones! It was once a cottage, you know. This was the garden — it's all nettles, now, but I expect they grew potatoes and cabbages."

Debbie was interested. It was nice to think of people living here, ordinary people; she said, "I wonder if there's anything left. *You* know, Mark, hidden treasure or anything."

"Hidden treasure!"

"Not really *treasure*," she explained, "but just *something*. Let's look about, shall we?"

Mark was not particularly keen to hunt for treasure but he smiled and agreed and the two of them poked about in the ruins of the house. They looked for a long time because, somehow or other, the fascination of hunting for treasure gripped them. Mark found an old knife with a broken blade, and Debbie found a spoon.

"Look, Mark!" she cried excitedly. "Look, a spoon!"

"What a frightful looking thing!" Mark said.

It was rather frightful, for it was bent and completely black and encrusted with dirt.

"It's silver," cried Debbie.

"No, it isn't."

"Yes, it is. I'll take it home and clean it. Can I have it, Mark? Can I have it for my very own."

"Of course," said Mark, smiling at the request.

"Even if it's silver?"

"It isn't silver."

"But if it *is*," said Debbie urgently.

"You can have it if it's gold," replied Mark laughing.

Debbie sighed with pleasure. She put it in her pocket and they walked on. Somehow or other the mere fact that people had lived here — people who used spoons — made the woods seem less empty. It was the vast space and emptiness of the Dunnian Woods that frightened her. She said so to Mark and Mark seized on the word at once.

"Empty!" he exclaimed, "but the woods aren't empty! They're full of all sorts of birds and animals . . . look there's a rabbit, Debbie!" he cried as a little grey streak fled across their path.

"I know there are a few rabbits —" Debbie began.

"There are hundreds," he declared. "You don't see them because they live underground . . . hundreds and thousands of them in their little holes, all lined with soft stuff like birds' nests. And then there are squirrels. If you sit very quietly you see them peeping at you out of the trees. That's why I like coming to the woods by myself, because there's so much to see . . ."

He talked on, telling her all sorts of interesting things and Debbie felt better every moment. Suddenly she thought: I wish I could give Mark something . . . but of course she couldn't. Mark had all he wanted and she had nothing to give.

"What are you thinking about?" Mark asked.

"Nothing," replied Debbie quickly.

"But you *do* think about things. What do you think of all the time? Do you like being at Dunnian?"

"Yes."

"No, you don't," he said. "You wish you were back with your mother."

Debbie hesitated. She wasn't sure. She looked back at her old life and suddenly, for the first time, she realised its drawbacks. She remembered the anxieties, the worries, the constant nagging to which she had been subjected ("Debbie, you've boiled the eggs as hard as stones!" "Debbie, you've forgotten to dust the mantelpiece!"), and she remembered, too, how her head had ached after sitting up late and how often she had felt sick and miserable.

"You do, don't you?" urged Mark.

"No, not now."

"Good," said Mark smiling at her.

"I wish I was cleverer," she said slowly. "I wish I could do lessons as well as Edith. I wish I had curly hair."

Mark didn't laugh. He said, "I like you better than Edith. You're my favourite sister."

This was wonderful. It was going to help a lot. It was going to make all the difference in the world. Mark liked her.

They walked on for a little and then Debbie heaved a sigh. "If only you didn't have to go away to school I believe I could be quite happy," she declared. "I wish you could stay at home."

"So do I," replied Mark in a gruff voice. "You needn't think I like it, Debbie . . . sometimes I feel I just can't bear it another moment . . . but I've got to bear it. All boys have to go to school so — so I've got to bear it, Debbie," and then he found himself telling Debbie all

120

about school, and all about the troubles and trials which had made his first term at school a perfect nightmare . . . about the boys who made your life a burden, and about the nights when you lay awake and thought of Dunnian. Mark had meant to keep his troubles to himself, to stick it out and tell nobody, so he was rather surprised to find himself telling Deb.

CHAPTER
FOURTEEN

Humphrey and Mark

The years passed but Dunnian showed little signs of change. There was electric light in the old house now, and four bathrooms, and there was a new garage behind the stables which held two cars, but Dunnian had assimilated these modern improvements without losing character or dignity. Several of the old trees had fallen and had been replaced with small ones which would grow to noble proportions long after Humphrey was dead. The drive had been widened a little but the lawn was as smooth and green and velvety as ever. When Humphrey returned at Christmas time in the year 1914 for his first "war leave" he found the place as peaceful and beautiful as ever — it was only in the children that he found change. They grew so quickly, they seemed to move on suddenly; suddenly one found that their heads came higher up on one's own body and there was less need to stoop when one spoke to them; suddenly one found in them new words and thoughts.

Mark was at Loretto now, it was a splendid school and not too far from Dunnian — Mark liked it a good deal better than Welland House. He had developed into a grave, thoughtful boy, but there was a latent twinkle in his eye and he had a sense of humour much livelier than either of his parents. He was a very "special" person to Humphrey, firstly because he was such a splendid companion and secondly because Humphrey felt the necessity for making up to Mark for what he had lost. Humphrey was still unreconciled to the fact that Dunnian was to belong to Celia when he was dead; sometimes he blamed himself for accepting Aunt Celia's decision so tamely, and sometimes he wondered whether things would have been different if he had insisted upon a proper "Dunne" name for his eldest son. If Mark had been Henry or Humphrey or William, Aunt Celia might have left the place to him — so Humphrey thought, and he blamed himself accordingly.

It was a good Christmas leave in spite of the war, they had a Christmas tree — one of their own small firs which Johnson brought in from the woods — and they all helped to decorate it with coloured balls and tinsel and little candles. Even Celia helped, she was four and a half now, still tiny, but as pretty as a picture and as perky as a robin. The other girls were like Alice but Celia was a Dunne.

"Oh, pretty!" cried Celia, when the decorations were finished and they all stood back to admire their handiwork. "Oh, pretty tree — I think a squirrel would like to make his nest in you!"

"Silly!" exclaimed Joyce. "A squirrel would be frightened of it. Silly baby!"

Humphrey half-expected tears, but Celia was not a cry-baby and although she was so much smaller than the others she was quite able to stand up for herself. He

123

found it very interesting — and sometimes a little alarming — to see his children's characters developing before his eyes. Alice had been an excellent mother when they were all small, but now he thought she was apt to spoil Edith, to cosset her and make much of her and imbue her with the sense of her own importance as "the eldest Miss Dunne." He was so perturbed about this that he tackled Alice about it, but he did not get much satisfaction for his trouble.

"Edith is so sensitive," said Alice with a smile. "Edith has such a tender heart. You don't understand girls, darling. Girls are quite different from boys. They need encouragement, you know."

"She's a little sulky, sometimes," Humphrey pointed out, "and she's apt to be selfish with the others."

"It's just her way," replied Alice quickly. "Really and truly she's got a very sweet nature."

That afternoon there was a children's party at Dunnian. The Raeworths came (Andrew and Angela and Mildred), and the Murrays from Timperton and the Sprotts and a few others as well. It was delightful to see them all dressed up in their pretty frocks, flitting about the old house like a swarm of butterflies, it was entrancing to hear their happy laughter and the cries of astonishment which greeted the appearance of the tree. Humphrey dressed up as Father Christmas and distributed the presents, and enjoyed himself thoroughly in his unaccustomed rôle; he was very much amused when Celia came forward to receive her gift and announced gravely: "I think you must be a relation of

124

mine, Mr. Christmas. You're very like my Daddy if it wasn't for your beard."

It was a satisfactory leave in every way, and, although it was necessarily short, Humphrey felt he had accomplished a good deal. He and Mark had moved on a step further in their friendship. They took out a gun and shot some rabbits on the moor and Mark made a good start at shooting. After dinner they went out together into the crisp, cold night and looked at the stars through Humphrey's telescope. Like most sailors Humphrey knew a good deal about the stars, and he found that Mark was interested in them, too. Humphrey would smoke his pipe and they would talk or be silent together in friendly understanding.

The days soon passed and Humphrey returned to his ship. He was a captain, now, in command of a cruiser, so his responsibilities increased. When he was at sea Dunnian seemed like a dream and his family seemed like a part of the dream, vague and insubstantial.

At Jutland, when a shell hit the *Glory* with a sickening thud, Humphrey thought of Mark. Quite suddenly, and while he was giving the necessary orders in a cool, firm voice, Humphrey realised that he should have told Mark about Dunnian; that Dunnian was to be Celia's house when he was dead. Mark was old enough to know and Humphrey wanted to explain the whole thing ... it would be a pity if he had left it too late.

The old *Glory* was out of the fight but she managed to stagger home, she staggered into Rosyth and dropped anchor above the bridge. Humphrey was dead tired but before he went to sleep he sent off a wire to Loretto asking Mark to meet him at Hawes Pier on the following day.

The day was fine and as Humphrey stepped into the ship's boat and was rowed over to the pier he scanned it eagerly to see if Mark had come. Would he be there? Would they have let him come? Yes, there he was! Humphrey's heart turned over in his breast as he caught sight of the slim figure in the grey flannel suit standing upon the stone jetty waiting for him. He waved, and Mark waved back ... another few minutes and Humphrey had sprung out of the boat and was shaking hands with his son.

"Is everything all right, Mark?"

"Yes, Dad, rather, everything's fine."

"They let you come!"

"Of course — I explained — they didn't make any fuss at all. Gosh, it's grand to see you, Dad!"

"It was just a sudden idea —"

"A splendid idea —"

They walked up the pier together, their hearts bursting with pride and happiness. (*What a son to have!* thought Humphrey, glancing at the bright, eager face which was now almost on a level with his own. *What a father!* thought Mark, as he walked beside the blue-and-gold clad hero. Gosh, I wish the fellows could see him!)

"If they hadn't let me come," Mark was saying. "Well, I should just have *come* all the same. They couldn't have kept me from coming — wild horses couldn't. I got a train from Musselburgh and changed at Edinburgh. It was quite easy."

Soon they were sitting in the queer old-fashioned dining-room of the Hawes Inn having lunch together and Mark was looking about him with interest and excitement.

"You're thinking of David Balfour," said Humphrey smiling.

"Yes, of course I am — you always know what I'm thinking, don't you, Dad?"

It was early, so the dining-room was empty and Humphrey was able to tell Mark all about the battle — or at least about the *Glory's* part in the action. He illustrated his story with spoons and forks and cruet stands, moving them about to show Mark what had happened.

"That's the *Glory*," said Humphrey, and ever after, Mark associated the old *Glory* with a mustard pot. "That's the *Glory*, you see. We were following the line . . . the *Valiant* was just here . . ."

"Was it a victory?" Mark wanted to know.

"It would have been if we hadn't lost them in the fog," replied Humphrey a little doubtfully.

"They ran away so it must have been a victory," Mark pointed out.

"Time will tell," replied Humphrey. "We don't know enough yet to be able to say for certain. We lost more ships but — as you say — they avoided further action." He sighed and rearranged the spoons. "I wanted to talk to you about things," he added.

"Yes, Dad."

"You see, I couldn't help thinking. It's war and there may be another show — and — and we can't be sure that it won't be the old *Glory's* turn to go up next time. You see what I mean."

Mark saw.

"That's why I wanted to talk to you," Humphrey said.

"Yes," said Mark. "Yes." He looked out of the window and saw the *Glory* lying at anchor in the sparkling water. The scene was a trifle blurred.

"It's about Dunnian," Humphrey said. "Dunnian belonged to Aunt Celia — you know that, of course — and she left it to me for as long as I'm alive, but after that it goes to Celia."

"To Celia!"

Humphrey nodded. "It was Aunt Celia's idea. She was a queer old lady and that was what she wanted. She was born in the house and she lived in it for ninety years and she wanted another Celia to have it."

"What a funny idea!"

"Yes. Perhaps I should have told you before."

"Why?" asked Mark in bewilderment.

"Well, didn't you — I mean perhaps you thought it would be yours."

"Mine?" asked Mark.

"That would be the usual thing," Humphrey pointed out. "I mean you're my eldest son — but Aunt Celia had this queer idea and so —"

"Yes, I see."

It was very difficult, far worse than Humphrey had expected. He decided that he must take the next fence with a rush — it was the only way. "So you see," said Humphrey very quickly. "You see, Mark, if anything happened to me Celia could turn you all out of the house

128

when she is twenty-one. I don't suppose she would do it, of course, unless she married, but she would be entitled to do it if she felt inclined."

"Celia!" exclaimed Mark again. "But Celia is just a baby."

"You have to look ahead," said Humphrey desperately. "We *must* look ahead, old fellow. There isn't much money except what goes with the house and it goes to Celia, of course. I wouldn't be saying all this if it wasn't for the war, but we've got to look ahead . . . just in case . . ." I *shouldn't* be saying it at all, he thought, as he saw Mark's face whiten. It's ghastly to upset him like this. He's only a child when all's said and done . . . but I might be killed any day. He thought of the *Queen Mary*, of that frightful explosion and the burst of flame which had followed it. Humphrey would never forget that sight as long as he lived.

"Yes, of course," said Mark huskily.

"So that's how it stands," continued Humphrey, trying to speak quite cheerfully. "And that's why you'll have to think very seriously and try to decide what you want to do."

"I have been thinking about it, Dad. I think I should like to be a doctor. Would that be all right?"

"I suppose so," said Humphrey in surprise, for somehow he had never thought of this. "It's a long training, but once you were qualified you would be independent. You really think you'd like it?"

"Yes, I'm sure I should."

"You had better go ahead, then. It's a great thing to know your own mind, to have a definite goal and go all out for it — that's the way to succeed."

"Would it take too much money, Dad?"

"No," said Humphrey firmly. "No, there's a little money — enough to see you through. It might not run to Oxford or Cambridge —"

"I thought of Edinburgh."

"Fine — it would be near home, too."

Mark was silent for a few moments and then he said, "What about the others?"

"Your mother has a little money of her own, not much of course, but — but she would get a pension if . . . and Billy wants to go into the service, doesn't he?"

Mark nodded.

"Don't worry, old chap," said Humphrey. "I wouldn't have told you all this, but I felt I would rather tell you myself than leave you to find out about it later. I'm not dead yet, you know."

Mark smiled faintly.

"Don't worry," repeated Humphrey. "And of course don't talk about it to any one — except Mother, of course. You can talk about it to Mother if you like . . . now then, how about coming aboard."

"Coming aboard!" echoed Mark in amazement. "You don't mean I could come aboard the *Glory*, do you?"

"Why not?" asked Humphrey smiling.

It was a sudden idea of Humphrey's to take Mark aboard and it was a very good one, for Mark was so excited at the privilege of being on board a ship which had just taken part in a battle that he forgot his troubles;

his face lost the strained expression, which had worried Humphrey so much, and became boyish and eager. Some of the officers were on board and were very kind and cheerful, they showed Mark the scars which had been sustained by the ship and one of them presented Mark with a shell splinter which he had found in his cabin. Mark was interested in everything and Humphrey saw that he was making a very good impression on everyone who spoke to him. Humphrey could not help wishing that Mark was going into the service; it would be easier from a financial point of view, but it never crossed his mind to try to influence Mark for he wanted Mark to be free and make a success of his chosen profession.

CHAPTER
FIFTEEN

Celia

With a hop and a skip and a jump Celia went down the garden path. Old Johnson was digging, he was turning over the rich brown earth in long straight drills. He stopped digging when he saw Celia and leant on his spade and smiled at her. Johnson was fond of all the children but he liked Celia best — a wee crack with Celia was one of his chief pleasures.

"They were telling me there's going to be a party," Johnson said.

"It's Edith's birthday, that's why. She's fifteen."

"You're all growing up."

"Not fast enough," said Celia, shaking her head. "Mark is seventeen, you know. He would be in the war if he was older." She hesitated and then added, "And you would be in the war if you were younger."

"That's so," agreed Johnson.

"I think they're silly not to have you," continued Celia thoughtfully. "You could dig the trenches for them."

"So I could," he agreed.

"You're *very* good at digging, Johnson."

"I've been at it a long time," he pointed out.

Celia nodded.

Having finished with that subject in a satisfactory manner Celia started another. "Nannie's going," she said.

"So they were saying," replied Johnson. "I was surprised to hear it, mind you, for I thought she was a fixture."

"She likes babies," Celia said in an aggrieved tone of voice. "She would rather go and look after a nasty howling baby than stay here with me. It's funny, isn't it?"

"It sounds daft to me," declared Johnson.

"It *is* daft," agreed Celia. "That's just what it is — *daft*."

"Are you getting another nurse?"

"No, Becky's going to keep an eye on me," said Celia gravely.

"You'll like that."

"Yes, I shall. Becky isn't nearly so strict and she's a lot more interesting, but all the same," said Celia, and there was a tremor in her voice. "All the same — I think I shall — miss Nannie — a lot."

There was a little silence. A robin hopped on to Johnson's spade and watched them with bright, beady eyes.

"And how is the Captain?" asked Johnson suddenly.

"Very well," replied Celia with the little sharp nod which always reminded Johnson so forcibly of old Miss Dunne. "Very well indeed, thank you, Johnson. Of course we don't know where he is because he isn't allowed to tell us. You see I might tell you and you might tell Downie and Downie might go down to the Black

Bull and get drunk — *that's* how the Germans hear where our ships are, you see."

Johnson chuckled. He said, "What about *me* going down to the Black Bull and getting drunk?"

This was considered a good joke and Celia laughed delightedly.

"So you think there's German spies in Ryddelton?" Johnson inquired.

"Of course there are," replied Celia, suddenly grave. "There are spies everywhere, you know, so we've got to be very careful."

"About this party," said Johnson. "You'll not bring a horde of children into my garden, I hope."

"I won't bring them, replied Celia with a mischievous look. "It isn't my party, you know. I hate parties just as much as you do."

"If they come here they'll get more than they bargained for," murmured Johnson. "If they come here, trampling on my beds and breaking down my bushes . . ."

"I never have a party on *my* birthday," Celia pointed out.

"That's true enough," allowed Johnson.

"How's Doris?" inquired Celia anxiously. "Have her puppies been born yet?"

"Yesterday," replied Johnson. "Two dogs and a bitch — you'll be wanting one of them most likely."

"Oh, Johnson — if they'll *let* me!"

"They'll let you if you go about it the right way. One of the dogs is a beauty, I just thought when I saw him: That's the one for Miss Celia, I thought."

"Oh, Johnson!" cried Celia, clasping her hands.

"You'll see them on Thursday," Johnson continued, nodding encouragingly. "You come down on Thursday morning and I'll let you see them . . ."

There was another silence. Celia had perched herself on the handle of Johnson's barrow. She had picked up an unripe pear and was biting into it with her small sharp teeth — every now and then she shuddered.

"You'll have collywobbles," Johnson warned her.

"I never do," she replied. "I can eat anything at all. Nannie says my inside is made of leather."

"Who's coming to the party?" asked Johnson.

"The Raeworths, of course, and Tessa and Oliver Skene. They're staying at Ryddelton House."

"That'll be Colonel Skene's children," said Johnson. "They'll be nice friends for you."

"They're too old to be any fun," Celia replied.

"Different people enjoy themselves in different ways."

Celia nodded. The subject did not interest her much. "How do you like my dress, Johnson," she inquired.

"It's not bad," he said. It was the height of praise, and Celia knew this and was suitably gratified.

"It's cherry-coloured," said Celia, looking down at herself complacently. "I like cherry colour, it makes me feel happy. I like nice new clothes."

"See and not spoil it," Johnson said.

Oddly enough this warning was not really necessary, for Celia, although she was a bit of a tomboy and enjoyed romping and climbing trees, took good care of her clothes and scarcely ever tore them. Suddenly there was the sound of a car coming up the drive and Celia cocked her head and listened. She said, "That'll be the Skenes."

"I wouldn't wonder," agreed Johnson, adding a trifle regretfully, "You'd better get back."

"Why?" asked Celia. "I mean they won't want me and I'm enjoying myself talking to you."

"You'll be wanted," Johnson told her.

She strolled off, but instead of returning to the house she climbed into an old cedar which grew just outside the garden wall. There she sat like a large tropical bird, roosting in the branches. It was her favourite perch. The tree was so high that she could look over the tops of the smaller trees and see the terrace. They were all on the terrace, her long-sighted eyes picked them out quite easily: Mark, tall and lanky in his grey flannels, Tessa Skene in white. Another boy, taller than Mark, was sitting on the stone balustrade, smoking a cigarette and talking to Edith and Joyce — that was Oliver of course. It was fun seeing them without being seen and Celia hugged herself with delight ... What was the good of standing there talking! Why didn't they play a game or explore? When Celia found herself in somebody else's garden she wanted to run about and see things.

The Raeworths were arriving now, Angela and Andrew and Mildred. They came out of the house with Deb and shook hands all round. It looked so silly that Celia rocked with silent laughter.

"Hallo!" exclaimed a voice just below her. "Hallo, Monkey-Face!"

It was Billy, of course. Billy disliked parties as much as Celia. He had managed to escape before the guests arrived.

"Come up!" called Celia. "It's *awfully* funny. They look so silly shaking hands with each other."

"They'd look sillier if they rubbed noses," declared Billy as he climbed up beside her.

"They won't find us here," said Celia as she moved along the branch to let Billy past.

"He was smoking," said Billy. "Oliver Skene was smoking."

"I know, I can see him from here. He's rather nice, isn't he?"

"No, I don't like him . . . move up a bit farther."

"He's nicer than Tessa, anyway."

"They're both gumboils," said Billy emphatically as he climbed on to a thick branch above Celia's head and settled himself astride it in a comfortable position.

There was only two years difference in age between Billy and Celia, and the latter was so strong and wiry and bold that she made a good companion for a boy. They climbed walls and trees together, they dammed burns and sometimes went fishing. All these activities were quite legitimate, of course, but some of their activities were not. Celia was on for any kind of mischief which Billy could devise — and Billy had a fertile brain.

While Celia and Billy were still sitting, perched in the branches of the tree, the party of children had moved from the terrace on to the lawn. They had decided to play hide and seek but the details of the game still had to be settled.

"We'll go in pairs," said Tessa Skene who always knew what she wanted. "We'll toss for partners, shall we, who's got a coin?"

Oliver produced half a crown and began to toss, saying, "Heads I go with Edith, tails I go with Joyce . . . tails it is!"

"That's not the way to do it!" cried Tessa.

Oliver took no notice of the objection. "Heads Andrew and Tessa, tails Andrew and Edith . . . heads this time," said Oliver.

He continued to toss and to settle the fate of his companions; it was rather amusing and gave him a pleasant sense of power. Andrew and Tessa disliked each other so he had arranged a pleasant afternoon for them. Edith could have little Mildred Raeworth as a partner; it would serve her right for being so high and mighty.

Mark and Debbie had been coupled by Oliver and were walking away together when Tessa ran after them. "Look here," she said. "It's better to divide up the family. I'll go with Mark and Debbie can have Andrew as a partner — you don't mind, do you?"

"Of course not," replied Mark.

Debbie said nothing, for she minded a good deal. It would have been lovely to have Mark as her partner.

"I'll go with Andrew," said Edith hastily. "Debbie can go with Mildred."

"I don't see what use there was in tossing," said Mildred Raeworth crossly.

Oliver and Joyce went off together in the direction of the garden.

"It was heads, really, wasn't it?" said Joyce with a little chuckle.

"Was it?" asked Oliver in pretended dismay. "Was it really? I thought it was tails."

"I don't mind," declared Joyce, smiling up at him.

He smiled back. Joyce was only a kid but she was very pretty and most amusing, far more amusing than her stuck-up sister or the simpering Raeworth girl . . . that was why Oliver had chosen her, of course.

"Where are you going to take me?" he asked, for Joyce was leading him down a path in a purposeful manner.

"To the garden," she replied. "There are plums on the south wall."

"Lead on, Macduff," said Oliver cheerfully.

Meanwhile Mark and Tessa were making off in the opposite direction. He knew exactly where they would hide. He looked at her sideways as they walked along: dark shiny curls and a rose-leaf complexion and greeny sort of eyes. Her eyes were the colour of green leaves with sunshine on them, thought Mark. She was smaller than Edith for her head barely reached his shoulder but somehow she seemed older than Edith, more poised and finished and controlled.

"Are you going to be here long?" Mark asked.

"Only a week," she replied. "I've got to go back to school, isn't it sickening?"

Mark had to go back to school, too, but a week was quite a long time, perhaps she would come over again. He hoped she would.

"How old are you?" she asked.

"Seventeen," replied Mark.

"I'm sixteen," said Tessa. "I wish I were older. My cousin is driving an ambulance in France. What do you like doing best?"

"Fishing, I think."

"I like acting," she declared. "We did a play at school — it was for the Red Cross. We did *A Midsummer Night's Dream*."

Mark had never taken part in school theatricals but he knew and liked most of Shakespeare's plays. "What part did you take?" he asked with interest.

"It was Helena," she replied. "It was silly, wasn't it? I should have been Hermia, of course."

"Yes," agreed Mark, looking at her. "Yes, you should have been Hermia."

"I get so tired of girls," continued Tessa. "Girls, girls, girls all day long. I expect you get tired of boys, don't you?"

She chattered on and Mark answered as best he could. He was a little shy for he was not used to girls — other than his sisters — and he was all the more shy because he wanted so much to make a good impression. They were in the woods now and the woods were quiet and full of shadow, the foliage of the trees was heavy, it hung drooping in the hot sun.

"Will you be here next holidays?" Mark asked. "Will you be here for Christmas? It's always fun at Christmas, especially if there's skating or tobogganing."

"We might," she replied doubtfully. "I don't know. We generally go to our other grandmother for Christmas."

CHAPTER
SIXTEEN

Billy and Celia

The rain was coming down softly, filling the burns, washing the foliage of the trees, and sinking into the ground where the roots of plants were waiting to suck it up. It was fine growing rain, Johnson decided, viewing it with pleasure. It would bring on the vegetables and revive the drooping flowers. Alice, also, was pleased to see the rain, for Dunnian depended upon a spring for its water supply and sometimes, in a long drought, the spring was insufficient for the needs of the big house. The children were not so pleased; rain was all very well in term time but in the holidays it was a bore and they were aware that when it started to rain like this — slowly and gently and inexorably — it might go on for days without stopping. It was quiet in the nursery. Mark was working with his stamps; Debbie was curled up on the window seat, reading and listening to the distant voice of the Rydd Water — the Rydd was talking loudly to-day. Edith and Joyce had got out a box of scraps and were cutting them up on the nursery table, making new clothes for their dolls. They were still interested in dolls and enjoyed making new outfits for them. Billy seemed at a loose end. He wandered about disconsolately and then, after a hasty look round, he drifted out of the door. Celia followed him. She found him standing at the top of the stairs with his hands in his pockets. He smiled at her and said, "Shall we slide down the bannisters or what?"

"Let's explore," said Celia eagerly. "Let's explore the attic. We always meant to, didn't we? This is just the sort of day —"

They went up the narrow little stair together and tried the attic door. It was locked, of course, but the door was warped and by dint of a little manipulation on Billy's part they managed to open it.

"Gosh!" exclaimed Billy looking round in surprise. "Gosh, what an enormous place!"

The attic stretched from end to end of Dunnian House beneath the large slate roof. It was low-ceiling and lit by small windows which peered out under the eaves. The whole of the floor-space was filled with furniture which had been discarded by various generations of Dunnes over a long period of years, discarded in favour of newer and more modern furniture. Some of the stuff was broken and some of it was worthless, but other pieces were in good condition and would have rejoiced the heart of a connoisseur. There were chairs and cupboards and dressing-tables, there were chests and boxes and trunks, there were rolls of carpet which exuded a pleasant smell of moth-cake. There were two four-poster beds and any number of pictures framed in heavy gilt leaning against the walls. The place was not really very dirty for Becky looked after it herself, coming up at intervals to clean and open the windows.

Celia began to push her way between the furniture, looking at it with interest. She found a spinning wheel and set it in motion. "Look, Billy!" she exclaimed. "Look, it's like the picture in the Sleeping Beauty. It's a spinning-wheel."

Billy had found a musical box, he wound it up and it emitted a thin, sweet tinkling tune.

For a while the two children were intent and busy. They opened chests and peered in at old forgotten finery, at tiny shoes and fans and lace; they opened cupboards and found albums full of photographs of people they had never seen or heard of ... ladies in crinolines and poke bonnets; gentlemen in striped trousers, with whiskers on their cheeks; children with smoothly brushed hair and frilly drawers which showed beneath their voluminous skirts ...

"*Aren't* they funny!" cried Celia, laughing delightedly. "Look at *this* one, Billy — it's a boy and he's wearing petticoats!"

There were pictures of Dunnian, too, but instead of the big trees which surrounded the house now, there were small, thin trees and shrubberies.

Presently this employment palled on Billy and he looked round for something else to do. "There's a lot of wood, here," he said. "It's a waste, isn't it? I could make a lovely boat out of it — a model boat to sail on the Rydd ..."

"Make one for me, too, and we can have races," said Celia eagerly.

They had found tools in one of the chests and, although the tools were a little rusty, they were still serviceable. Billy made another tour of the attic (this time with a definite object in mind) and presently he found exactly what he wanted. There were half a dozen chairs piled up in a corner, chairs with thick wooden legs which would suit his purpose admirably.

"I suppose Mummy doesn't *want* this chair," said Celia with momentary anxiety as the saw bit into the wood.

"It wouldn't be here if she wanted it," Billy pointed out.

This was true, of course, and Celia abandoned care and took her part in the work of destruction with an easy mind. The first model boat was not very successful, but the second and third were better. Celia was, now, quite as keen as Billy, she sawed off the legs and helped to shape the hulls.

"We won't bother about the details," Billy declared. "But we must have masts and sails . . ."

"We can cut up a handkerchief for sails," said Celia happily.

Although they were not actually conscious of wrong-doing they kept their activities a secret — for grown-ups had such funny ideas about things. The boats, when not in use, were kept in Billy's drawer beneath his underclothing and they were conveyed to and from the river hidden beneath coats and jerseys. Celia and Billy obtained a great deal of pleasure from the boats. Various adjustments were necessary but when these were made the boats sailed none too badly on a pool below the waterfall. They were named after His Majesty's battle-cruisers: the *Lion* and the *Tiger* and the *Princess Royal*.

One day when Billy had been sent with Becky to Edinburgh to pay a visit to the dentist, Celia was sailing her boat by herself. It was an admirable day for sailing, the breeze was light and the *Tiger* responded to it gracefully . . . suddenly Celia looked up and saw Edith standing on the other side of the pool, watching her.

"What are you doing, Baby?" asked Edith.

Celia hated being called Baby — nobody ever called her Baby except Edith — so she did not reply. She made a grab for the *Tiger* but it eluded her and sped across the pool to the opposite bank where Edith was waiting for it.

"What an extraordinary looking thing!" exclaimed Edith, picking it out of the water and examining it.

"It isn't extraordinary," declared Celia. "It's my boat. It sails beautifully."

"Where did you get it?"

"I made it, of course," cried Celia, and she ran round the edge of the pool and seized it out of Edith's hands.

Edith went away after that, and Celia continued her game . . . but somehow or other the fun had gone out of the game; somehow or other Celia was a little worried, a little anxious.

When she went up to the house for dinner Nannie was waiting for her at the door with a curious expression on her face. "What have you been up to, now?" Nannie wanted to know. "Where's that boat? Give it to me, Celia — your mother wants to see it."

"But, Nannie, it's my boat —"

"Yes, I dare say. You come along and tell your mother about it." Nannie took the boat and ushered Celia into the drawing-room. "Here she is," said Nannie. "And here's the boat."

"It's mahogany!" said Alice, taking it and looking at it in amazement. "Celia, where did you get this piece of wood?"

"In the attic," replied Celia shortly.

"What were you doing in the attic?"

"Looking about."

"It looks to me as if it was a leg of a chair," said Nannie.

"It was just an old chair," said Celia hastily. "Nobody wanted it."

"Did you cut the leg off a chair?" asked Alice in horror-striken tones.

"It was just an *old* chair," repeated Celia, but with much less assurance, for she was beginning to realise that she and Billy had perpetrated a major crime.

"Oh, *dear*!" said Alice, turning over the wood and looking at it more closely. "It's the leg off one of those valuable mahogany chairs — how could you have done such a thing! You naughty little girl!"

"Just an old chair," said Celia, swallowing hard. "Just a silly old chair nobody wanted —"

"It's Daddy's chair. It's one of a set. We put them up in the attic because there wasn't room for them, but that doesn't mean we don't want them. Oh dear, how naughty you are! Daddy will be *very* angry when he hears about it."

"Did Billy help you?" asked Nannie, with sudden suspicion.

"I sawed it off myself," replied Celia in quavering tones. "I sawed it off with a saw . . ."

"You must never do such a thing again," said Alice sternly. "It's very naughty indeed, it's destructive. You must go straight to bed and stay there for the rest of the day. Put her to bed, Nannie."

Nannie hesitated. She said, "Celia, are you sure you did it yourself? I don't see how you could have done it yourself — sawed it off and all."

"I did," declared Celia. "I sawed it off with a saw."

Nannie led her away and put her to bed. She peeled off Celia's clothes and folded them up and put them on a chair. No words were exchanged until Celia was arrayed in her nightgown and had climbed into bed.

"I'm glad you're going away," said Celia as she turned her face to the wall. "I hope *that baby* will cry all night . . . I hope it will be sick . . ."

Nannie gave a muffled snort of laughter and hurried away.

Billy and Becky returned at tea-time. Billy came up the stairs and along the passage whistling cheerfully; his visit to the dentist had been painless and he had bought a new knife . . . Celia heard him and called to him as he passed her door for she was exceedingly anxious to have a word with him before he spoke to any one else.

"Hallo!" said Billy, looking into her room. "Hallo, Monkey Face, are you ill?"

"It's the boats," replied Celia in a conspiratorial whisper. "They've found out about the boats and they're awfully cross. Those chairs belong to Daddy and cost a lot of money."

"Gosh!" exclaimed Billy in horrified accents. "Gosh, I'm for the high jump!"

"No, it's all right," said Celia eagerly. "That's why I wanted to talk to you. Nobody knows you were there — so don't say anything."

"Nobody knows I was there!"

"No, I didn't tell them."

"But what did you say? Did you say you'd made it yourself?"

"Not exactly," replied Celia, wrinkling her forehead in the effort to remember what she had said. "They didn't *ask* who made the boat, they only asked who had sawed off the leg of the chair; I said it was me — and so it was. I sawed off the legs, didn't I?"

"I showed you how to do it —"

"Oh, I know, but it doesn't matter. I don't mind being sent to bed *a bit*."

Billy looked at her with admiration and affection — she really was a brick. "It was most frightfully decent of you," he declared. "It was just about the decentest thing I ever heard of . . . but it won't do. I'll have to tell them it was my fault."

"No!" cried Celia, raising herself in bed. "No, Billy, you're not to do it — you'll get spanked."

"I know," agreed Billy with a sigh. "I know that as well as you do, but it can't be helped."

"It can be helped — don't be a goat, Billy."

"It's you that's the goat," he replied. "I couldn't let you take the blame when it was my idea."

"It was my idea, too."

"It wasn't," said Billy firmly. "It was my idea and I'm going straight to Mummy to tell her about it."

"Oh, Billy!" cried Celia, bursting into tears. "Why can't you leave it alone! It's over now — I've been in bed all the afternoon — it will be such a *waste* if you get punished, too."

Billy hesitated, but only for a moment. "I couldn't — honestly," he said. "I'd feel such an awful swine."

Billy's interview with his mother was not a pleasant one, and his interview with Mark was painful (for Mark wielded a pretty strap and took his duties *in loco parentis* with conscientious thoroughness). The incident of the mahogany boats was now closed; it had been unfortunate in some ways but it had far-reaching consequences which were not unfortunate at all — and perhaps were worth the destruction of a valuable chair. The bond between Billy and Celia was strengthened into a loyal friendship which would last all their lives.

PART 3

Young People in the House

CHAPTER
SEVENTEEN

June, 1923

"You're Mark Dunne, aren't you?"

"Yes. Oh, hallo, Oliver!"

"It's odd meeting you like this!"

It was rather odd. Mark had been spending a week in London and had gone into Harrods to buy a present for his mother. He was trying to decide between a small bottle of scent and a large bottle of bath salts.

"Haven't seen you for years," Oliver was saying. "Not since the war . . . I got in at the end of it, you know."

"I just missed it."

"You were lucky. It was pretty nasty really. What are you doing now?"

"Medicine. It's tremendously interesting."

"Rather you than me. It's a frightful grind, isn't it?"

"What are you doing, Oliver?"

"Nothing," said Oliver, laughing. "Nothing at all and yet I'm always busy. I haven't decided what I want to do. How does one decide, Mark?"

Mark grinned. He liked Oliver and admired him, for Oliver was everything that Mark was not. Oliver was gay and careless, he was always laughing; he treated life as a very good joke.

"I was wounded, you know," continued Oliver. "It wasn't particularly nice but it got me out of the mess — then, when I recovered, the jolly old war was over and I was high and dry. Fortunately the family seems to like paying for my bread and butter — it's lucky, isn't it?"

Mark did not take this explanation at its face value. He remembered hearing that Oliver had been very badly knocked about. He had a vague idea that Oliver had distinguished himself by winning the M.C.

"I expect you have to take things pretty easy," Mark said.

"Oh, I don't know," said Oliver vaguely. He looked about and added, "What are you doing here?"

Mark remembered his dilemma — scent or bath salts — the young lady behind the counter was still waiting patiently for him to decide.

"Scent," said Oliver, when the matter had been explained to him. "Scent every time. *Rêve D'Amour*, that's the stuff."

Mark bought it at once, of course. *Rêve D'Amour* cost about twice as much as he could reasonably afford, but that could not be helped. They came out of the shop together and stood for a few moments looking up and down the street.

"It was odd meeting you," said Oliver. "All the odder because Tessa and I are off to Ryddelton on Wednesday."

"I'm going on Thursday."

Oliver laughed again. "You may be there before us. We're going by road, Tessa and I."

"What fun!"

"Yes, it will be, rather. I've got a new car — passes everything on the road — a perfect gem. Look here, Mark, how would you like to come with us?"

"Really?"

"Yes, of course, there's plenty of room. We're going to spend a night at Wetherby — it's about half-way —"

Mark did not hesitate for long. In fact he only hesitated long enough to make sure that Oliver was in earnest.

"I'd love to come," he declared. "Yes, I can easily get away on Wednesday —"

Going home to Dunnian was always tremendously exciting but this time it was more exciting than ever. The three of them sat in the front seat (there was ample room for three slim young people); Tessa was the jam in the sandwich. Mark had not seen Tessa since that party at Dunnian . . . it was six years ago or very nearly . . . but she was just the same, gay and pretty and friendly. They talked and laughed, and sometimes, when the car was buzzing along the Great North Road, they lifted their voices in song.

"We must keep Oliver amused or he'll go to sleep," Tessa explained. "Then we shall end in the ditch. It doesn't matter if people think we're mad. They don't know who we are."

"It never matters," Oliver pointed out. "If strangers see you behaving like lunatics it doesn't matter because they don't know who you are; and, if your friends see you behaving like lunatics, it doesn't matter because they know who you are."

155

"You've hit on a very profound thought, Oliver," Tessa declared.

The second day was even better than the first for Mark had lost the remains of his shyness and they were getting nearer to Dunnian every moment. They lunched at Otterburn, climbed over Carter Bar and greeted Scotland with whoops of joy. On they went, diving into the valley, snaking down the long hill into Jedburgh.

"We must have fun this summer," Oliver declared. "We must have picnics. We can buzz into Edinburgh and dance —"

"I've got to do some work," said Mark.

"Nonsense!" cried Tessa.

"I've got to," Mark told her. "Of course I shan't work all the time —"

"Of course not," she replied.

Until now the country had been unfamiliar to Mark but now they were passing through "known country" and at every turn in the road he saw hills and woods and little farms whose features he remembered.

"You're very silent all of a sudden," Tessa said.

"It's Dunnian," replied Mark. "I always get excited . . ."

Oliver laughed but Tessa seemed to understand. "I don't wonder you love Dunnian," she said in a low voice.

"You must come over as often as you can."

"I take that as an invitation," she told him. "You'll be sick of the sight of me before the summer's over."

"That isn't very likely," murmured Mark.

"I'm longing to see Edith again," Tessa continued. "I haven't seen Edith for ages. Has she changed much?"

"She's grown up, of course," replied Mark without much enthusiasm — somehow or other he felt annoyed at the mention of Edith's name.

"How like a brother!" laughed Tessa. "Can't you tell me what she's like? Is she as pretty as ever?"

"Joyce was the pretty one," put in Oliver. "She was a most attractive little girl. I suppose she's grown up, too."

"We're all grown up," said Tessa. "It's tremendous fun, isn't it? Tell me about Edith's fiancé."

"I didn't know Edith was engaged!" Oliver exclaimed in surprise.

"Yes, she's engaged to a fellow called Rewden," said Mark. "They live over at Sharme. He's a good bit older than we are. As a matter of fact I don't know him, it all happened last term."

"Douglas Rewden of Sharme!" exclaimed Oliver. "He's a bit of a catch, isn't he?"

"I suppose he is," said Mark uncomfortably. He did not like the suggestion that his sister had "caught" Rewden.

"Of course he's a catch," declared Tessa. "Grannie says all the girls in the neighbourhood are tearing their hair."

There was a little silence after that. For the first time Mark felt out of tune with his companions . . . but he tried to assure himself that it was just their way of talking, it meant nothing at all. I'm old-fashioned, thought Mark, perhaps I'm a bit of a prig. After all one ought to be pleased that Edith is making a good marriage . . .

* * *

Douglas Rewden was dining at Dunnian, so he was there when Mark arrived. There was not much time to take stock of him in the bustle and fuss, the kisses and questions and laughter with which members of the Dunne family were wont to greet each other, but after dinner, when Alice and the girls had gone and Mark and Douglas were left sitting at the table with the port between them, Mark was able to take a good look at his prospective brother-in-law. He was tall and well made with fair hair plastered down on his somewhat narrow head. His moustache was fair, too, and his eyes were a curiously pale blue. He was colourless and uninteresting to look at and he was equally uninteresting to talk to — so Mark found. Golf and bridge were the two subjects in which he was interested, and as Mark was no good at either the conversation languished and died.

"We'd better make a move," said Mark, rising. "You'll be wanting to make the most of your time with Edith."

Rewden rose at once and they went into the drawing-room.

As was natural Rewden made a bee-line for Edith who was sitting on a sofa doing some wool work. She made room for him to sit down beside her, and he sat down. Mark had joined the rest of the family and was busy answering their questions and asking questions himself, but every now and then he glanced towards the sofa somewhat anxiously. It was obvious that Rewden admired Edith — and indeed she was very easy to admire — but they did not seem to have much to say to each other and Mark could not believe that Edith was

fond of him. Edith was an intelligent young woman,
what could she see in a nincompoop like Rewden?

"It's lovely, isn't it?" Alice said in a low voice,
nodding towards the engaged couple. "Dear Edith, I'm
so glad she has found the right man. He's charming,
isn't he, Mark, such nice manners and so good-looking."

"He's a good deal older than Edith," said Mark in the
same low tone.

"That doesn't matter," replied Alice smiling. "You
young people are so funny about age. To me Douglas
seems quite young — a mere boy — but, just because
he's older than you are, you talk as if he had one foot in
the grave."

"When will Dad be home?"

"Not until the autumn, I'm afraid," said Alice sadly.
"Of course we can't have the wedding without him.
Douglas is *very* impatient, but I told him quite firmly
that we must wait."

"Dad knows about it?"

"Oh, of course! I wrote to him at once. He doesn't
know Douglas, but I told him all about it and he's very
pleased. It's a pity we couldn't have the wedding in the
summer, but it can't be helped."

"I'm going to be the chief bridesmaid," said Joyce,
smiling. "Edith hasn't made up her mind how many
bridesmaids she's going to have —"

"Six, dear," said Alice. "She must have six . . ."

"I think she should have seven," said Joyce. "Then I
can walk by myself in front of the others. I'm the *chief*
bridesmaid, you see."

"But Joyce, six would be better —" Alice began.

"No, seven, Mother," said Joyce. She began to enumerate them, and Alice agreed and disagreed — it was all quite ridiculous, Mark thought; he bore it as long as he could and then he rose, saying that he would take the dogs for a bit of a walk before he went to bed.

"You needn't bother," said Joyce. "Debbie always gives the dogs a run . . ."

"Debbie can come too . . . or else have a holiday," replied Mark, smiling at his cousin.

This was such a foolish remark that Debbie did not bother to answer it, she was on her feet in a moment and ran off to get her coat.

"Debbie is very useful," said Alice. "I don't know what I should do without her, really, and when Edith and Joyce are married it will be so nice for me to have Debbie to keep me company."

"Is Joyce thinking of matrimony?" asked Mark in surprise.

"Not yet, of course," replied her mother, "but she's sure to marry one of these days . . ."

"Of course I shall," said Joyce.

Mark could not help smiling as he called the dogs and went towards the door. Apparently it had never crossed his mother's mind that Deb might marry . . . and why shouldn't she? thought Mark. Debbie had improved in looks tremendously in the last few months. She was still thin, but not so delicate — her hair was smooth and glossy, and her skin, though darker than that of her cousins, had warmed to a peachy hue. Her eyes had always been lovely, soft and grey and shaded by dark lashes. He would be a lucky man who chose Deb for a wife, thought Mark, as he watched her come running down the stairs to join him, her face aglow with pleasure.

"Where shall we go?" asked Mark.

"Let's walk down the river," she replied.

"Have you put on thick shoes?"

"Of course I have."

She was eager to be gone, for at any moment the drawing-room door might open and Joyce come out — she wanted Mark all to herself.

They talked of various matters as they walked along. Mark told her about his work and of his hopes for the future. His qualifying exam was in the autumn and he must do well. If he did well he might be offered a post in one of the big hospitals — it would be splendid if he could do well enough to be chosen for that.

"You will," said Debbie confidently.

"I *shall*," he replied with determination. "I must work hard this vacation — I really must."

They were silent for a few minutes, walking along by the stream. The dogs were hunting rabbits and water rats, they were having a grand time.

"What do you think of Rewden?" said Mark at last.

"He's very nice," said Debbie.

"Would you care to spend your whole life with him?"

Debbie looked up in alarm. She cried, "Oh Mark, don't you like him?"

"There's nothing to dislike about him," replied Mark thoughtfully. "At least I found nothing — there's nothing to like either —"

"Perhaps Edith sees something that we don't see."

161

"Perhaps she does."

"That must be the reason," Debbie declared, and it was obvious from the way she spoke that she had given the matter a good deal of thought. "You know, Mark, people must see things to like in each other — things that are invisible to outsiders — otherwise nobody would get married at all."

"That's quite true," he replied with a sigh of relief. It was the first piece of comfort he had received and he was so grateful to Debbie that he slipped his arm through hers and gave it a little squeeze. Deb had always been his "favourite sister" and she still was.

CHAPTER
EIGHTEEN

Mark and Tessa

Tessa had not forgotten her promise to come over to Dunnian, and the following morning she and Oliver arrived in the car. It was Edith she wanted to see — and Joyce, of course. The three girls strolled off down the garden arm in arm, their heads close together, and Mark watched them from the library window. He had settled down to work but his books seemed very dull this morning and he could not fix his thoughts. In a few moments Oliver came out of the house. Oliver saw the girls and waved and ran after them. They all disappeared from Mark's view but not from his thoughts and he found himself wondering which way they would go. Perhaps they would cross the river by the stepping stones and go up through the woods . . . it would be lovely in the woods this morning. It would be warm and fragrant. The hot sun on the pines would bring out the sweet resinous smell. Shafts of sunlight would fall between the trees making pools of yellow light . . . Like the first Celia Dunne, Mark had this odd faculty of seeing Dunnian with his inward eyes, seeing it clearly and truthfully. (Sometimes in the middle of a lecture on anatomy, or physics, the dusty class-room would disappear and instead he would see Dunnian, the trees, the lawns, the gardens, and would hear the soft murmur of the Rydd.)

Mark ran his fingers through his hair and sighed and tried to fix his thoughts on the printed page. He managed to banish his visions and studied hard for a while . . . and then he heard voices and saw Tessa and Joyce coming back across the lawn. This time he could not resist the temptation to join them; he closed his book and jumped out of the window.

"Pink frocks," Joyce was saying eagerly. "I think Edith is right. Blue would suit me, of course, but it wouldn't suit you —"

"Pale grey would be so much more uncommon," Tessa urged. "I mean a sort of silvery grey — and bouquets of pink carnations."

"Where are all the others?" asked Mark. He was sick of the subject of Edith's wedding. They were all crazy about it.

"We lost them in the wood," replied Joyce, her face clouding a little. "It was silly, really, because I was going to take Oliver to see the garden. He said he wanted to see it, and then —"

"What about a walk?" asked Mark.

"We've just been for a walk," said Joyce crossly.

"But it wasn't a very long one," said Tessa, smiling.

This sounded quite hopeful and Mark's hopes were fulfilled with extraordinary ease. In a few minutes he and Tessa were walking across the lawn together.

"I thought you were working this morning," Tessa said.

"I tried to," replied Mark. "But, you see, when I come back to Dunnian I feel I must go out and see the place. After I've seen it properly I shall be able to settle down."

"Yes, of course," she agreed. "I think Dunnian is perfect. Ryddelton House is bigger but it isn't nearly so nice. There have always been Dunnes here, I suppose."

"For hundreds of years. I thought I would take you to see the old peel tower where my ancestors used to live. I don't think they can have been very comfortable, but they were very secure."

"I'd love to see it. Ryddelton House is comparatively new. Oliver will have it some day."

"I wondered —"

"Yes, Oliver will have Ryddelton. That's why we're here this summer. Grannie wants Oliver to learn to look after the place. The factor is going to show him the ropes."

Mark gave a little sigh. Sometimes he felt a little sad that Dunnian would not be his. He said, "It's nice for Oliver, isn't it. I expect there's a lot to learn. There's a great deal of land, isn't there?"

"Quite a lot," she nodded. "Oliver finds it quite interesting, but it's terribly dull for me. I don't like Ryddelton and Grannie is so stuffy. It's frightful to think I've got to put up with Grannie's fads and fancies all the summer."

Mark felt a trifle embarrassed, for he liked old Lady Skene and he felt that it was not quite right to speak of her slightingly.

"She's such a sight," continued Tessa, smiling. "That awful red wig — and it's always a bit crooked — those appalling clothes!"

"I think she's rather wonderful," said Mark

"You wouldn't if you had to live with her."

"She's old," said Mark, who had made up his mind that he must voice his opinions. "She's old but she's alive and interesting. She does so much good in the neighbourhood —"

Tessa laughed. "She likes to have her finger in every pie if that's what you mean."

It was not what he meant but he did not pursue the subject for suddenly he saw how foolish it was to argue with Tessa about her grandmother. Here they were, together, walking across Dunnian Moor — surely they could find something better to talk about!

Tessa had evidently come to the same conclusion: "Isn't the air marvellous!" she exclaimed. "You're higher than we are at Ryddelton and the air seems quite different."

This changed the course of the conversation and they talked of all sorts of matters which interested them, and found agreement.

"I don't know where we're going and I don't care," said Tessa suddenly. "We shall get into an awful row if we're late for lunch, but who cares about that."

"We're there," replied Mark, laying a hand on her arm and pointing.

They were standing at the top of a high sloping bank covered with thick grass and boulders. Below them ran the Rydd Water — it was slow and quiet here —

166

slipping along smoothly with scarcely a ripple upon its silvery breast. Beyond the little river there was a small flat plateau ringed with trees and bushes and at one side of this plateau rose the ruined tower of Dunnian.

"Oh!" exclaimed Tessa. "Oh Mark, it's a stage!"

"A stage?" asked Mark in bewilderment.

"Yes, look at it, Mark. Look at that flat piece of ground and the trees and bushes all round it. Can't you see — it's a perfect natural stage."

Mark had not thought of it like that, for the Old Peel Tower was part of his life, and the flat piece of ground belonged to it. To Mark it spelt romance, the romance of past Dunnes who had lived there, who had been born and bred in the place, who had held it by strength of arms against their foes. He had hoped that Tessa would see it as he saw it, he had hoped she would sense the atmosphere of the past. His head was full of stories about the old Peel ... it would have been nice to sit down on the bank and tell Tessa some of the stories.

"Can't you see what I mean?" asked Tessa a trifle impatiently.

"Yes, it's like a stage," admitted Mark.

"It's a marvellous stage," she declared. "You could use the old tower as a dressing-room, couldn't you?"

"I suppose you could."

"It's lovely," said Tessa with a little sigh. "It's quite lovely. Let's do *A Midsummer Night's Dream*, shall we?"

"You don't really mean it, do you?" asked Mark in alarm.

"Of course I mean it."

"But, Tessa —"

"I love acting. It will be tremendous fun."

"Tessa, it's — it's a historical place," said Mark. "I mean —"

"But *they* wouldn't mind," declared Tessa, looking at him with wide eyes.

"Who wouldn't mind?"

"The ghosts," said Tessa. "Poor ghosts — they would like it. I know they would."

"Really, Tessa —" began Mark, but he could not help smiling.

"Besides, we apologise to them," said Tessa earnestly. "We apologise to them at the end of the play. You remember, Mark:

> 'If we shadows have offended
> Think but this (and all is mended)
> That you have but slumbered here
> While these visions did appear.'"

Mark laughed. He said, "That certainly is a handsome apology to the shadows of my ancestors, but all the same —"

"It will be something to *do*," interrupted Tessa eagerly. "It will be a lovely thing to do. Ryddelton is so dull, isn't it?"

Mark did not think it was dull.

"Oh, but it *is*," declared Tessa. "It's terribly dull — but if we could have a play the time would pass like lightning. Let me see now, there's you and Oliver and Edith and Joyce and me — of course Oliver and I would have to come over here every day and rehearse the scenes."

This was certainly a great inducement and for the first time Mark wavered. He said, "But Tessa, I'm supposed to be working."

"You shall have a *small* part. Oh, what fun! Oliver will love it. He's terribly keen on theatricals and very good, too. We'll make him Demetrius —"

"But there are dozens of people in *A Midsummer Night's Dream!*"

"We'll do scenes from it — just a few scenes. We'll do the scenes which take place in the wood. Let me see — you had better be Lysander, I think."

"Honestly, Tessa —"

"Don't be stuffy," she implored. "You know, Mark, when I want a thing I want it terribly — I just have to get it."

"Do you?"

"Yes, now listen: the audience will sit on this bank, of course. They can sit on rugs. We'll give the money to the Lord Roberts Memorial Fund."

"What money?"

"The gate-money, stupid. Heaps of people will come, people from the town. We'll run a bus from Ryddelton . . . Look!" she cried, catching hold of his arm. "Look at the stage, Mark! Think of how beautiful it will be! I don't suppose the play has ever been done in such a perfect setting before."

Her eager face was so lovely that Mark was swept away. All at once the thing seemed feasible.

He laughed.

"You will!" she cried. "Oh Mark, what a dear you are! Let's go down and decide about everything."

They went down the slope together and crossed the river by some broken stepping stones — Tessa skipped across them like a mountain goat — and soon they were standing upon the little plateau looking about them and discussing ways and means.

The "stage" was even more perfect on closer inspection — so Tessa declared. The turf was short and smooth and there were a few big rocks which would do for sitting on. The bushes were thick and made splendid wings. At the entrance to the old tower there were some fallen stones which must be cleared away and some nettles which must be cut, but a man could do all that was needed in a few hours. Now that Mark had consented to the idea he was almost as keen as Tessa, for if they were going to do it at all they must do it properly.

Tessa stood on the "stage" and tested it for sound. "It won't do if there's an echo," she explained; but there was no echo at all; her voice floated across the little river as clear as a bell.

> "And in the wood where often you and I
> Upon faint primrose beds were wont to lie,
> Emptying our bosoms of their counsels sweet
> There my Lysander and myself shall meet . . ."

It was so beautiful that tears rose to Mark's eyes. "Oh, Tessa!" he said huskily.

She turned and smiled at him, holding out her hands.

"Oh, Tessa, how lovely you are!" cried Mark.

CHAPTER
NINETEEN

Deb

Deb had been looking forward to this summer eagerly, but now the summer was here and it was not going as she had expected. She was not enjoying it much . . . it's because of the play, thought Deb. When the play is over everyone will settle down . . .

She had never heard the beginning of the idea, but all at once everyone was talking about the play — it ousted the wedding as a topic of conversation. They were all delighted at the idea of acting a play but unfortunately they were not unanimous as to what the play should be. Edith wanted a modern comedy and was backed up by Oliver; Tessa was determined to have scenes from *A Midsummer Night's Dream*; Aunt Alice was eager that they should act a play but she wanted one with music, and especially with songs in it for Joyce — Joyce was having singing lessons and it seemed a pity to waste this opportunity to show off her voice.

"She has such a pretty voice," declared Alice, smiling at her second daughter affectionately.

"Could we do *Faust*?" asked Joyce, who had suddenly visualised herself as Marguerite, singing the "Jewel Song" to an enraptured audience.

"My dear girl," said Mark impatiently. "What on earth do you think we are? Who ever heard of amateurs attempting *Faust*?"

"It must be something we can do out of doors," said Tessa. "It must be *A Midsummer Night's Dream*."

"It's so hackneyed," declared Oliver.

"It's the sort of thing school-children do," said Edith.

The battle raged for several days and then all at once it was over. Tessa knew exactly what she wanted, so she won. The others were still hunting for a modern comedy (with good parts for five people) which could be played out of doors without any artificial properties, but their efforts grew more and more feeble.

"It's no good," said Oliver at last. "We can't find anything suitable."

"There isn't anything suitable," Tessa declared. "If you don't want *The Dream* you'll have to write a play yourself."

She was so sure that they would "come round" that she was already at work upon the play, moulding it to her requirements. She eliminated Act I, because it had to be played indoors, but took some of the speeches out of it and grafted them into Act II. Some of the speeches were too long (in Tessa's opinion) so she cut them down. She found her self-appointed task very fascinating.

They were all having tea on the terrace at Dunnian when the matter was finally settled. The whole family was there including Douglas Rewden who had come over from Sharme to discuss arrangements for the wedding and was somewhat surprised to discover that this hitherto absorbing subject had been shelved.

"Now that it's settled we must go ahead," said Tessa happily, and she explained her ideas. Debbie discovered that she was to be Oberon and Celia was to be Puck. Celia would make a very good Puck, thought Debbie, but she was not so sure of her own ability to play the Fairy King. She had not expected to be included in the cast . . .

"Of course you must be in it," said Mark. "You can do it beautifully, Debbie. We need you."

"I suppose you've cast us all," said Oliver with a grin. "May I ask what character I'm to represent."

"You're Demetrius," replied Tessa. "Mark is Lysander."

"I shall be Helena," said Edith and Joyce together with one voice.

"I don't know —" began Tessa.

"You're engaged," said Joyce quickly. "It's my turn to have some fun. I want to be Helena." She struck an attitude and declared:

> " 'I will not trust you, I;
> Nor longer stay in your curst company.' "

"I'm the eldest," said Edith.

"I think Edith had better be Helena," Oliver said.

"Then I shall be Hermia," declared Joyce.

"I don't think that would do," said Tessa firmly. "I must be Hermia because I'm small and dark. You know the bit where Lysander says: 'Away, you Ethiope' . . . and Helena says: 'Though she be little she is fierce.' Hermia is always small and dark."

"Joyce would make a splendid Titania," said Oliver, smiling.

"I won't," declared Joyce. "Titania is such a fool. I'll be Oberon and Debbie can be Titania if she likes."

"Yes, of course," said Debbie quickly. She did not mind what part she had as long as the others were satisfied.

"Are you sure, Deb?" asked Mark.

"I'd *rather* be Titania," replied Deb, nodding.

"That's settled, then," declared Tessa who was anxious to get things straight and never lost an opportunity of fixing a point firmly in everyone's mind. Deb wondered, afterwards, how often she had heard Tessa say, "That's settled, then," before passing on to some other debatable point.

"What about Quince and Bottom and all of them?" asked Oliver.

"We can't have them," replied Tessa. "There's nobody to play them."

"There's Rewden," Oliver said. "Rewden could be Bottom and then we could have the bit where Titania wakes up and sees Bottom. It's awfully good theatre and it would amuse the townspeople."

Deb was horrified at this suggestion for she had read the play and was aware of the extravagant things she would have to say to Mr. Rewden. (She had been told to call him Douglas but she had not accomplished this difficult feat). How could she possibly put her arms round his neck and say that she would "Kiss thy large fair ears, my gentle joy" . . . ?

174

Celia had read the play, too, she leant across and whispered, "Deb, his ears *are* large and fair."

"Hush," said Deb sternly.

"What about the fairies — Peasblossom and the others," someone inquired.

"We can do without them. I'll take out all that," said Tessa, turning over the pages of her book and making rapid notes.

"You'll need one fairy at least," said Edith. "Perhaps Mildred Raeworth would do, she's very small for her age."

"It ought to be called 'Tessa's Dream,'" said Oliver laughing.

"I'm only taking out a few little bits —"

"I'm sure you're doing it beautifully, dear," said Alice kindly.

"I mean," explained Oliver. "I mean, if any of the audience has ever seen or read or heard of William Shakespeare's play he may feel that he's been cheated and want his money back."

Alice said with a bewildered air, "I'm sure Tessa will give him his money back if he wants it."

They all laughed. Alice was not aware that she had said anything funny but she smiled as if she had meant to. She found it increasingly difficult to understand the young — and especially difficult to understand Oliver. When they were all talking together like this it was almost as if they were talking in a foreign language with which she was only partially acquainted. She sighed and thought of Humphrey. Humphrey was so easy to understand.

"I'll be Bottom," said Billy suddenly. "You've forgotten me but I want to be in it. We did that play at Welland House so I know all about it."

"Really?" inquired Oliver, who disliked Billy and never lost an opportunity of baiting him. "You know *all* about it, do you? How lucky for us to have your knowledge at our disposal. Perhaps you would tell us what it's all about."

"I thought you knew," replied Billy in surprise. "You were talking as if you did. It's about two lots of lovers who get lost in the Wood of Arden — near Athens, you know. It's Midsummer Night, of course, and the fairies are having a party. The lovers have come a long way and they're very tired so they lie down and go to sleep. Well then, you see, Puck comes along and goes round scattering magic poppy dust in people's eyes and when they wake up they fall madly in love with the first person they see — and of course it's the wrong person. They all get tangled up like anything — it's a very funny play."

Oliver was completely silenced by this masterly *résumé* of the plot and it was left for Alice to say, very fondly: "You certainly seem to know all about it, Billy."

"Yes," he agreed. "Yes, I do. I was Puck in the school play, but I'd like to be Bottom now if nobody minds. It will be fun wearing the donkey's head. Douglas had better be Theseus. You'll need Theseus to explain everything at the end when the lovers get unmagicked and fall into each others arms."

"I'd rather be Demetrius," said Douglas with a glance at Edith.

"Demetrius!" exclaimed Tessa in alarm. "But Demetrius is the most important part in the play. Have you had much experience of acting?"

"Er — no," replied Douglas, "but if Edith is going to be Helena I'd better be Demetrius —"

"It's a big part," said Tessa.

"It's only a play, Douglas," said Edith.

"There's a tremendous lot to learn," said Oliver.

Douglas looked from one to the other with a doubtful sort of air.

"Of course, if you insist," said Oliver casually. "If you really insist upon it the part is yours . . . but I warn you there's a tremendous lot of stuff to learn."

"And you're so busy," added Edith, smiling at him.

"Oh, well," said Douglas helplessly. He saw that everyone was against him — even Edith — so it was no use pursuing the matter further.

Several days passed. The discussions and the arguments went on and on, but gradually something began to emerge from the chaos, something rather exciting, Deb found. Deb had learnt her part quite easily — she was word perfect — and, as Billy knew his part already, they began to practise together and had great fun. She rather enjoyed making frantic love to Billy — Billy dressed up with a donkey's head hiding his fair round face.

The others were rehearsing, too, for they all had a great deal to learn in spite of Tessa's blue pencil. They went about with rapt expressions upon their faces, muttering their lines over and over. Tessa was not only the editor and one of the principal actors, she was

177

producer as well, and she ruled her small company with an iron hand.

"Don't stand there," she would say. "Come forward and speak clearly. Remember it's the open air and people won't be able to hear ... that's wooden, Joyce. Do it like this —" and Tessa would step forward and show how the thing should be done.

Sometimes her decisions were questioned by the other actors, who had their own ideas of how their parts should be played, but Deb noticed that, after the point had been discussed and debated, the others usually gave in and allowed Tessa to have her way, and Deb was obliged to admit that Tessa was usually right. "That's settled, then," Tessa would say — and somehow or other it was.

Gradually the play took shape; the date was fixed and notices were sent out to be displayed in the shop windows in Ryddelton. Tickets began to sell almost at once, for a great many people thought it would be amusing to go over to Dunnian and see the young people acting — it was well worth a shilling, including the bus fare. People were coming from the big houses as well: the Farquhars and the Murrays from Timperton, the Johnsons from Carlesford and all the people from round about Ryddelton.

No scenery was needed, for nature had provided that, but dresses had to be made or altered to suit the wearers and Becky sewed industriously in the old nursery at the top of the house. Deb went up and helped her whenever possible, for there was a good deal to do, and, besides, she liked to help Becky; it was quiet and peaceful in the old nursery, they sat there together for hours on end, chatting about one thing or another or sitting in silent amity. Every now and then one of the actors would pop in to see how they were getting on, to try on a doublet or make suggestions about a dress.

One afternoon, when Deb and Becky were hard at work, the door opened and Tessa walked in. She was the person who had given the dressmakers more trouble than all the other members of the cast put together. Her dress had been altered half a dozen times.

"What's wrong now, I wonder," murmured Becky in an undertone.

Deb smiled, for these *sotto voce* remarks of Becky's always amused her. They were so characteristic of Becky. Sometimes the subject of the remark was intended to hear it, and sometimes not, but if Becky were asked to repeat the remark she usually said something quite different.

Tessa took no notice of Becky — there was no love lost between them — "Hallo, Debbie!" she said in a cheerful tone.

"Hallo!" responded Deb, without enthusiasm.

"I've been looking for you, Debbie," Tessa said.

"Have you?" asked Deb in some surprise, for as a rule Tessa took very little notice of her.

"Yes, I wondered where you were," said Tessa, perching herself on the edge of the table and swinging her legs.

"Miss Deb is here most afternoons," said Becky. "It's a pity other people can't do a bit of sewing sometimes."

Tessa made no reply to this except to glance at Becky with a supercilious air.

"I want to talk to you," she said to Deb. "It's about the play, of course. We want Andrew Raeworth to take the part of Egeus, and we can't very well ask Andrew without asking Angela. You see that, don't you."

"Yes," said Deb.

"Of course Mildred is going to be the fairy — but we haven't got a suitable part for Angela."

"Couldn't Angela be the fairy?" asked Deb.

Tessa laughed. "Can you *see* her!" she exclaimed. "She's far too big, for one thing."

Deb said nothing.

"You aren't particularly keen, are you?" Tessa inquired.

Deb hesitated and then she said slowly, "You mean you want Angela to be Titania?"

"You don't mind, do you? I mean you just took the part because Mark said we needed you . . . but, now, we don't need you."

"What does Mark think about it?" asked Deb.

"I've told you," replied Tessa impatiently. "We don't really need you now. You'll be quite glad to get out of it, won't you?"

"Did Mark say that?"

"Yes, of course. You don't mind, do you?"

Deb did not answer at once. She was busy making a tuck in Billy's costume, but at last she said, "No, I don't mind, Tessa."

"That's settled, then," declared Tessa, jumping off the table.

There was a little silence after she had gone. Becky asked for the scissors and Deb passed them to her.

"It's not right," said Becky suddenly. "You shouldn't let them do it."

"I don't mind, not really," replied Deb in a low voice. "If Mark wants to have Angela in the play —"

"It isn't him at all," declared Becky. "You know that as well as I do. It's not his doing — it's hers. She twirls him round her finger."

"I know."

"It's not right," repeated Becky emphatically. "It's neither good for you nor for them. Why should you be the one to take a back seat?"

Becky waited a moment but there was no reply.

"You ought to make an effort," Becky continued. "You ought to take your proper place. People can't see you if you always stand in the shade."

"If they don't want me —"

"They ought to want you. They *would* want you if they had any sense. Some people don't know what's good for them."

"But, Becky —"

"It's not only the play," continued Becky doggedly. "It's bad enough in all conscience putting you out of the play with your part all learnt and your dress made and everything — but that's not the worst. The worst is she's always putting you out and always will unless you can stand up to her."

Deb knew this already, only too well. "I can't, Becky," she said in a very low voice.

"No, I don't suppose you can," agreed Becky, looking across the table at Deb's lowered head with deep affection.

"You *can't* stand up for yourself. Maybe you wouldn't be you if you could do it, but it's a pity none the less . . ."

"Becky, don't say anything —"

"Of course not. It's none of my business . . . it beats me what Mr. Mark can see in her."

"She's very pretty."

"Flashy," Becky said, somewhat unjustly, "She's flashy, and men are fools."

Now that she was no longer in the cast Deb had more time to spare for her usual duties. She sewed with Becky, sat with Aunt Alice and took the dogs for walks. The others were all so busy with rehearsals that she saw very little of them, but she noticed that Mark's manner to her had altered a little. He had always had a "special smile" for Deb, but now the smile was less spontaneous . . . He was busy, of course, working all the morning, shut up in the library with his books, and rehearsing his part in the afternoon, but Deb had hoped that the evening walk with the dogs would continue and she was bitterly disappointed when she found that the evening walks were "off." Mark went out with the dogs by himself or else he retired to the library and left Deb to take them. She knew — or thought she knew — the reason for this change in Mark. The reason was Tessa. Tessa did not like her. Tessa was taking him away. She was taking him away completely, not even a little bit of friendship was to be left to Deb.

One afternoon Deb took the dogs and went down to the tower to watch the rehearsals, she was early and the stage was empty. It was a very hot day and she sat down on the bank in the shadow of a rock and waited for the actors to appear. How lovely it was! The sun was golden, the air clear, the grass green and cool. Down below was the little river and beyond was the stage, ready and waiting for the play. Deb was almost asleep when she heard voices and suddenly Oliver and Edith appeared on the stage — they had come to rehearse together.

"We'll go over that bit in Act II," Oliver was saying. "We'll take it from: 'I love thee not, therefore pursue me not.' You don't put enough fire into your part, Edith."

"It seems so awful," said Edith with a light laugh.

"What do you mean?"

"I mean it seems so awful for me to follow you all over the place and keep on saying that I love you."

"I enjoy it," declared Oliver.

"I don't," she replied. "It goes against the grain when I have to say: 'I am your spaniel and, Demetrius, the more you beat me I will fawn on you.'"

"Miss Dunne is not used to pursuing," said Oliver, laughing.

"Oh, well, you know what I mean."

"I know exactly what you mean — but we happen to be acting a play. You aren't Miss Dunne and I'm not Mr. Skene."

"No," said Edith. She hesitated and then added: "At first I thought I couldn't go on with it — Helena seemed

183

so — so shameless and — and despicable ... but of course we're both in a spell of magic —"

"Exactly," agreed Oliver, taking out a cigarette and lighting it. "It's just the poppy dust — I love you madly all the time. Perhaps you would feel better about it if you kept that firmly in mind."

Edith laughed.

"Would you feel better?" he asked.

"I might — or I might not," she retorted.

"I should like to try to make you feel better."

"How would you do that?"

"We'll rehearse the part where I wake up in my right senses — that ought to do the trick."

Oliver lay down beside a rock. He looked very odd lying there in his ordinary clothes and Deb could not help smiling. Edith looked odd, too, standing in the middle of the stage waiting for him to wake up and look at her. There was a little silence and then Oliver sat up and stretched himself. He yawned and looked all round (It was well done, Deb thought), his eyes fell on Edith and he rose slowly, holding out his hands. His voice rang out in gladness and surprise:

"Oh, Helen, goddess, nymph, perfect, divine!
To what, my love, shall I compare thine eyne?
Crystal is muddy. O how ripe in show
Thy lips, those kissing cherries, tempting grow!
... O, let me kiss
This princess of pure white, this seal of bliss!"

They were standing quite near each other as Oliver finished, and suddenly he stepped forward and took her in his arms . . . and kissed her.

"But that isn't in the play," declared Edith, struggling feebly.

"It ought to be in the play," replied Oliver emphatically. "When I say I'm going to kiss a girl I always do it straight off. In fact I usually do it without making a song and dance about it first. I could have given Demetrius some useful tips . . ."

"You *are* awful," declared Edith, who was busy tidying her hair.

"We'll tell Tessa to put it in the play," said Oliver gravely. "She's taken so many liberties with the script that one more wouldn't make much difference . . . and it would give me so much pleasure," he added persuasively.

Edith laughed.

"I shall be willing to rehearse the scene as often as you like," Oliver continued. "If fact I think we'd better do it again, now."

"No, thank you," said Edith, still laughing.

"Why not?"

"If there's any more nonsense I shall let Joyce take the part."

"You wouldn't be so cruel!" Oliver exclaimed.

Edith laughed again. There was a thrill of excitement in her laughter. She said, "I know what you are, Oliver. You don't mean a word you say."

"Are you sure?" he asked. "Are you sure I don't mean it? Perhaps I'm trying to find out what *you* mean. Edith, look at me —"

"Hush, someone's coming," Edith said.

Deb had watched and listened spellbound, but now the spell was broken and she realised that she ought not to be listening to this piece of by-play, this play within a play. They did not know she was there; they had not seen her sitting in the shadow of the rock. Her mind was in a turmoil. She wished that she had not seen so much. She wished with all her heart that she was somewhere else. What was she to do? Should she rise and show herself or should she stay where she was and wait for them to go away?

Fortunately, at this moment, Mark and Tessa appeared. "Hallo, are you rehearsing?" Mark inquired.

"Let's do Act III, Scene 2, where we all talk together," said Tessa, taking off her hat and putting it on a rock.

The others agreed to the suggestion and the rehearsal started without more ado.

CHAPTER
TWENTY

Midsummer Night's Dream

"It's going to rain," said Alice. She had said it at least six times and each time Deb had answered, "The glass is quite steady, Aunt Alice." She repeated it again, patiently, for she knew exactly how Aunt Alice felt — it would spoil everything if it rained.

"I'm glad you aren't acting, dear," said Alice. "We'll walk down together, you and I, and it will be a great help to have you. I like to have someone to help me."

Deb smiled. She was very fond of Aunt Alice. Suddenly she felt quite glad that she was not in the play. She had been disappointed at first for it had seemed such a waste of time to have learned all the speeches, but it was not really a waste for she would never forget the beautiful words. They would be with her always, safely in her head:

"And never, since the middle Summer's Spring
Met we on hill, in dale, forest or mead,
By pavēd fountain or by rushy brook

Or on the beachēd margent of the sea
To dance our ringlets to the whistling wind . . ."

Deb said the words over as she ran to get Aunt Alice's coat. They gave her a lovely feeling of freedom and space. Almost she could feel the cool sea breeze whistling through her hair.

"You're such a comfort to me, Debbie," said Aunt Alice, as they walked across the moor. "I'm not as strong as I used to be and I dare say you've noticed I get a little muddled sometimes. I think I should feel better if Humphrey were here. Sometimes I almost hope they won't make him an admiral. It would be so lovely to have him at home all the time, wouldn't it?"

"Lovely," agreed Deb.

"We've been married twenty-four years, but I don't suppose we've spent more than four years together, all told," Alice continued sadly. "Children are very nice and I'm glad we have them, but sometimes I can't help being a little envious of people who are free to follow their husbands round the world."

"It *is* hard," Deb said sympathetically. She thought of her mother as she spoke. Her mother had handed her over to the Dunnes and had followed the drum. She was still following it and Deb scarcely ever heard from her now. Occasionally a letter came, a bald "duty letter," conveying the information that Joan was at Peshawar or Simla or Deira Doone and was having a gay time. Even when Joan and her husband came home on leave they did not seem very anxious to see Deb. Their lives had flowed in another direction and there was no point of contact.

Aunt Alice was still talking. "You know, dear," she said. "You know it's a very curious thing (I was just thinking about it last night): I wasn't at all anxious to have you when your mother married and went to India . . . and now I couldn't get on without you."

"You've been perfect to me," Deb said, and she gave Aunt Alice's arm a little squeeze.

"It's *very* curious," repeated Aunt Alice thoughtfully.

By this time Alice and Deb had reached the crest of the hill and, looking down, they saw that people were arriving fast, walking up the path by the river in little groups and taking up positions on the bank.

At the bottom of the bank there were two rows of chairs, the "reserved seats" which had been sold for half a crown. These chairs were filling rapidly. It was very strange to see so many people gathered together in this quiet spot, stranger still to hear the buzz of talk and laughter. Deb wondered what the owls were thinking of it, and the old jackdaws which always built their nest in the highest part of the tower.

"How do you do," Aunt Alice said. She was nodding and smiling to her friends, to Mrs. Wilson of the fish-shop in Ryddelton and to Lady Craig of Timperton Grange. "How do you do . . . so good of you to come," said Aunt Alice to each in turn. "How do you do. I hope you have brought a rug . . . I do hope you won't catch cold . . . the young people enjoyed getting it up . . . so lucky it's fine, isn't it?"

Deb following close at her heels and carrying a rug and a cushion for her to sit on, said the same things — or almost the same. "So nice of you to come . . . I hope you'll enjoy it. Yes, we thought it would be rather fun; it's such a perfect setting for the play. No, I'm not acting in it."

They settled into their seats, but not without a good deal of fuss. Lady Skene had disposed herself comfortably in the wrong chair with a rug wrapped round her legs and a sable cape round her shoulders. Any one looking at her might have received the impression that she expected a blizzard to interrupt the proceedings. She was so carefully wrapped up and so securely settled that nobody had the courage to suggest that she should move and this necessitated a good deal of rearrangement amongst the holders of the other reserved seats. However, after some trouble, the thing was managed and everyone was satisfied.

The audience was ready now. It sat back and waited more or less patiently for the play to begin. The stage was empty, green and silent and mysterious. Between the audience and the stage the little river pursued its way — it was like a sword (thought Deb) a shining sword, separating the world of everyday from the fairy wood where all sorts of strange events were about to happen.

Suddenly the notes of a bell floated across the water and almost immediately Celia appeared, dressed as Puck, followed by Mildred Raeworth as a fairy.

"How now, spirit, whither wander you?" cried Celia in her clear ringing voice . . . the play had begun.

Celia was good — there was no doubt of that — she was the spirit of mischief personified. She was gay and impudent . . . and she was enjoying herself immensely.

The audience settled down to listen. Perhaps the audience realised from that very first moment that this was something out of the common in amateur theatricals. Deb realised it. She had watched some of the rehearsals, of course, but there was always some hitch in the rehearsals, something that broke the continuity and destroyed the illusion. There was no hitch now, the play ran smoothly, it was beautiful and exciting, there was real magic here.

The play continued. Here were Oberon and Titania . . . Here were Demetrius and Helena, playing their parts in the entanglement with a good deal of spirit and fire. Deb thought that there was very little to complain of in the manner of Helena's wooing . . . it was obvious that Edith had been able to overcome her scruples fairly easily.

And, now, at last, here were Lysander and Hermia, wandering in together with their arms round each other's waists.

"Fair love, you faint with wandering in the wood;
And, to speak troth, I have forgot our way . . ."

It was Mark's voice, clear and vibrant and full of loving solicitude. It was Mark, not Lysander, not a puppet in a play . . . and Tessa was no puppet either. It was Mark who said to Tessa: "My heart unto yours is knit; so that but one heart we can make of it." It was Tessa who replied: "Good night, sweet friend: Thy love ne'er alter till thy sweet life's end."

They stood there, talking to each other in the little glade. They were young and beautiful and in love. Their voices were clear and yet quiet — as if they were talking to one another alone, unseen, unheard by any one. They *were* talking to one another, heart to heart.

Deb's own heart seemed to turn over in her breast as she listened. It was so painful that she scarcely knew how to bear it. She had known before, of course — she had known that they were in love — but there is a difference between knowing something and seeing it enacted before one's eyes.

Later, when the poppy-dust had done its work and the lovers were separated, it was no less painful. It was no comfort to Deb when Lysander declared: "Not Hermia but Helen, now, I love," for this was only the magic spell, this was only midsummer night madness. It was Hermia that he loved with all his heart. It was Hermia he would marry.

Deb was so enthralled by the strange painful beauty of the play that she lost all sense of time and place. The minutes flew; she felt as if she were alone in the woods watching the drama unfold before her eyes, and it was not until the very end when Puck came forward to make his valedictory speech that Deb came to herself and realised where she was.

"If we shadows have offended,
Think but this (and all is mended),
That you have but slumbered here,
While these visions did appear."

Deb had slumbered — though not very peacefully —
but she was awake now. She slipped away from Aunt
Alice's side for she felt she could not bear to take part in
the talk, nor to listen to the congratulations which would
follow. She pushed her way through the crowd which
already was on the move, rising, collecting rugs and
cushions and surging down the path. Two young men in
front of her were discussing the play with complete
frankness.

"It was magnificent but it wasn't Shakespeare," one
of them was saying.

"I don't think Will would mind," replied the other.

"No, I don't believe he would. The setting was
perfect."

"It was the Skene girl who re-wrote it, I believe."

"Must be clever."

"Yes, and damn' pretty into the bargain."

"She didn't cut down her own speeches."

"Not she. Hermia walked away with the play."

"The others were pretty good too. I thought Helena —"

"The eldest Dunne girl was Helena. She's engaged,
you know."

"To Demetrius, I suppose."

"She ought to be —"

Deb pushed on. She was behind a fat woman now.
The fat woman was saying in a bewildered sort of voice:

"But I always thought there were funny men in that play."

"There was Bottom," said her companion.

"I thought there was a man called Snug."

"That's in another play —"

"No, I'm sure. I was waiting for the funny bits all the time, and then —"

"They took the funny bits out," said a third voice. "It was a pity, really."

"I didn't know you were allowed —" the first woman said aggrievedly.

"Perfectly lovely," said another voice full of warm approval. "I wouldn't have missed it for anything. That's how the play ought to be acted — by young, beautiful creatures in a real wood."

Deb was out of the crush now. She ran up to the top of the hill. It was ten o'clock, but it was not really dark — the sky was light, the earth was grey, there were no clouds, no shadows — Deb threw herself on the ground and lay there for a long time with her face against the cool turf . . . presently she must go down into the world again and take up the burden of her life . . . but not just yet. Somehow, somewhere she must find strength and courage to go on.

CHAPTER
TWENTY-ONE

Conversations

Mark woke with a feeling of flatness. It was all over. He had not expected to enjoy it but it had been tremendous fun. They had all worked together and they had *made* something — it was not perfect, of course, but it was worth while — now the cord which had bound them all together was broken and they were scattered. That was what Mark felt. It had been lovely saying those words to Tessa . . . "How now, my love, why is thy cheek so pale" . . . "Gentle Hermia, may I marry thee?" Somehow he knew she had understood that he really meant the words, that they expressed his own deepest feelings.

Mark leaned out of his bedroom window. It was very early but the birds were awake, twittering in the bushes, singing in the trees. Mark's heart sang with them. "My love . . . my fair love . . . may I marry thee?"

He was going to see her this afternoon, for she and Oliver were coming over to tea. He must get her alone and find out if she *really* understood. Of course he could not say anything definite to Tessa yet, he was not even qualified, he had nothing to offer her, but they were both young. Tessa would not mind waiting . . . he would work like a Trojan and pass his exam with honours. He would work ten times harder than ever before . . .

It was not very difficult to get Tessa alone, for the others were busy adding up the money and congratulating themselves upon the large pile of shillings which had been taken by Johnson at the gate.

"I'm no good at arithmetic," Tessa said and she walked out into the garden; Mark followed her and, together, they went down the path between the trees.

"It was fun, wasn't it?" said Tessa. "I enjoyed it terribly much."

"So did I," said Mark. "It was even rather fun pretending to hate you, Tessa."

She smiled up at him: "Was it pretence?"

"You know it was," he said.

There was a little silence and then Tessa said, "We're going away to-morrow."

"Going away!"

"Yes, Oliver and I ought to have gone back to London last week, but of course we waited for the play."

"I see," said Mark. It was a great temptation. He would have given anything to be able to say: "Gentle Hermia, may I marry thee?" — the words were there on his lips — but it would not be right. It would not be fair to bind her. He must wait.

"Will you miss us?" Tessa inquired. "I hope you'll miss us. It's nice to be missed."

"I shall miss you horribly."

Tessa sighed. She said, "I hate leaving this place. I should like to settle down and live here for ever and ever. It's so lovely."

"Yes, it is," agreed Mark. "I feel just like you. Dunnian seems like a part of me — if you know what I mean. Sometimes I wish that Dunnian —"

"Oliver is sorry to leave here, too," said Tessa, interrupting him. "There's a very potent attraction at Dunnian — perhaps you've noticed it."

"You mean — Joyce?" asked Mark in surprise.

She laughed but did not answer.

Presently they began to talk of the play. It was an inexhaustible subject of conversation. "You do think it was a success, don't you?" Tessa asked. "You aren't sorry I persuaded you to have it."

"It was splendid," Mark replied. "I enjoyed every moment of it."

"Everyone played up like anything, didn't they?"

"Yes, the only flop was Angela — but of course it must have been difficult for her being dragged in at the last moment."

"Poor Angela!" exclaimed Tessa laughing. "I'm sorry for Angela, you know. Her one ambition in life is to grab a husband — anything in trousers would do. She pursues her game madly and rolls her eyes; no wonder the men sheer off!"

"Oh, I say," said Mark uncomfortably.

"It's perfectly true."

"No — honestly. Angela is rather a dear. I've known Angela for years and years, we used to do our sums together. She isn't a *bit* like that."

"Have it your own way," said Tessa casually.

Mark was silent. He could not bear to hear Tessa talk in this fashion, it was not worthy of her . . . but he

197

comforted himself with the reflection that this kind of talk was not really natural to Tessa but was "put on" — just as her dress was "put on." Her dress might be unbecoming but that did not alter her nature nor make him love her less.

Mark began to work harder than ever now. He worked late at night, poring over his books, and making copious notes in his neat small writing. He was thus engaged when Deb opened the library door and looked in.

"Shall I take the dogs out?" she asked.

"No, come and talk to me," replied Mark, flinging down his pen. "My head is buzzing; I can't do any more to-night."

She came and sat down on the hearth-rug and held out her hands to the fire. "It's cold to-night," she said. "The wind has gone into the east."

"I want to talk to you about things," said Mark.

She smiled and waited. It was nice that Mark wanted to talk to her. Mark had been . . . not quite so friendly, lately; but now he was smiling at her in the old way, so everything was all right.

"It's about Oliver," said Mark. "Oliver and Tessa have gone."

"Yes," agreed Deb. She tried to make her voice sound regretful, but it wasn't easy.

"It's funny," continued Mark slowly. "It's funny, really. I thought — I don't know if you noticed — I thought he was fond of Joyce."

"Joyce?" asked Deb.

"Yes, I thought so. Didn't you?"

"I thought —" began Deb, and then she stopped.

"What did you think?" asked Mark.

"I didn't think he was fond of Joyce."

"Well, I did," declared Mark, "and what's more I think Joyce is — is fond of Oliver. She's rather under the weather, isn't she?"

"Yes."

"What do you think can have happened?"

Deb did not answer. She had taken up the hearth-brush and was busy sweeping the grate, making it neat and tidy.

"I don't know what to do," continued Mark. "If Dad were here — but of course he isn't. Oliver is a good fellow, isn't he?"

"He's very good-looking," said Deb, after a little pause.

"I mean he wouldn't do anything shabby, would he?" asked Mark a trifle anxiously.

"You know him much better than I do," Deb replied.

Mark sighed and lay back in the big chair. He said, "I wish I knew what to do. It's a comfort to be able to talk to you about it. I can always talk to you about things. You're my favourite sister, Deb."

Once, long ago, these words had filled Deb with delight, but they sounded different now. She did not want to be Mark's favourite sister.

"I can talk to you about *anything*," repeated Mark. "You always understand. I wonder if you understand what I feel about Tessa."

"I think so," said Deb in a very small voice.

"Wasn't she marvellous as Hermia?"

"I thought you were marvellous as Lysander."

"I wasn't really acting," said Mark.

Deb had known this, of course, but to hear him say it made it more definite, more real, more painful. Deb told herself that if only Mark had set his heart upon someone else she would not have minded — if it had been Angela or Jean or *any* of the other girls — but Tessa was the wrong person for Mark; Tessa was ruthless, she was selfish and deceitful, she was no more like Mark's conception of her than a tiger is like a kitten. Some day Mark would find out what Tessa was really like . . . but he would find out too late. Oh, Mark, why are you so blind? She will break your heart!

Fortunately Deb had the sense to know that it was useless to say anything. She held her peace.

"She's so sweet," Mark was continuing. "There's something about her . . . she's so beautiful and good and kind . . . of course I haven't said anything to her yet, because — well — because I must have something to offer her, but I'm almost sure she likes me. I think it will be all right, don't you?"

"Yes," said Deb. She was quite sure Tessa intended to marry Mark. Her intention had been obvious from the beginning.

Mark smiled. He said, "You see everything, quiet little mouse that you are!"

There were other conversations going on in Dunnian that evening. The house seemed to be listening to them. The voice of the Rydd Water was very soft and low.

"I don't think it's fair," Joyce was saying. Joyce had come into Edith's bedroom to say good-night and she had stayed to talk.

"What isn't fair?" asked Edith with a yawn.

"You have everything," Joyce replied. "You take everything and leave nothing for me. You've always done that."

"I don't know what you mean."

"You *do* know," declared Joyce in trembling tones. "You know quite well. You're engaged to Douglas — almost married — why can't you be content with that?"

"Content?" asked Edith. "I never said I wasn't content —"

"Oliver has always been my friend," said Joyce tearfully. "He always liked me best — and then you —"

"I can't help it if people like me," said Edith smiling. She was sitting in front of her mirror and, as she spoke, she took up her brush and began to brush her hair. It was thick and golden, the colour of ripe corn, and she gave it a hundred strokes with the brush every night of her life.

"One . . . two . . . three," said Edith, drawing the brush through her hair.

"I wish you'd listen," said Joyce.

"I *am* listening. What do you want to tell me?"

"You might let me have a chance now and then," said Joyce, trying to control herself and speak naturally. "You're so selfish and — and unkind. I should have been Helena in the play."

"Oliver said —"

"I know, but you could have refused. It wasn't right for you to take the part. Douglas didn't like it, and I don't wonder."

"It was only a play, silly."

"People are talking."

"Who cares?"

"Douglas cares."

"I'm not married to Douglas, yet." There was a queer expression in Edith's eyes as she said these words.

"You don't mean —" began Joyce in dismay.

"I don't mean anything," declared Edith hastily. "As a matter of fact I'm so sleepy that I don't know what I'm saying. You had better go to bed."

Joyce went towards the door and paused with her hand on the handle: "Edith," she said. "Have you had a letter from Oliver?"

"No, why should he write to me?" said Edith.

In Alice's bedroom a third conversation was taking place. Becky was there, she was heating some milk on the electric radiator. Alice always had a glass of hot milk before she went to sleep and Becky usually had some too. They both enjoyed the little quiet time together, sipping their milk and talking about the day's doings. It was a habit which had originated when Celia was born and had never been abandoned.

"They're all so cross," Alice complained. "I suppose it's the reaction or something. I never remember a time when they were *all* cross, Becky."

"I can, then."

"Can you?"

"Yes, when they had measles," said Becky nodding. "They were all as cross as cross could be. There was no pleasing any of them."

"But they haven't got measles now, so —"

"They're in love," said Becky.

"They can't all be in love."

"Can't they?"

"No, of course not. Even Debbie is a little impatient — *she* can't be in love. Edith and Joyce quarrel all the time; Mark is sulky. It's *very* unpleasant."

"It will wear off," said Becky comfortingly.

"But what's the reason for it?"

"I told you —"

"You don't really mean they're all in love, do you?" asked Alice in some alarm. "It was just a joke, wasn't it, Becky?"

"Yes, just a joke."

"You frightened me," declared Alice, lying back on her pillows. "You frightened me horribly. I couldn't bear it if they were all in love at the same time and Humphrey not here. You know, Becky, I can't cope with them now. They don't tell me things. It was so much easier when they were small."

"It always is. Tantrums and stomach aches are soon cured."

"Gregory's mixture," agreed Alice, nodding. "I believe it would do them good *now*, but of course they wouldn't like it if I suggested it." She sighed and added: "I wish Humphrey were here."

"So do I," said Becky.

"Do you think Mark is fond of Tessa?"

"It looks like it, I must say."

"She's a sweet girl," said Alice. "Pretty and clever and sweet."

"I don't care for sweets much, myself," said Becky in an undertone.

"What did you say, Becky?"

"She's not good enough," said Becky.

Alice smiled. She said: "Of course you think there's nobody good enough for Mark, don't you, Becky?"

Becky did not reply.

CHAPTER
TWENTY-TWO

Humphrey

Humphrey managed to get leave. He walked into the drawing-room one evening when they were all sitting round the fire.

"I thought I would surprise you," he said.

"Humphrey!" cried Alice, rising and upsetting her work-basket on to the floor. She was in his arms in a moment, half laughing and half crying.

They were all here — all the family — Humphrey seized his daughters and kissed them; Celia clung round his neck; over her head Humphrey's eyes sought Mark's — and they smiled.

"This is splendid!" Humphrey said. "This is what I like — all being together —"

"How did you manage to get away?"

"How did you come?"

"Have you had dinner?"

"How long can you stay?"

He laughed and said, "Have pity on me! I flew from Marseilles and I've got two months' leave."

"Lovely!" said Alice, blissfully.

"Yes," agreed Humphrey. "It's about time I had some leave. It's about time I came back to look after my family. What's all this about a wedding?" He smiled at Edith as he spoke but she did not smile back

"He's such a dear," declared Alice. "He's so quiet and easy to understand. You'll like him, Humphrey."

"I hope so," Humphrey said, smiling more broadly than before.

"Of *course* you'll like him," said Alice. "There's something about him — he's a little shy but *charming* when you get to know him!"

"He seems to have charmed Edith very successfully," laughed Humphrey.

As usual Humphrey was feeling the strangeness of being at home, of being at Dunnian in the midst of his family, of hearing the light voices of his womenfolk. He felt even more strange than usual this time, more out of touch with their lives, but perhaps that was due to the fact that he had not been home for so long. They were "grown up" now, thought Humphrey, looking round the circle of faces. They were men and women. Billy was independent and self-confident, well started on his career. Only Celia was still a child, and even she had grown and developed since he had seen her last. She was different from the others, of course, for she was small and neatly made . . . she was more like Aunt Celia than ever. Humphrey was proud of his daughters, and he had reason to be proud for they were all remarkably good-looking: two large and fair and blue-eyed — like Alice — and one small and dark and merry. What a stir they would create if he could transport them to the ward-room! Parker was supposed to be an authority on

206

women — what would Parker think of his daughters, wondered Humphrey.

"Such a lot to arrange," Alice was saying. "The date hasn't been fixed — we were just waiting to hear from you before fixing the date —"

"Dad," said Billy. "Dad, I want a tail coat. I want to be an usher. I'm not too young, am I?"

"Daddy," said Joyce. "Don't you think pink would be nice for the bridesmaids' dresses?"

"You'll have to get a new topper, Dad."

"You'll have to give away the bride, you know."

"The reception must be here, of course."

They were all talking at once and Humphrey found some difficulty in keeping track of all the suggestions and demands. He managed to disentangle one of the suggestions and to answer it. "Of course the reception must be here," said Humphrey, raising his voice slightly. "There hasn't been a wedding at Dunnian for something like eighty years. Isabel was the last Miss Dunne to be married from the house — Debbie's great-grandmother."

Deb was smiling at him across the room. (He thought: she's improved enormously. She's pretty in her own quiet way and there's something very attractive about her . . . but she doesn't look well . . .)

"That's very interesting," Mark said.

"Quite a lot of presents have come already," said Alice. "We put them in the east bedroom. Edith will show them to you — such lovely presents, Humphrey!"

"Lucky girl!" said Humphrey, smiling at his daughter.

Once again Edith refused to smile back.

(I'm out of touch, thought Humphrey. I mustn't tease Edith. People are often a bit prickly when they're in love.)

"Daddy," said Celia suddenly. She was sitting on a stool beside him and leaning against his knee. "Daddy, I want to ask you something."

"What do you want to ask?" inquired Humphrey, smiling at her affectionately.

"I needn't go to school, need I?" Celia said.

"She ought to go to school," declared Edith. "Joyce and I went to school, and Celia ought to go. She's getting spoilt at home."

"Celia isn't spoilt," said Alice quickly.

"I don't want to leave Dunnian," Celia explained. "I wouldn't mind going to school if I could take Dunnian with me."

The others laughed at this, but somehow or other Humphrey understood. "We'll see," he said. "Mummy and I will talk it over. We won't send you away from Dunnian if you feel very strongly about it."

"I feel *very* strongly about it," said Celia gravely.

"If only you could have been here for the play!" exclaimed Billy. "Gosh, you would have liked it, Dad. I was Bottom, you know. It was tremendous fun."

"I was Puck," said Celia.

They all began to talk at once and to tell him about it.

The evening passed pleasantly but all the same Humphrey was glad when "the women and children" went to bed and he and Mark were left together for a quiet chat. Mark had opened the door for his mother. He came back to the fire and stood on the hearthrug looking down at Humphrey.

"Sit down," said Humphrey. "I can't talk to you up there. You've grown into a perfect giant."

Mark sat down without speaking.

"This is nice," said Humphrey. "This is like old times. Is everything all right?"

It was the usual question. It was the question Humphrey always asked when he came home from sea. Long ago when Mark was quite a small boy he had been given to understand that it was his business to look after the family in his father's absence. Mark had liked it. He had felt important and responsible. It had been one of those things which had bound them closely together ("Is everything all right, Mark?" "Yes, Dad, everything's fine.") but to-night Mark did not make the usual reply. He hesitated.

"There's nothing wrong, is there?" asked Humphrey in sudden anxiety.

"I'm not sure," said Mark.

"What's the matter?"

"I'm not sure," repeated Mark. "It may be nothing at all. It's about Edith, really. I can't help wondering if she really likes Rewden."

"Don't you like him?"

"Not awfully," said Mark uncomfortably.

"What's wrong with the fellow?" It was Humphrey's quarter-deck voice, crisp and incisive, a voice which demanded a plain answer to a plain question, and this was what Mark could not give. There was nothing *wrong* with Rewden — not really.

"He's sort of — colourless," said Mark vaguely.

"I don't know what you mean. If Edith likes him — aren't they fond of each other?"

"I don't know. That's the whole trouble," said Mark.

"You'll have to explain."

"I can't. I don't want to say too much. It's just — well — Edith doesn't behave as if she were very fond of him."

"I can't bear people mooning and making eyes at each other in public."

Mark laughed, but it was not a very mirthful sound. "Mooning!" he exclaimed. "You won't see much mooning there."

"I don't want to."

"I know," agreed Mark, "but there is a sort of medium."

Humphrey was worried when he went up to bed. He was worried not only about Edith and her "colourless" young man but also, strangely enough, about Mark. There was something missing in Mark, that gaiety of spirit which lay beneath his quiet manner was slightly dimmed . . . and, somehow, Humphrey had not felt that close companionship with Mark . . . he had felt as if something stood between him and his son, shutting them off from each other. Debbie, too, had seemed unlike herself . . . and Joyce was not as spontaneously gay as usual . . . of all the family only Alice was the same. Alice was always the same — his dear, beautiful Alice.

She lay in his arms with her head on his shoulder.

"Alice, is everything all right?"

"Yes, darling, of course. I've missed you horribly . . . but everything's all right now you're home. We won't send Celia to school, will we?"

"Not unless you think she should go."

"I don't," said Alice. "Dunnian is hers, really — it will be hers when you and I are dead — so I don't think it's right to send her away, do you?"

"Perhaps not."

"She doesn't know, of course."

"She mustn't know until she's twenty-one," said Humphrey firmly.

There was a little silence and then Humphrey said, "Alice, you're quite pleased about this marriage, aren't you?"

"Yes, of course, darling."

"Do you think Edith is fond of him?"

"Yes, of course, darling. I told you in my letter —"

"I know."

"I always tell you everything, Humphrey."

"I know. I love your letters. They're a part of you —"

"And your letters," said Alice sleepily. "Darling letters, Humphrey —"

Douglas Rewden came over to Dunnian the next morning and Humphrey interviewed him in the library. Humphrey had not intended the interview to be formal but somehow or other it was . . . they were both shy and embarrassed. Rewden did not smoke and he refused a drink, saying that, although he was not a teetotaller, he had not much use for the stuff.

"Oh, well . . ." said Humphrey, putting down the decanter regretfully. He felt he ought to be glad that his future son-in-law neither smoked nor drank, but somehow he was not. It would have been easier if they could have had a drink together, it would have been "more matey."

"You and Edith seem to have — er — fixed it up," said Humphrey smiling in what he hoped was a friendly manner.

"Er — yes," agreed Rewden. "Edith and I — er — er."

"Yes, quite," agreed Humphrey.

"Mrs. Dunne said you were pleased."

"Yes — oh yes, of course. I mean if you and Edith —"

"Yes," said Rewden.

There was a short silence. Humphrey began to feel quite desperate. "Are your people pleased?" he asked.

"Oh, yes," said Rewden without enthusiasm.

"That's all right, then."

"Of course my mother is a little — er — er — but she knows I've got to marry sometime."

"Perhaps she's sorry to leave Sharme."

"She isn't leaving," replied Rewden. "I'm letting her stay on at Sharme. Edith and I will spend most of our time in London."

"Business?" asked Humphrey.

"Er — no. As a matter of fact I don't — er — care for business. I've got a house in London, of course."

"I see," said Humphrey. He was disappointed, for he had hoped Edith would be settled near Dunnian. Sharme was only thirty miles from Dunnian.

"I like London," Rewden said. "You get good bridge in London."

"I shouldn't care to live in London, myself."

"Why not?" inquired Rewden, raising his fair eyebrows in surprise.

"It doesn't matter," replied Humphrey hastily. "I mean if you and Edith — well, that's all that matters, isn't it?"

"Of course," said Rewden.

There was another silence, a very embarrassing one. Humphrey searched about in his mind for something to say but he could find nothing.

"What about the wedding?" asked Rewden at last.

"The wedding?"

"Yes, we were waiting for you, but now you're here. There isn't any sense in waiting, is there? Can't we fix the date?"

"That's for Edith to decide," said Humphrey.

"We were waiting for you," repeated Rewden in a tired voice. "There's no sense in putting it off. I should like it to be next month."

"That doesn't give much time!" exclaimed Humphrey.

"It's better to get it over," Rewden said.

This was a queer thing to say . . . or perhaps it was only a natural thing badly worded. Humphrey gave Rewden the benefit of the doubt. He remembered that when he was engaged to Alice he had been very anxious to hasten on the wedding. It was natural for a man to be impatient . . . but somehow Rewden did not give one the impression of an impatient lover, eager to be united to the woman of his choice. He seemed tired and slightly bored, his voice was flat and uninteresting. Humphrey had not understood what Mark meant when he said Rewden was "colourless" (it had seemed a stupid word to describe a man) but now he realised that it was a strangely apt description.

"You'll have to talk to Edith about the date," Humphrey said.

"Yes," agreed Rewden.

Silence fell again. Humphrey felt he would like a drink (a drink would have helped a good deal; the mere fact of rising and pouring it out would have been a relief and a distraction) but you couldn't sit and drink by yourself, it wasn't a bit the same.

"Is that all you wanted to say?" asked Rewden.

"No," said Humphrey, pulling himself together. "No, not quite. I'm afraid there's no money, Rewden."

"I know," replied Rewden. "Mrs. Dunne told me. It doesn't matter. You can't have everything." He conveyed the impression that it mattered a good deal and that he was being magnanimous.

Humphrey did not like it.

"Women with money are usually plain and uninteresting," added Rewden.

This sounded better — by implication — but Humphrey was still a bit ruffled. He remembered his interview with Alice's father; how respectful he had been! How anxious to make a good impression!

"I hope you'll settle something on Edith," Humphrey said. It took a good deal of nerve to say it, but Mr. Wanlock had told him he must.

"Oh!" said Rewden in surprise. "I was going to give her an allowance, of course, but —"

"I should prefer a settlement."

"Oh, well — if you want it — I'll speak to my lawyer. It seems a bit unnecessary."

"I should prefer it," repeated Humphrey firmly.

When Rewden had gone Humphrey sought for Edith and found her in the east bedroom arranging her presents on a large table which had been put there for the purpose. Humphrey felt that it was his duty to speak to Edith, but it was not a pleasant duty. It was because he dreaded it that he rushed upon it with undue haste.

"Edith, I want to speak to you very seriously," he said.

She looked up and he saw from her face that she was alarmed. Perhaps he had spoken too sharply.

"It's all right," he assured her. "There's nothing of be frightened of."

"You've seen Douglas," she said somewhat anxiously. "What did he say?"

"Nothing very much," replied Humphrey. "He wants the wedding to be soon — but that's for you to decide."

"There's no hurry, is there?"

"No, of course not."

"Was that all Douglas said? He didn't say anything about the play, did he?"

"Not a word," replied Humphrey.

She looked relieved. She was smiling. Humphrey hesitated and then he said: "I suppose you're quite sure you want to go on with it?"

"Go on with what?" asked Edith.

"You're sure you want to marry him?"

Edith hesitated, but only for a moment. The hesitation was scarcely perceptible — she covered it with a laugh. "Of course I do," she said. "What a funny question!"

"Edith, are you certain?" urged Humphrey. "I know it would be difficult and a bit unpleasant if you changed your mind; but it would be better to do that than to marry him unless you're quite sure about it. We'll stick by you and see you through . . ."

"But Daddy —"

"Are you really fond of him, that's the question."

"I wouldn't have said I would marry him if I hadn't been fond of him, would I?"

"No," said Humphrey doubtfully. "But you might have changed your mind."

"I suppose Joyce has been talking!"

"Joyce! What has Joyce got to do with it?"

"Nothing, of course," said Edith crossly. She had taken up a gold and platinum bracelet set with diamonds and was trying it on her arm — it was Lady Skene's present.

Humphrey looked at her. He saw that her face wore a sulky mulish expression, it was an expression which Humphrey had seen before. When Edith put on this expression it meant that she intended to keep her own counsel and go her own way. She had worn it when she was a child — when Humphrey had caught her eating sweets in bed and had asked her where she had got them. She had not answered then and she would not answer now. You could get nothing out of Edith when she wore that mulish expression.

"I want you to be happy," said Humphrey. "That's all, Edith. I want you to be happy. Are you sure you can be happy with Rewden?"

"Of course," said Edith firmly. (She intended to be happy. She was making a brilliant marriage; she would be rich; she would live in London; she would have a splendid time. Oliver should never have the satisfaction of knowing that he had touched her heart.)

CHAPTER
TWENTY-THREE

The Wedding Reception

Dunnian House was full of flowers; chrysanthemums and dahlias in the hall and late roses in the drawing-room. It was a quiet house; the Rydd filled it with a gentle murmur, but soon the guests would arrive and the voice of the Rydd would be drowned in a buzz of talk and laughter. Becky had not gone to the church for she had things to do — things which could not be done till the very last minute. She went round the house looking at all the arrangements with an eagle eye and giving instructions to the maids.

"Move that jar of chrysanthemums into the corner," said Becky. "We'll have someone knocking it over if we don't look out . . . and roll up that rug . . . and put a chair over there."

"There's a chair there already."

"I know. Lady Skene will sit there — unless I'm much mistaken — and she'll want another beside her for whoever's talking to her. Did you put hairpins on the dressing-table for the ladies? They won't use them, of course, but there had better be some there . . ."

Becky had scarcely finished her alterations and was still in the billiards room pottering about amongst the presents and rearranging them for the third or fourth time when the bride and bridegroom drove up to the door in a new car — a present from the bridegroom's mother — and got out looking cool and collected. Becky hurried to meet them but already Edith had gathered up her train and walked in. The next two cars were full of bridesmaids; Joyce and Celia, Deb and Angela, Jean Murray and Felicia Rewden (a cousin of the bridegroom), they all went into the drawing-room and stood there looking at the cake. They were happy and excited and they all knew each other well — except Miss Rewden, of course. She knew nobody and gave the unfortunate impression that she was glad to have it so.

"Stand here, Douglas," Edith was saying. "Celia, spread out my train . . . no, not like that; Joyce had better do it."

"Shall we stand in a group?" Angela inquired.

"Yes, but you can move about later. It looks silly to stay in a group . . ."

Humphrey was now arriving with Mrs. Rewden and her younger son; and Alice with Mark and Billy . . . and then the guests began to pour into the drawing-room, thick and fast, the Murrays, the Macfarlanes, the Sprotts and scores of other families, all talking and laughing cheerfully, all agreeing that the bride was one of the prettiest they had seen, that the church was beautifully decorated, that the day was splendid and that Dunnian House was a perfect house for a wedding reception. Old Lady Skene had taken up her position in the most comfortable chair; her sight was worse than ever and, even with thick lensed glasses, the faces of her fellow guests were undistinguishable blurs, but she had managed to get hold of Mrs. Raeworth . . . Evelyn was such a good-natured creature.

"Sit down beside me," said Lady Skene. "Tell me who's here. Who's that girl in the pink frock talking to the Rewden boy?"

"Joyce," replied Evelyn Raeworth sitting down beside her old friend and preparing to be her eyes.

"Of course," nodded Lady Skene. "What it is to be blind! Pretty girl, isn't she? Oliver had rather a penchant for Joyce at one time."

"Why aren't they here — Oliver and Tessa, I mean."

"Oh, hadn't you heard? They've gone to New Zealand. It was all arranged quite suddenly. Jack had to go so he decided to take the children. It will be a lovely trip for them."

"Tessa was to have been a bridesmaid, wasn't she?"

"Yes, but she couldn't do both and the New Zealand trip was too good to miss. They went off last week and they aren't coming back until the spring — so they'll be away all winter," added Lady Skene a trifle enviously.

"Why didn't you go with them?"

Lady Skene chuckled. "My dear, I'm eighty-five! If a woman can't settle down comfortably at home when she's eighty-five I don't know when she can. Where's Alice?"

"Over there near the door in a silvery sort of frock and a chinchilla fur."

"Oh yes, I see her now. Sweet creature, Alice . . . looks young to have all those big children, doesn't she?

Is that Mark standing beside her? Mark is a pet. I've always liked Mark best of the family."

"That's lucky, isn't it?" said Evelyn, smiling.

Lady Skene grinned back at her mischievously. "You mean he and Tessa . . . but of course nothing is settled yet, they're much too young."

"Deb is my favourite," declared Mrs. Raeworth.

"Debbie!"

"Yes, she's a dear. As a matter of fact I've only just discovered Deb for she manages to hide herself pretty successfully, but now that I've found her I'm going to drag her out of her lair. I'm determined to paint her for one thing."

"I should paint Joyce if I were you. She's prettier."

Evelyn Raeworth said nothing.

"Do you see Harriet Murray anywhere?" asked Lady Skene.

"Yes, she's talking to Alice — black and white silk and black fox furs."

"Tell her I want to speak to her, Evelyn."

Mrs. Raeworth smiled and departed to carry out her mission, she was quite used to being ordered about by Lady Skene.

"Selma!" cried Mrs. Murray, hastening up and taking the vacant chair. "Selma, my dear, I never saw you! I might have known you would be ensconced in the most comfortable corner in the room. What a squash, isn't it? Everybody's here. I'm enjoying myself tremendously."

"I haven't seen you for ages, Harriet."

"I've been ill," replied Mrs. Murray gravely. "I haven't seen a creature. It's been *too* dreary. Dr.

Anderson has been ill, too, so I had to have his assistant — quite a nice young man, but he doesn't understand my tummy."

"Dr. Anderson is always ill," declared Lady Skene.

"I know. I told him he ought to get a partner — someone really good. Timperton is *full* of people with tummies — I can't think why."

Lady Skene seemed to understand this somewhat ambiguous statement. She replied: "It must be the water, Harriet. You should get a thingummy-jig to put in your cistern. It takes all the chalk out of the water, or something."

"I'm sure it can't be the water," Mrs. Murray declared. "Ian never drinks it and his tummy is worse than mine."

"Celia!" cried Lady Skene, catching hold of Celia's frock as she passed. "Celia, come here and talk to us. I want to hear all about everything."

"Would you like to see the presents?" asked Celia, looking down at Lady Skene and smiling. "I'll take you to see them if you like."

"No," said her ladyship firmly. "I've seen hundreds of displays of presents. It's a barbarous custom to display them — a form of blackmail. How many sugar sifters have they got?"

"Twelve," said Celia. "Twelve sugar sifters and eleven sets of silver cruets and fourteen butter dishes. Of course we've scattered them about," declared Celia gravely. "We haven't put them all together, you know."

"You should have put them all together," said Lady Skene. "It would serve the butter-dish-people right.

Everyone goes and looks at the presents with the sole object of seeing their own contribution, and whether it is properly set out for all the other people to see."

"Yours isn't."

"Isn't it?"

"Edith is wearing it," said Celia. "There's just a card saying: "Lady Skene, gold and platinum bracelet set with diamonds."

Lady Skene chuckled. "Very proper!" she said. "That'll teach the butter-dish-people what's what ... Let's look at you, child. Come nearer ... h'm, you're more like old Celia than ever. When are you going to get married, eh?"

"I'm thirteen," replied Celia grinning. "You can't get married till you're fourteen and any way I don't want to."

"You don't want to be a bride in white satin and have all the county sending you butter dishes?"

"Oh, I suppose I shall get married *some* day," said Celia thoughtfully, "but, if I do, it will have to be someone — different."

"They're all different, my dear."

"But I mean *quite* different," said Celia vaguely. "I mean someone like — like young Lochinvar." She looked at Lady Skene as she spoke to see if Lady Skene was laughing at her, but no, she was perfectly grave.

"Young Lochinvar has come out of the west," said Lady Skene, nodding. "Say it to me, child."

Celia said it in a low clear voice:

"Oh young Lochinvar has come out of the west
In all the wide border his steed is the best
And, save his good broad-sword, he weapons
    had none;
He rode all unarmed and he rode all alone."

"Very nice," said Lady Skene. "Very nice indeed. We must keep our eyes open for young Lochinvar; he would make an admirable husband for you."

At this moment Mark approached, edging his way through the crowd with a tray of glasses.

"Mark, this is lovely," said Lady Skene. "Give me a full one, I adore champagne. Mark, why haven't you been over to see me, lately? Yes, I'll have a piece of cake as well."

"I've been working," replied Mark. "And of course we've been busy with the wedding and all that. Have you heard from Tessa?"

"A postcard from Marseilles — you've had a letter, I suppose."

"No, not even a postcard."

"Foolish girl!" exclaimed Lady Skene. "Why doesn't she write to you? If you were my young man I should write to you every day."

Mark laughed. The implication that he was "Tessa's young man" was extremely pleasant.

"You had better throw her over and have me instead," continued her Ladyship gravely. "As a matter of fact I'm looking about for a nice young man to walk out with."

"I shall be delighted," declared Mark with equal gravity. "What about to-morrow afternoon?"

224

"You won't come."

"I shall — at three o'clock precisely."

She chuckled delightedly: "Get away with you!" she said.

It was now time for the speeches but, fortunately, the speeches were short. When they were over and the healths had been drunk with acclamation, the noise of chatter broke forth with renewed energy.

Humphrey still had Mrs. Rewden on his hands and saw no prospect of release.

She was not "colourless" like her son, but neither was she any easier to get on with.

"This is the first time I've been here," said Mrs. Rewden, gazing round through a pair of tortoiseshell lorgnettes.

Humphrey was aware of this, of course; he and Alice had invited Mrs. Rewden several times but their invitations had been refused. "We were so sorry you couldn't come before," said Humphrey.

"It's a pretty house," she said in lukewarm tones. "This is the drawing-room, I suppose; it's small, isn't it? We have two drawing-rooms at Sharme. I find a second room very convenient. I suppose you haven't thought of throwing out a bow-window?"

"No, I haven't," replied Humphrey firmly.

"I like a bow-window."

"So do I — in the right place. This would be the wrong place, I'm afraid. It would spoil the symmetry of the façade; it would be an *excrescence*," said Humphrey a trifle heatedly.

"You might enlarge the room by throwing another room into it," Mrs. Rewden suggested.

"I don't really want to enlarge the room," Humphrey replied. "It's crowded to-day, of course, but we don't have wedding receptions at Dunnian every day of the week."

Mrs. Rewden looked at him in surprise. "No, of course not," she agreed, "but it's very convenient to have a large room in the house. You needn't use it when you're alone."

"We use our drawing-room," replied Humphrey. "We use it constantly. This is a family house, Mrs. Rewden."

"Yes, that's what it looks like," she said in disparaging tones.

Humphrey had come to the end of his tether now, in fact he was in grave danger of becoming rude. He signalled frantically to Alice and she came to the rescue at once.

"Have you finished your little talk," asked Alice, smiling sweetly. "Perhaps Mrs. Rewden would like to see the presents . . . Mark will take you to see them . . . Mark, you'll take Mrs. Rewden, won't you?"

Mark put down his tray and accepted the burden with a good grace. He had been watching his father and was aware that it was high time he was relieved from duty.

Having disposed of her most important guest Alice looked round to see if everyone else were happy — yes, everyone was talking hard, there were no stragglers. They all knew one another, of course, that's what made it so comfortable. Alice exchanged a few words with Mrs. Murray and complimented her upon Jean's appearance; she asked Mr. Raeworth if his chrysanthemums were doing well; she approached Mrs. Macfarlane and inquired after her son; she remembered that Mrs. Sprott's husband had sprained his ankle and inquired after the injured joint with solicitude. "So sweet," said everyone, after she had moved on. "So pretty and kind. Edith is very good-looking, of course, but she'll never be as nice as her mother."

Alice's eyes roved the room. Where was Joyce? Ah, there she was, talking to Douglas Rewden's brother! Celia was handing plates of cake — and probably eating a good deal more than her share; but it did not matter. Celia could eat anything without ill effects. Billy was nowhere to be seen, but Alice knew that he could look after himself. Edith was looking a little pale — but very beautiful — perhaps it was time Edith went upstairs to change.

Joyce went upstairs with Edith. It was Joyce, Edith wanted, and no one else. "I hate a whole lot of people fussing round my room," said Edith somewhat ungraciously. In spite of the fact that they quarrelled a good deal and that Edith was apt to be selfish and demanding the sisters were very fond of each other — they always had been.

"You looked marvellous," said Joyce, as she unpinned the veil. "Everyone said so. Wilfred Rewden said he had no idea he was getting such a beautiful sister."

"You seem to get on with him."

"He's rather nice — rather fun, really. He said he was going to stay with you in London."

"So are you," said Edith. "Don't forget that."

"Is it likely!" Joyce exclaimed.

"We'll have a marvellous time," said Edith, as she slipped out of her dress. "Balls and operas and everything. You can stay the whole winter if you like."

"Edith!"

"It will make it easier for me," said Edith thoughtfully (she never bothered to pretend her motives were altruistic). "Yes, you had better stay the whole winter if they'll let you."

"I'll *make* them let me," Joyce declared.

The dressing went forward apace and, when Deb looked in to say that Douglas was ready and the car was at the door, Edith had reached the stage of putting on her hat, arranging it carefully on her shining hair in front of the looking glass.

"Oh, Debbie, have you got a needle?" cried Joyce. "Quick, Debbie, there's a button off her glove."

Deb seized the glove and ran away to find a needle and thread. She almost collided with Alice in the doorway.

"Darling, are you ready? How sweet you look!" said Alice coming in.

"Mother, I told you not to come!" exclaimed Edith.

"I *had* to come," said Alice, going forward and kissing Edith fondly. "I had to see you just for a moment, my darling. Oh, I do hope you'll be happy, Edith — I'm sure you will. Douglas is so —"

"I told you not to come!" said Edith in a trembling voice.

"But why —"

"Because I can't bear it, of course," said Edith, and suddenly she sat down on the bed and burst into a flood of tears.

"Edith, darling —"

"I knew I couldn't bear it," cried Edith, wringing her hands. "The only way I could — could go through with it — was not to think about it."

"Edith!"

"I can't," cried Edith, weeping as if her heart would break. "I thought I could, but I can't — I can't go away — with *him*."

It was a frightful moment but Alice was perfectly calm. "Darling, I know what you're feeling," she declared, wiping Edith's tears and motioning Joyce away. "Darling, I know so well. I felt *just* the same, darling —"

"Mummy, Mummy!" cried Edith clinging to her. "I can't go — what *ever* shall I do!"

"Poor lamb," said Alice. "Of course you're a little upset at the idea of leaving home — it's quite natural — but you'll be so happy with dear Douglas that you'll forget all about us. There now, be a brave girl and dry your eyes . . . I felt *just* the same, darling."

"You didn't," sobbed Edith. "You don't understand a bit. I hate him — he bores me to distraction — how can I go away with him — alone! Oh, Mummy, why did I ever say I would marry him!"

Joyce, surveying the scene, wide-eyed with dismay, understood a good deal better what Edith was feeling. "But, Edith, it's too late now —" she began in horror-stricken tones.

"Hush, Joyce," said Alice. "You don't understand at all . . . there, there," she added, patting Edith's back in exactly the same soothing manner as she had patted it when Edith had a tooth out at the age of eight. "There, there, Mummy understands; but you needn't be frightened, you know. Douglas is so kind and thoughtful, it will be quite *all* right."

"Mummy, I can't —"

"Come now, be a brave soldier," said Alice firmly and cheerfully. "Be a brave soldier, Edith. They're all waiting for you, my precious, all waiting to see the beautiful bride . . . dry your eyes, that's Mummy's brave girl; here's a clean handkerchief, darling."

Somehow or other Edith was soothed and restored, her eyes bathed in cold water and her cheeks carefully powdered. Alice did not repeat the mistake of kissing her daughter, she pushed her gently but firmly out of the door and handed her over to her newly acquired husband who was waiting impatiently on the landing.

Alice was smiling fondly as she leaned over the bannisters and watched the couple run downstairs (in a hail of roseleaves and silver-paper horse-shoes) and vanish out of the door. "She has *such* a tender heart," murmured Alice to no one in particular.

PART IV

Grown-up People in the House

CHAPTER
TWENTY-FOUR

Billiards

Celia and Debbie were walking across the moor with the dogs. There were always dogs at Dunnian; they were descendants of old Boris, carefully bred by Johnson — brown and white spaniels with long ears and silky coats which shone with daily brushing. To strangers the Dunnian dogs looked alike, but to their intimate friends they were all quite different in appearance and personality. Penny had an affectionate nature, she was always ready to be petted and loved; Peter was more independent, needing a firm hand to keep him in order; Dinah was merry and playful, she took your bedroom slippers and hid them behind the curtain, but you could not be angry with her for it was only a joke.

"Do you remember the play?" asked Celia, pausing on the crest of the hill and looking down at the "stage."

"Of course. It's only a year ago," said Deb smiling.

"Yes, but it seems much longer. Everything is so different now, isn't it?"

Deb agreed. Before Edith's marriage the house had been full of comings and goings, there were tea-parties and tennis parties and young people dropping in at all hours of the day, but now Edith had vanished from the scene and Joyce had vanished too (she had spent the winter in London with the Rewdens and there was no talk of her coming home.) Mark had qualified brilliantly and had obtained a post in a London hospital; he had not been home for months . . . Dunnian was very quiet now, it was a house of women, Debbie and Aunt Alice had been alone most of the time, it would have been unbearably quiet without Celia, but fortunately Celia was firmly fixed at home. She was doing lessons with a governess who bicycled over from Ryddelton every day. Humphrey had spent the winter in the Mediterranean and had just returned, looking brown and fit. He was a rear-admiral now and his family was very proud of him. Deb was even more glad than usual when Uncle Humphrey came home for she was a little worried about Aunt Alice — it had been a long, dull winter for her and she seemed languid and depressed.

"Let's go down to the Peel," said Celia. "I want to see if the jackdaws are here this year."

They began to climb down the bank.

"Oliver and Tessa are back," continued Celia. "They're staying with old Lady Skene. Did Mummy remember to tell you she had asked Oliver to dinner?"

"No, she didn't," said Deb.

"He rang up," explained Celia. "Mummy asked him to dinner to-night. I told her not to forget to tell you."

"It's all right," replied Deb (who was doing the housekeeping now). "We're having quite a good dinner. Clear soup and roast chicken and a chocolate soufflé."

"Oliver is jolly lucky," declared Celia. "It will be nice to see him again, won't it?"

Deb did not reply. It made no difference to her whether she saw Oliver or not, he was quite outside her orbit. The two girls had reached the river by this time and calling the dogs they began to cross by the stepping-stones . . . and just as they reached the other side a man emerged from the ruins and came towards them.

"Hallo, talk of an angel . . ." cried Celia gaily.

"Hallo!" exclaimed Oliver. "Does that mean you were talking about me? You were talking prettily, I hope."

"Neither good nor evil," returned Celia. "We were merely discussing what you were going to have for dinner."

Oliver laughed. He shook hands with the girls in a friendly manner. He had not noticed them much last year because they had been overshadowed by Edith and Joyce, but now he saw that they were rather attractive. Celia, though still a child, was forthcoming and friendly; Deb was reserved and shy; but, all the same, they were alike — they might have been sisters rather than third cousins, thought Oliver.

"I came here to remember the play," Oliver said. "It was good fun, wasn't it?"

"Tremendous fun," agreed Celia.

"Everyone acted well — except Angela. We should have stuck to you," said Oliver, smiling at Deb.

"I don't expect I would have been any better," Deb replied.

They all began to walk along by the side of the river with the dogs careering madly up and down and round about. Celia was almost as ambulatory as the dogs, she was looking for birds' nests, climbing trees, pushing through the bushes. Sometimes she was ahead of the others and sometimes far behind.

"It was naughty of you to let us down over that Titania business," said Oliver smiling down at Deb in a friendly fashion.

"Let you down?" asked Deb in surprise.

"Never mind, it's over now. It was stage fright, that's all. I know the feeling well. Suddenly you go hot and cold all over and you feel you can't bear it."

Deb did not understand what he meant ... Tessa couldn't have told him the true facts of the affair ... but it was no use raking it all up, the whole thing was over and done with.

"I shouldn't have thought you would suffer from nerves," said Deb gravely.

"I'm very nervous, really — very highly-strung," replied Oliver seriously — like many people of his temperament he enjoyed discussing himself — "You'd think, to look at me, that I was full of brass but as a matter of fact I'm not like that at all. I'm awfully shy. You wouldn't believe it, would you?"

Deb admitted that she found it difficult to believe.

"I control myself, of course," continued Oliver who had begun to enjoy himself immensely. "I don't wear my heart on my sleeve. It doesn't *do*."

Deb agreed with him there (for years she had hidden her heart successfully from all the world) and, because she could agree sincerely, she raised her head and smiled at Oliver for the first time. She had a pretty smile which lit her small grave face like a sunbeam . . . her soft grey eyes were dewy with youth and innocence.

There was a moment's silence and then Oliver went on talking, he told her about the trip to New Zealand and of some of the interesting things he had seen. "It's most awfully interesting to see new places," Oliver declared.

"It must be," responded Deb a trifle enviously.

Deb usually found conversation difficult, she preferred to listen while other people talked; so they got on very well indeed. By the time they reached the garden Deb was willing to admit that Oliver was improved, that — in fact — Oliver was quite nice, and she said as much to Celia as they went up to the house together.

He was nice at dinner, too, cheerful and chatty, deferential to his host and attentive to his hostess. Humphrey had been to New Zealand so they had a good deal in common — they discussed the climate, the inhabitants and the origin of the Maoris.

"It ought to be called New Scotland," Oliver declared. "Not only is the country very like Scotland — on a different scale — but it's brimful of Scots. I felt quite at home, more at home than in any other country I've visited."

Humphrey had felt the same. It was all very pleasant and agreeable.

"Did you see Edith when you were in London?" Alice asked.

"Only once," replied Oliver. "Tessa and I met them coming out of the opera — Joyce was there too — they looked very well, I thought."

"I wish Joyce would come home," said Alice with a sigh.

"She's having too good a time in London, I expect," said Humphrey, smiling.

"I suppose you heard —" began Oliver, and then he stopped.

"Heard what?"

"Oh, nothing much. It was just something Tessa said —"

"About Joyce?"

"She's very pretty, you know," said Oliver smiling. "She's been going about and meeting people so you ought not to be surprised if you hear she has a good many admirers — one very attentive admirer — I expect you'll be hearing about it, soon."

Naturally Joyce's parents were anxious to hear more and Oliver was persuaded to be more explicit. He knew and liked the man and assured Humphrey that he was good-looking and eligible.

After dinner they all went into the billiards room and the two men had a game — a very close and exciting game — while Deb marked for them

"I miss the girls — and Mark, of course," said Humphrey with a sigh. "I enjoy a game of billiards but there's nobody to play with unless I ask Raeworth to come over."

"Why doesn't Deb play?" Oliver inquired.

It was quite a natural question, but Humphrey could not answer it except to say that Deb had never been taught.

"Why hasn't she been taught?" asked Oliver.

Humphrey had no idea

"I always mark," Deb explained. "I like marking. There always used to be plenty of people to play."

"But there aren't plenty of people, now," said Oliver, smiling at her. "Come on, Deb. I'll give you a lesson."

Deb was a little dubious about it. She declared that she was not good at games . . . she would spoil the game for others . . . she might cut the cloth . . . but these excuses were swept aside as things of no account.

"It would be very nice if you could give me a game now and then," said Humphrey. "I think it would be a good plan for you to learn."

Deb was by no means the first girl who had received billiards lessons from Oliver, and the lessons had always been enjoyed by teacher and student alike. It was extremely pleasant (Oliver had always found) to have this admirable excuse to lean over his pupil, to take her hands in his and arrange them carefully — the left hand on the table, the right hand on the cue. To-night was no exception to the rule. Deb's hands were soft and delicate, her hair was fragrant and shining . . . as he stooped over her and arranged the position of the cue he noticed her ears, small and pink like shells.

"You must start right," said Oliver gravely. "You must assume the correct posture . . . raise your left hand a little more to make the bridge . . . like this, Deb."

Deb had watched so often that she knew a good deal about the game and it was not long before she was hitting the ball fair and square and cueing it straight to the point on the cushion indicated by her instructor.

"She must learn to put on side," said Humphrey who had been watching the lesson with interest.

"Not yet, sir," replied Oliver gravely. "It's most important to get her cueing perfect before she begins to put on side. I'll come over to-morrow morning and give her another lesson."

"But I couldn't think of bothering you!" cried Deb in dismay.

"No bother at all," replied Oliver. "I'd like to do it — and you really ought to learn. It will be so nice for the admiral if you can give him a game."

"It *would* be, of course," said Deb doubtfully. "But I'm sure it will be a bother for you —"

"No bother at all," repeated Oliver emphatically.

The next day was wet, the rain came down in sheets, and Deb was sure that Oliver would not come. She was busy in the flower room, rearranging the vases and filling them with fresh water when Oliver walked in.

"Hallo, have you forgotten about your lesson?" he inquired.

"No, of course not, but it was such an awful day I was sure you wouldn't come."

"It's just the right sort of day for billiards," Oliver assured her.

Deb dried her hands and followed him to the billiards room and the lesson began. She found it most interesting to-day, for she was allowed to put on side — Oliver explained the way it worked and illustrated his lecture with easy strokes.

"It's wonderful," said Deb. "I've watched hundreds of times but I never really *saw*. You make it seem so easy."

"It is easy when you know how," replied Oliver smiling.

They spent the morning practising nursery cannons and Oliver stayed to lunch.

On Wednesday the clouds had cleared — it was a perfect day. Oliver came over at the same time, but after they had had a little practice they decided to go out and strolled into the garden.

"I wish Ryddelton House was this size," said Oliver regretfully. "Ryddelton is too big and the property is enormous and difficult to administer. I'm learning all about roofs and drains and what not, and I find it very dull."

"It ought to be interesting," said Deb, rather shyly.

"In what way?" asked Oliver.

"Making improvements," explained Deb. "Going round and seeing what's wanted, building new barns. That's a lovely barn you're building near the old mill."

"You've seen it, have you? Yes, it's quite a good barn — and we're building a silage tower on the home farm."

Deb smiled and said, "You *are* interested, really."

"I might get interested if I had someone to help me," said Oliver gravely. "I think the reason I find it dull is because I've got nobody to talk to — nobody who cares a rap about the improvements I'm trying to make."

"What a pity!" said Deb.

On Thursday the billiards lessons were interrupted — Oliver had to go to Edinburgh for two nights — but Deb practised by herself and on Saturday, when Oliver came over to tea, he was loud in praise of her progress. There was just one thing wrong (Oliver said) she was not holding her cue quite correctly. He bent over to show her the right way . . . and kissed her on the tip of her ear.

"Oliver!" cried Deb, tearing herself away and gazing at him in dismay.

"Darling," said Oliver earnestly. "Darling Deb, I'm so sorry, but I couldn't help it. I couldn't, really . . . you're so sweet."

"Oliver! Please!"

"You're the sweetest girl in the world. You knew I'd fallen in love with you —"

"No."

"You must have guessed."

"No."

"Well, I have. Head over heels . . . I'm simply crazy about you."

"Don't, Oliver," said Deb, drawing back. "Please don't —"

"Deb, darling, please listen to me —"

"I don't want to — you've spoilt it —"

"No, Deb —"

"Yes, I thought you were different, but you're just the same."

"I *am* different," declared Oliver. "You don't understand. I've never been really in love before — I want to marry you."

"Oliver — we don't — we don't *know* each other, even!" cried Deb in horror-stricken tones.

"Listen, Deb," said Oliver. "Just listen to me for a few moments. I know it's too soon to ask you — I meant to wait — but I couldn't help it. I know you're afraid to say 'yes,' but don't say 'no,' Deb. We'll wait a bit. We'll go on just the same."

"We can't do that," she declared. "Besides you don't mean it."

"Don't mean it!" exclaimed Oliver in surprise.

Deb was so upset that she scarcely knew what she was saying. "No, you don't mean it," she told him. "That's the way you always talk to girls."

"I've never asked a girl to marry me before," replied Oliver emphatically.

She was silent. Somehow or other she knew he was speaking the truth.

"Honestly," he said. "Honestly, Deb. I've played about a bit but this is quite different. Won't you believe me?"

"Yes," she replied in a low voice. "Yes, I believe you, but it's no good —"

"Why?"

"We scarcely know one another."

"I feel I know you quite well."

She shook her head.

"Well, that's easily remedied," said Oliver cheerfully. "We'll go on as we are and get to know one another better."

"No, it's no good. We aren't the same sort of people," said Deb in desperation.

"All the better. I'm sick of people like myself . . . Deb, I know we'd be happy together . . ."

"No," she said with a catch in her breath. "No, we wouldn't. We don't like the same sort of things . . ."

"We'll wait," said Oliver again. "It's too soon. I was all kinds of a fool to frighten you. We'll pretend it hasn't happened . . ."

Deb could stand no more. She escaped and ran out of the room and left Oliver standing at the table with the cue in his hand. She was more upset than she had ever been in all her life, she was almost sick with fright. When she reached the privacy of her room Deb locked the door and flinging herself on the bed she buried her face in the pillow. She lay there for a long time with her heart pounding madly in her ears . . . it was so unexpected it was such an extraordinary thing to happen. Even now she could scarcely believe it was true. She had enjoyed learning to play billiards and had thought it was very kind of Oliver to spend so much time and trouble over the lessons, but it had never crossed her mind that he meant anything by his attentions. They had had jokes together, of course, but that was just Oliver's way — it was the way he had treated Joyce and Edith and probably half a dozen other girls as well. Deb had said she did not know Oliver, but she knew him well enough to guess that his path through life was strewn with broken hearts. Why did he want to marry *her*, Deb wondered. He could have married any of the other girls — he could have married Joyce or Edith — she knew this perfectly well. It seemed very strange that the one girl Oliver wanted to marry should be absolutely determined that she would never marry him . . . "Never," whispered Deb, pressing her face into the pillow. "Never, never, never . . ."

CHAPTER
TWENTY-FIVE

Persuasion

Deb thought it was all over. She had given Oliver to understand exactly what she felt. She had said "no" quite plainly and had not held out the slightest hope that she would change her mind. She was sorry for Oliver, of course, but it could not be helped . . . and he would soon get over his disappointment and fall in love with someone else. One thing was certain, thought Deb, Oliver would not come over to Dunnian any more. She had shown him her feelings too plainly. She was a little anxious in case Uncle Humphrey and Aunt Alice might notice the sudden cessation of the billiards lessons . . . she would have to think of something to say when they asked her the reason of it.

But Deb found there was no need to make excuses for Oliver's non-appearance. Oliver came over the very next morning. He walked in, smiling cheerfully. Deb was amazed to see him; she was uncomfortable and embarrassed; she could neither speak to him naturally nor look him in the face.

"Another billiards lesson!" exclaimed Uncle Humphrey, smiling.

"Yes, sir," agreed Oliver. "Deb's coming on very well. She's got a straight eye and a steady hand. I bet you couldn't give her fifty up, sir."

It was most extraordinary, thought Deb. How *could* Oliver behave as if nothing had happened?

The fact was Oliver had not taken Deb's refusal seriously. He knew that he had surprised and shocked her but he believed she would come round and he would get what he wanted in the end. Oliver had always got what he wanted so it was difficult for him to envisage failure. He wanted Deb all the more because he had not been able to get her easily (most girls were too easy, Oliver had found). Oliver had spoken the truth when he said that he was sick of people like himself. He had had a surfeit of smart, chattering, self-confident society girls and he found Deb a welcome change. He had been in love before but this time it was different for this time he wanted marriage. Deb would make a good wife. She was sweet and kind and peaceful. He would not grow tired of Deb. He could "see" himself settling down at Ryddelton with Deb and being happy in her company when the first frenzy of love was over — this was something he had never been able to envisage before.

Oliver wanted to marry Deb and he set about winning her with all the charm he possessed. He did not pester her with attentions, he did not force the pace. He came over to Dunnian and talked to her and gave her billiards lessons; sometimes he met her on the moor when she was out with the dogs and joined her for a walk. At first Deb was very shy with Oliver and avoided him whenever she could, but it was not easy to avoid him without being rude, and Oliver was so friendly and thoughtful and kind that she could not bring herself to be rude to him.

Matters were in this perplexing condition when Mark unexpectedly arrived home for a short holiday. He was pale and thin for he had been working hard.

"Town doesn't suit me," said Mark, when his parents commented on his appearance.

"I knew it wouldn't," declared Humphrey. "It doesn't suit me either. I feel cramped and I always eat too much. Three days in London and I'm nothing but a rag. I don't know how you've managed to stand it so long."

Oliver was expected to dinner that evening (which was nothing very extraordinary) and when Mark heard this news he rang up Ryddelton House and suggested that Tessa should come too. They came over together in Oliver's car.

Deb had not seen Tessa for a long time, and she noted without enthusiasm that Tessa was prettier than ever. Tessa was gay and friendly and beautifully dressed and her eyes shone like stars. Mark could not keep his eyes off her — and no wonder.

"How did you like New Zealand?" Mark asked when they had seated themselves at the dinner-table and started their meal.

"It was marvellous," declared Tessa. "I enjoyed every moment of it. I almost wept when we had to come away . . . didn't I, Oliver?"

"You quite wept, if I remember rightly," replied Oliver with a smile.

Deb could not help wishing that the Skenes had remained in New Zealand — both of them, for the rest of their lives — if they liked it so much it seemed a pity that they should have come away and left it . . .

"Mark is terribly thin!" exclaimed Tessa suddenly.

"It's the hospital work," replied Humphrey. "I think he should give it up and try to get something else."

Mark smiled. He had not been feeling well and he knew he required a good long holiday . . . how lovely it would be if he could spend a few months at home! Tessa was to be at Ryddelton all the summer, and Tessa was lovelier than ever.

"It's no use working yourself to death," continued Humphrey, looking at Mark with affectionate anxiety.

"You'll just get ill," said Tessa, nodding. "That's what will happen, Mark."

"I'll think about it," replied Mark slowly. "Of course the hospital work is splendid experience so I should be rather sorry to give it up."

"But, Mark!" cried Tessa. "It's quite impossible to stay in London all the summer!"

"Lots of people do," said Deb suddenly.

It was so seldom that Deb made a remark of this nature that everyone looked at her in surprise.

Oliver seemed pleased. He laughed and said, "As a matter of fact I believe several million people manage to support life in London all the year round."

"Debbie knew what I meant," said Tessa crossly.

It was rather fun to have "drawn" Tessa, but it was not worth it, really, for Deb did not like Oliver's championship any more than the reproachful glance she had received from Mark. She wished she had not spoken.

After dinner they went into the billiards room and Oliver tried to persuade Deb to take part in the game.

"Debbie always marks," said Tessa, as she chose a cue and chalked it in a professional manner.

"Not always," said Oliver with a little smile.

"I'm not good enough," said Deb. "Besides, you have four without me. I think I shall go and sit with Aunt Alice in the drawing-room."

"Who's going to mark, then?" Tessa inquired, but Deb had gone.

The Skenes left early so there was time to take the dogs for a walk before going up to bed. Deb was in the hall, struggling into her coat, when Mark came out of the drawing-room. "Wait for me," said Mark.

"Aren't you tired?"

"No, I want a breath of fresh air . . ."

They walked down the drive together with the dogs running and jumping and circling round their feet. It was nearly dark but the moon was rising above the tops of the trees like a silver ball and the air was warm and scented.

"Shall we walk down to the side gate?" asked Deb.

"That will suit me," agreed Mark.

For a while there was silence. It was so lovely to have Mark at home, so marvellous to be walking along beside him like this. Deb had been frightened and miserable but now that Mark was here things would improve. She would be able to hide from Oliver behind Mark's broad back.

"Deb," said Mark suddenly. "What's this I've been hearing about you?" His tone was playful and affectionate, and he took her arm as he spoke.

"Hearing about me!" echoed Deb in dismay.

"About you and Oliver. He's an awfully good fellow, you know. You like him, don't you?"

"Yes, I *like* him."

"He's *very* fond of you, Deb."

"I know," said Deb in a small voice.

Mark hesitated. "Of course if you don't love him it's no use," said Mark.

"No," agreed Deb. "No, it's no use at all." She felt unutterably relieved to find that Mark understood. She felt happier and more comfortable than she had felt for days — Mark understood, so it was all right. It was rather naughty of Oliver to have told Mark, but perhaps it was just as well; Mark was on her side, he understood, he would help her. "You see," continued Deb, looking up at him and squeezing his arm. "You see I couldn't help it happening because I never thought for a moment — I was very sorry about it."

"Yes, I'm sure you were."

"I wish you would explain to him, Mark. I told him it was no use but I don't think I can have made it quite plain enough. You'll tell him, won't you?"

Mark hesitated again. At last he said, "You like him, Deb. Don't you think you might get to love him in time?"

"Never!" cried Deb, stopping and taking her hand off Mark's arm. "Never, never —"

"Deb! That isn't like you! He's desperately in love with you. He wants you to give him a chance — that's all. He's willing to wait. Just give him a chance to — to —"

"No, Mark. It wouldn't be any use —"

"But why?"

"Because — because I know it wouldn't. It's much kinder to say so at the very beginning, isn't it?"

"That depends," replied Mark, smiling down at her affectionately. "You see Oliver is quite willing to take the risk. He wants to be friends with you. He thinks that if you got to know him better you might change your mind — and I think so too. I *know* you, Deb. You're such a funny little creature, you're frightened of anything new. Do you remember how miserable you were when you first came to Dunnian . . . and then, gradually, you grew to love Dunnian dearly. You see what I mean, don't you?"

"Yes, but it isn't the same."

"I think you should give Oliver a chance."

"It wouldn't be any use," said Deb desperately.

"Have you thought about it?" asked Mark, taking her hand. "You would be settled quite near Dunnian, you know — quite near all your friends. Oliver succeeds to Ryddelton House when Lady Skene dies . . . it's a lovely place, Deb. Of course I know that doesn't really count compared with other things but — but —"

"It doesn't count," said Deb.

They walked on.

"You aren't in love with any one else, are you?" asked Mark, with sudden anxiety.

"It isn't anything like that," said Deb, turning away her head. "It's because we're absolutely unsuited to each other, because we have different thoughts and feelings and look at things from a different point of view. We should never be happy together, never."

Mark was silenced, but only for a moment. He said, "I know what you mean, Deb. Oliver is pretty lively and he likes having fun —"

"He behaved very badly to Edith — if you call that fun."

"To Edith!" exclaimed Mark. "You mean Joyce. I thought at one time he liked Joyce, but there was nothing in it, nothing at all. He loves you, Deb. He wants to marry you and settle down. All that sort of thing is over."

Deb said nothing.

"Tessa was talking about you," continued Mark, after a little silence. "She said I was to give you her love and tell you that she wants you as a sister. She spoke so nicely of you — but of course I could see she was surprised and hurt. She thinks the world of Oliver."

This was too much . . . it roused Deb and she replied with spirit. "Really, Mark, I never heard such nonsense. They never bothered about me before — either of them — I might have been a table or a chair for all the notice they took of me. Why should they be surprised because I didn't fall in love with Oliver all of a sudden and fling myself into his arms the moment he asked me? I had seen the way he behaved to Edith and Joyce and at *that* time I was less than the dust. I was utterly amazed when he began to take notice of me —"

Mark laughed and pressed her arm. "That's just it," he declared. "You're such a little mouse that people don't notice you. When they begin to notice you they realise what a darling you are — that's just what happened to Oliver."

Deb said nothing in reply and presently Mark began to talk about Tessa. This was a relief in one way but not in another.

Things had now reached a stage where it was impossible to conceal them any longer and Uncle Humphrey and Aunt Alice became aware of what had happened. Uncle Humphrey said very little, but Deb knew that he shared Mark's opinion and hoped she would change her mind (he liked Oliver; Oliver was a very good match; there was nothing against the marriage). Aunt Alice's feelings were mixed, she aired them constantly.

"Of course I don't want you to get married," Aunt Alice would begin — she always began that way — "I should miss you dreadfully, in fact I don't know what I should do without you."

"I'm not going to get married," Deb would assure her.

"No, dear — but if you *were* going to marry any one I would rather it was Oliver because you would be settled quite near."

"I don't intend to marry any one."

"You must marry some day. You wouldn't like to be an old maid, would you, Debbie? Oliver is very nice. He used to be rather inconsiderate and difficult to

253

understand, but he has improved immensely. It was nice of him to bring me that book, wasn't it? I just mentioned that I hadn't been able to get it from the library and the next day he went and bought it and brought it over for me. He would make a very good husband, I think."

"I'm sure he will — but not to me. I don't love him, Aunt Alice."

"No. Well, of course, it's no use if you don't love him, dear. Humphrey said I wasn't to press you — and of course I don't want to press you because I should miss you so deadfully —"

Deb did not thrive in an atmosphere of disapproval. Nobody pestered her, of course, and, once she had made her intentions clear, nobody tried to persuade her to alter them; but she was so sensitive that the mere fact of knowing that she was doing something her friends considered foolish made her miserable. It was at this moment that a letter arrived from her grandmother asking her to come to Bournemouth for a few weeks, and Deb decided to go. She had been asked before, several times, but she had never been able to make up her mind to leave Dunnian — it was different now. Perhaps if she went away for a few weeks Oliver would find someone else and everything would be quite comfortable again.

Oliver came over the evening before her departure and inveigled her into the library for a chat.

"You're running away," he said, smiling at her. "There's no need to run away from me. I shan't bother you, Deb."

"You *are* bothering me," she replied. "Everyone is bothering me."

"I'll tell them not to," said Oliver. "You know, Deb, I'm not asking you for much — just for us to be friends."

"If it were only that!"

"I've said it's only that."

"But you don't mean it."

"Deb, listen —"

"No, I won't," she declared. "We aren't suited to one another. I like you quite a lot but I don't love you and I don't want to marry you." Surely that was clear enough, thought Deb. Surely Oliver would understand that.

"You like me quite a lot — that's a good beginning," said Oliver cheerfully.

Deb laughed — she couldn't help it — and Oliver laughed too. Oliver really was rather a dear. She was aware that if she had been heart-whole she might not have been able to resist him. She thought suddenly: . . . if Mark and Tessa . . . *then*, perhaps . . . because, *then*, it wouldn't matter . . . *then*, nothing would matter any more and she would just have to try to build some sort of life for herself out of the broken pieces . . . and if Oliver were willing to have her on those terms . . . knowing everything . . .

"I'll wait," Oliver was saying. "I'll wait years if necessary, and, meantime, I'll be very very good. I've started to be good already and I'm up to my eyes in work connected with the estate. New roofs for the cottages, new drains — all that sort of thing pleases you, doesn't it? Think of all the things we could do if only you would help me — but, no, we're not going to say another word about it. We're just going to be friends."

In spite of the fact that Deb was leaving of her own accord her last view of Dunnian was blurred by a mist of tears. She was leaving everything and everybody that she loved and going to a strange place. She knew quite well that when she returned to Dunnian Mark and Tessa would be officially engaged — there was no doubt about it in Deb's mind — and they would not be happy, or at least not for long. Sooner or later Mark would find out what Tessa was like, but he would not find out until she became careless . . .

During the journey Deb gave rein to her misery but when the end of her long, tiring journey came in sight she made an effort to pull herself together, for it would not be right to arrive at Milton Terrace looking sad and woebegone. She was determined to be a bright and cheerful guest.

Henrietta Lacey was old, now — she was over eighty — but she was still full of energy and life, still interested in all that went on around her. She welcomed her granddaughter affectionately.

"At last!" she cried. "Here you are at last! I thought I was never going to see you, my dear. Let me look at you . . . yes, you're a real Dunne — very like what I was at your age. I dare say you don't believe that I was once a pretty young girl."

Deb found this quite easy to believe, for Henrietta was a very pretty old lady with a strong resemblance to the portrait of great-great Aunt Celia which hung in Mrs. Raeworth's studio.

"I shall take you everywhere," continued Henrietta, nodding portentiously. "We'll go to the concerts together — in the Winter Garden, you know — and I shall ask my friends to meet you. They aren't all old, like myself, so it won't be too dull for you. We're going to have a lovely time together . . ."

They did. Deb would not have believed it possible that she could enjoy this visit to her grandmother, but she found it extremely pleasant to be petted and fêted and proudly displayed. It was a new experience and it did her a lot of good.

They went out a great deal, for Henrietta was sociable and popular, but sometimes in the evening they sat alone in Henrietta's little drawing-room and sewed and talked . . . and gradually Deb was able to tell this old lady all her troubles (not in plain straightforward words, but by hints and implications), and Henrietta listened and nodded and occasionally dropped a word or two of good advice. There was wit and wisdom in Henrietta, and Deb recognised this, enjoying the one and profiting by the other.

They were talking about Mark one evening. "Mark has got a fixed idea of you," Henrietta said. "He doesn't see you clearly because he's too accustomed to you. You're his sister and that's all there is about it. When people get fixed ideas dynamite is the only thing to move them."

"Yes," said Deb thoughtfully.

"Don't take second best," continued Henrietta, shaking her head. "Just wait patiently and see what happens — but don't wait too patiently either. People are apt to take you at your own valuation . . . I mean if you lie down on the floor and look like a door-mat people can't be blamed for wiping their boots on you."

Deb laughed — but she knew it was true.

CHAPTER
TWENTY-SIX

Timperton

Mark was seeing Tessa nearly every day. He was almost certain that she loved him but he had made up his mind that it would not be fair to ask her to marry him until he had something definite to offer her. He could not marry Tessa and continue with his hospital work — that was impossible. He must resign his appointment and look for something else. One night, when his mother had gone to bed and he and his father were sitting in the drawing-room together, Mark opened the subject in a tentative manner.

"I thought you liked the job at the hospital," Humphrey said.

"Yes," said Mark. "Yes, I like it, but I think it's time now — I mean if I could settle in a country district — perhaps not too far from Dunnian."

"I should like that," said Humphrey. "It would be a great relief to my mind if I knew you were within reach. I'm a little worried about your mother —"

Mark was worried too. There was nothing definite the matter with Alice but she seemed languid and tired and sometimes very muddled in her mind. She was only about fifty years old but she looked — and seemed — a good deal older. Mark had noticed a great difference in her since last year.

"It would be nicer to be near home, and in the country," Mark said.

Humphrey nodded. "Of course it would. Not only because you like the country and want to be near home, but for other reasons as well."

Mark looked at him in surprise.

"You think I'm blind," declared Humphrey, with a chuckle, "but I can see as far as most bats and it wouldn't take very good eyesight to guess your secret. It's Tessa, isn't it? She's charming. I'd like to see you married to Tessa, old boy."

"I don't know how you've guessed! I mean," stammered Mark. "I mean — I thought — I didn't know — and of course I haven't said anything yet to — to Tessa, but I think — I think it will be all right."

"I'm sure it will be all right," nodded Humphrey.

"I wanted to see my way first," continued Mark. "I wanted to know what I was going to do. I couldn't go on at the hospital —"

"No, of course not. We'll buy a partnership."

"Dad!" exclaimed Mark. "That would be marvellous! Are you sure you could afford it?"

"Perfectly certain. Some of my investments have turned up trumps ... We'll look about — I know nothing about these things — can we advertise, or what?"

"Dad, it's most awfully generous of you. I've cost you so much already."

"Nonsense, what's money for? I'd like to see you comfortably settled."

"My idea was to go as an assistant —"

"No good," declared Humphrey. "No good at all. You must have something to offer Tessa. She's used to having things nice."

This was so true that Mark could make no further objections, nor did he want to. His heart was surging with delight, his face shone like the sun. If Humphrey had wanted repayment for his generosity he was well repaid when he looked at his son's face.

"Do you think I should ask her now?" said Mark eagerly.

"You're the best judge of that," responded Humphrey, smiling. "Personally I think I should wait. You'll have something definite to offer her when we've fixed up the partnership."

"Yes," agreed Mark. "Yes, I believe that's the right way to do it."

"Send in your resignation at once," advised Humphrey. "It will do you good to have a holiday before starting your new work. You haven't had a proper holiday for years."

Humphrey was not the sort of person to let the grass grow under his feet; he set about the task of finding Mark a partnership without more ado, and very soon his efforts bore fruit. He was all smiles when he called Mark into the library and handed him a letter which had come that morning.

"Here we are," said Humphrey. "Here's the very thing. Dr. Anderson wants a partner — he's the G.P. at Timperton."

"At Timperton!" exclaimed Mark.

"Yes, it's splendid, isn't it? We've had letters from Fife and Rossshire and goodness knows where else — and all the time there was *this* at our very door. It's almost too good to be true. Your mother knows all about Dr. Anderson — the Murrays swear by him. You had better take the car and go over and see him at once."

"Perhaps he wants someone older," said Mark, for to him the thing seemed *much* too good to be true.

"No, he doesn't," replied Humphrey. "Read the letter, Mark. He says his practice has grown too big for him and he wants a young active man as a partner — it's the very thing for you."

An hour later Mark was well on his way to Timperton, driving quickly with the wind whistling in his ears. He still felt dubious about the post, he would not let himself think about it — there must be some snag. Things did not happen like that, thought Mark, ripe fruit did not drop into one's mouth. He had enjoyed his hospital work but he had always felt an exile, not only an exile from his home but an exile from the country. Bricks and mortar, the smell of petrol and the bustle and noise of London depressed his spirit and sapped his energy. He had had constant headaches and he could not sleep properly. It was the country Mark loved, green fields and trees and hills, quietness, peace and plain wholesome country food — and he loved country pursuits: a day on the river with his rod, or on the hill with his gun.

Timperton was larger than Ryddelton, and it had grown a good deal in the last few years. There were villas and bungalows on the outskirts of the little town and bigger houses with lovely gardens on the hill. The main street was wide, for a market was held here once a month and farmers came in from the country and stalls were erected to sell vegetables and fruit and flowers. Down the middle of the street there were trees growing which gave a pleasant shade — and at the other end of the street stood the doctor's house.

Mark rang the bell and waited, fingering his tie. He was very anxious about this interview for so much depended on it. Humphrey had warned him not to be too humble for that would be a mistake — on the other hand it would be equally disastrous to be too brassy.

Dr. Anderson was in, he had just finished consulting and when Mark was shown into the consulting room he was washing his hands at the sink. He was tall and very thin with stooping shoulders and sandy grey hair and his eyes were light blue and keen and piercing.

"Well, what can I do for you?" he inquired, smiling kindly. "I don't think I've seen you before, have I?"

"No," replied Mark. "I'm not a patient. You wrote a letter to my father."

"Of course!" nodded Dr. Anderson. "You're Dunne. I didn't get the name. Sit down, I'm very glad to see you."

"I thought I'd come," said Mark, taking a chair. "Of course you'll want to see my credentials and go into everything thoroughly, but I thought it would be a good plan to come over and see you first."

"A very good plan," Dr. Anderson agreed.

They began to talk. Mark explained what he had been doing and why he wanted a change. "London doesn't suit me," said Mark.

"I hope you're strong," said Dr. Anderson, looking at him critically. "You don't look very strong."

"I'm perfectly fit," declared Mark. "I need a holiday, that's all. I don't suppose you would want me at once —"

"No," said Dr. Anderson doubtfully. "No, I dare say my assistant could stay on for a few weeks longer. It isn't so difficult in the summer; it's the winter that bothers me, really. The practice is large and scattered — there are farms up the glen — I really need someone experienced to take some of the responsibility."

"I'm not afraid of work," said Mark. "I've had a good deal of responsibility."

"Are you married?"

"Not yet," said Mark, blushing. "I hope — perhaps — soon —"

"Good," said Dr. Anderson. He smiled and all at once he seemed more human. Mark liked his smile.

"I'm not married," continued Dr. Anderson. "My two sisters live with me and look after things, but it's a good thing for a doctor to be married — especially in a small place like this; it saves a lot of bother."

Dr. Anderson sat down and began to talk more seriously. He talked well, describing the district and explaining how Timperton had grown and spread in the last few years and his practice with it. He showed Mark his books, his accounts and the ledger in which he kept a list of his patients — it was all extremely clear and business-like. "There's ample work for two doctors here," declared Mark at last.

"That's why I need a partner," replied Dr. Anderson. "The fact is this place is full of retired people, elderly people who have broken down in health and suffer from digestive troubles."

"Good!" exclaimed Mark, somewhat callously. "I mean," he added. "I mean I'm very much interested in the digestive organs, in fact I thought I might specialise some day."

"You'll get plenty of experience here."

"Good," said Mark again.

"I've been carrying on with an assistant," continued Dr. Anderson; "but I'm not as strong as I was and I must have someone able and willing to take some of the responsibility off my shoulders."

"Do you think I'm too young?"

"I don't think so. You have a serious air," smiled Dr. Anderson. "A serious air takes you a long way. You inspire confidence. I want someone young and up-to-date. I believe we could get on very well together."

Mark thought so too. He was very favourably impressed. Of course there were inquiries to be made on both sides and the price of the partnership to be arranged but Mark had a feeling that everything would be settled satisfactorily.

He was invited to stay to tea and to meet the doctor's sisters, Miss Anderson and Miss Mary Anderson. They were twins and so alike that it was difficult to know them apart — two small, round twittering women of the age usually described as "uncertain" — and they talked in chorus, agreeing with one another and with everyone else as well.

"It will be so nice for Alan to have you."

"He needs someone to help him."

"We must look for comfortable rooms for you."

"Perhaps Mrs. Walker —"

"Yes, she will be the best."

"So nice and clean —"

"And such a good cook."

Mark, when he could get a word in edgeways, explained that nothing was settled yet. He could not help smiling at the Misses Anderson's way of talking, for their voices — as well as their appearances — were alike, and if you had shut your eyes you might have thought it was one person speaking instead of two. He wondered if they had two minds, or only one mind between them; it was an interesting problem.

"Rooms are not satisfactory," Dr. Anderson was saying. "You should rent a small house — that gives you a proper status at once. It's very important in a country district like Timperton to have a proper status. My assistant lives in rooms, of course, but that's different. We must make it clear from the very beginning that you are a partner."

Mark saw the point. "Yes," he said doubtfully. "Yes, but what about a house — and servants — and all that?"

"As a matter of fact I happen to know of a house which might suit you —"

"The Browns'," cried the two Miss Andersons.

"Yes, the Browns'. It's small but well built and nicely furnished and it has a small garden facing south. They would let it for a couple of years, I think."

"You can see it!" cried one Miss Anderson.

"We'll go round after tea!" cried the other.

Mark thought there was no harm in seeing the house, it did not bind him in any way, so he signified his willingness to look at it and after tea he was escorted down the street by the doctor's sisters. They walked one on each side of him and continued to talk eagerly about the amenities of Timperton. There was a tennis club, there was badminton, there was an excellent golf course. They were sure he would be happy here. They would help him to move in, they would find maids for him, they would tell him the best shops. It was obvious that they were very anxious for him to come — and to come soon — but this was not surprising for Dr. Anderson was quite unfit to carry on alone.

The house was delightful. It was not large but it was pretty and comfortable and had individuality for it had been built by an architect for himself. The floors were of inlaid wood, and the doors and wainscotings were of unpainted wood, waxed and polished. On the ground floor there was a sitting-room and a dining-room — both of which had bow windows facing south and looking out on to the garden — and a small room at the back which would do as a consulting room. Upstairs there were two very nice bedrooms and a bathroom. The servants' quarters were at the back. Mark was charmed with the house; he drove home feeling very pleased with life. Everything was falling into place like the pieces in a well-made jig-saw puzzle; there was no snag anywhere. If the price of the partnership could be arranged — and he felt pretty certain that it could — he would be settled in a congenial post and could speak to Tessa with a clear conscience. They would not be well off, of course, but they would have enough to live on very comfortably. I'll telephone, thought Mark — who could wait no longer to tell Tessa his news — I'll ask her to meet me to-morrow at the Peel Tower. There's nothing to keep us apart any more.

CHAPTER
TWENTY-SEVEN

Thunderbolt

Mark was early for his appointment and Tessa had not arrived when he reached the *rendezvous*. He had not been to the Peel Tower since last year and he looked round at the old place with affection and respect. The staircase (which went up at one side and ended in a little square platform) seemed to have suffered a good deal of damage from the frost and snow of winter. Some of the stones had fallen from their places, others had been loosened and were balanced precariously on the edge of the wall, but Mark managed to climb up safely, and standing on the little platform he looked over the tops of the trees towards Ryddelton House. Yes, there was Tessa. He could see her in the distance coming towards him through the fields . . . and, because he was so impatient to speak to her, he could not wait for her to come but hastened down the steps and through the woods and jumping over the gate, ran to meet her.

"You seem in a hurry!" cried Tessa, waving her hand.

"I love you," said Mark breathlessly. "I want to marry you."

The next moment she was in his arms and he was kissing her.

"You *are* funny," said Tessa, laughing excitedly. "You *are* funny, Mark. We've been seeing each other for days and days. Have you only just discovered that you love me?"

"I've loved you for years — you know that perfectly well — but I couldn't ask you to marry me when I was working at the hospital."

"Have you resigned?"

"Yes, I've resigned. Dad is going to buy a partnership for me. It's with Dr. Anderson at Timperton. You'd like it, wouldn't you? We could have a dear little house of our own. I've seen the very house."

She smiled at him. "You seem to have arranged it all!"

"Darling, you're pleased, aren't you?" asked Mark a trifle anxiously. "I wanted to have things arranged so that I would have something to offer you. Of course it isn't really fixed, yet, so if you don't like the idea . . . or if you'd rather go somewhere else . . ."

"No," said Tessa slowly. "No, Mark, I think it would be rather nice — just for a little while. It would be fun to have a house of our own — just you and me —"

"It would be heavenly!" cried Mark and he kissed her again.

"When did you begin to love me?" Tessa asked.

"Ages ago," he replied. "Long before the play. I wanted to ask you, then — you knew that, didn't you? You knew I meant it when I said, "Gentle Hermia, may I marry thee?'"

Tessa laughed. She said, "Why didn't you ask me, then? You *were* an old stupid."

"Would you have said 'yes'?"

"Of course I would."

"But I couldn't," declared Mark, suddenly grave. "I hadn't even qualified. I had nothing to offer you at all."

"I think you had a good deal to offer me," said Tessa, laughing. She put her arm through his and they began to walk across the meadow. Neither of them had much idea where they were going.

"You *will* marry me," said Mark. "You really mean it?"

"Yes, of course. I've told you so about three times already. What sort of person do you think I am?"

"The most wonderful person in the world," Mark assured her earnestly.

"I'm not, really," she replied, "but, never mind, I like you to think I'm wonderful. I think you're rather a dear."

"Do you?"

"Yes, rather a funny dear . . . what did you mean when you said you had nothing to offer me?"

"I just meant what I said . . ."

Tessa gave his arm a little squeeze. "We needn't *pretend*," she said. "I hate shams and it's natural to look to the future. Some day Dunnian will be yours and you'll let me share it, won't you? I've always told you how much I love Dunnian."

Mark stopped dead. He felt as if he had been turned to stone. He could not answer her.

"Some day," repeated Tessa, smiling at him. "Not for years and years, of course, but it's natural to think of the future when you're young. Why shouldn't you be glad to think that some day Dunnian will be yours!"

"Because," he said hoarsely. "Because it won't be — mine — ever." It was not what he had meant to say. He had no words to express his feelings.

"It won't be?" she repeated in a bewildered tone.

"No," said Mark.

"But what do you mean? You're the eldest son."

"Yes, of course, but Dunnian isn't entailed. It doesn't come to me."

They were standing in the middle of the meadow, now, ankle deep in the sweet lush grass which was full of golden buttercups. The larks were singing and the sky was very blue — but to Mark it seemed as if a thick black cloud had come over the sun.

"I don't understand," said Tessa, and there was a new note in her voice, a strange sharp note which Mark had not heard before. "I don't understand. Who does it go to if it doesn't come to you? Can your father leave it as he likes?"

"No," said Mark dully.

"But that's dreadful!" she cried. "That's dreadful! I can't believe it!"

"I thought you knew."

"How could I know? How could I possibly know unless someone told me?"

"You knew I was studying medicine."

"Oh, that!" cried Tessa scornfully. "I knew *that*, of course, but I thought you were just amusing yourself —"

"Amusing myself!" he cried.

"Oh, you know what I mean," she replied, stamping her foot on the ground. "I thought you were just marking time until — until Dunnian was yours."

"Tessa!"

"You haven't played fair," she said angrily. "No, you haven't. Why didn't you tell me long ago?"

"I've told you — I thought you knew —"

"You deceived me —"

"Oh, Tessa, this is dreadful!" cried Mark. "What's happening to us?"

She took no notice. "It wasn't fair," she continued in trembling tones. "It wasn't right. You let me go on thinking — thinking that you — why didn't you tell me long ago?"

She was behaving like a child, unreasonably, illogically . . . she was just a child, really, and such a beautiful child. Her face was flushed and her eyes were sparkling with tears . . . suddenly Mark caught her in his arms and she did not resist him. They kissed each other for the third time, a long lingering kiss.

"Tessa, you do love me?"

"Yes," she sighed.

He was suddenly caught up to heaven. The sun was shining again in Mark's sky. "Darling, I knew it was all right," he whispered. "You've forgiven me, haven't you? We'll be so happy together."

He waited for a reply, but she said nothing.

"We'll be so happy that we won't — we won't mind about — about anything," Mark stammered. "We'll be so happy together."

She drew herself out of his arms and stood back. Her eyes were tearful but her mouth was firm. "I'll have to — to think about it," she said.

"But Tessa, if we love each other —"

"You've deceived me, Mark. That's what hurts."

"I didn't mean to," said Mark earnestly. "You know that, don't you? You know I didn't mean to. It was all a mistake, Tessa."

"Was it?"

"Yes, all a mistake. We love each other, don't we? This doesn't make any difference, does it?"

"I think it makes a good deal of difference."

"But, Tessa —"

"But, Mark, don't you see — we should be nobodies without Dunnian," Tessa said.

Mark did not go home to lunch. He went up the hill and sat there for a long time with his back against a rock looking at the fair spread of country with unseeing eyes, looking down at Dunnian with its lawns and gardens and terraces half-hidden amongst the trees. A little more than a year ago Deb had brought her troubles to this very spot . . . but Mark did not know that. His thoughts veered to and fro: at one moment he saw things from Tessa's point of view and the next moment from his own. It must have been a shock and a disappointment to Tessa — she was so fond of Dunnian. She loved him — he was sure of that — but she did not love him enough. *She did not love him enough to marry him without Dunnian tacked on*! She wanted Dunnian and she wanted the position that Dunnian would give her; she had seen herself as mistress of the lovely old place — not now, of course, but in the future. The prospect of living out her life as a doctor's wife did not appeal to her at all. She might change her mind, of course, but

Mark did not think it likely, for Tessa always knew exactly what she wanted and was not given to changing her mind.

Now that this dreadful thing had happened Mark could not think why he had never mentioned the fact to Tessa — the fact that Dunnian would not be his. (If only I had *told* her, thought Mark, biting hard on the mouthpiece of his empty pipe.) Why hadn't he told her? The answer was *because he never thought about it, himself*. He had never envisaged the place as his. It was a fixed fact in his mind that Dunnian would eventually belong to Celia. (Long ago when Humphrey had informed Mark of the provisions of old Aunt Celia's will Humphrey had impressed upon him that it was a secret; he could speak to his mother about it, but to nobody else. Nobody else was to know — Celia, herself, was not to know until she was twenty-one. She was to be brought up just like the other children, not treated differently nor set apart from the rest of the family. Mark had seen the wisdom of this decision and had subscribed to it, but he had never realised how it affected himself.) He saw, now, that he had been sailing under false colours — *everyone* must think that he was his father's heir . . .

Mark had been so happy. He had been so sure of Tessa, so certain that she returned his love and would marry him . . . the way had seemed so smooth, the sky had seemed so clear . . . it was a thunderbolt.

I should have asked her first, thought Mark. I should have made sure of the most important thing first. What good is the partnership without Tessa!

It was not much good. Mark wished with all his heart that he had not sent his resignation to the hospital for it would have been better to go back to London and work like a slave and try to forget what had happened.

Several days passed and there was no word from Tessa, no message, and at last Mark heard that she and Oliver had left Ryddelton and gone back to London . . . and with this news his last hope vanished. He was very miserable, he was angry and wounded and sad. Sometimes he blamed himself for what had happened, sometimes he blamed Tessa. Dunnian had lost its power to heal and soothe him for his confusion and grief were connected with the place. The sun shone and Dunnian glowed like a jewel, but it did not glow for him. He felt lonely — and that was queer because he had never felt lonely before (he had liked to be with people but he had always felt happiest alone). Now, suddenly, the world felt big and draughty. If he could have confided in his father it would have helped a good deal but there were all sorts of reasons why he could not do so . . . no, he could not tell his father what had happened. He could not have borne his father's sympathy nor to have to sit and listen to criticisms of Tessa, and, last but not least, he could not have borne his father's distress. Mark knew that his father had always wanted him to have Dunnian, and that for some reason his father felt himself to blame for the curious provisions of Aunt Celia's will. Mark knew that Humphrey was even a trifle ashamed of the "oddness" of the will (Humphrey did not like to feel that people were talking about his family) it was one of the reasons why he had wanted to keep the will a secret.

Humphrey would feel that *this* was his fault, too, he would be distressed beyond measure when he heard what had ensued from his desire to keep the family skeleton in the cupboard.

Humphrey asked no questions — he was too wise — but he could not fail to see that something was amiss, his eyes seemed to be saying, "Is everything all right, Mark?" — but Mark could not reply. The nearest Humphrey got to asking the all-important question was when the papers relating to the partnership came from the lawyers to be signed.

"You're sure you really want it?" Humphrey asked, with his pen poised in the air.

"Of course I want it, Dad," replied Mark. It was pride, chiefly, which made him say the words, for by this time pride had come to Mark's aid. He intended to make a life for himself without Tessa, and it would be a good life, too.

Mark was not the least surprised that everything went through without a hitch. It had seemed too good to be true; but, now, the snag had appeared. That was how Mark saw it.

The papers were signed and, a day or two later, Humphrey said good-bye and returned to his command in the Mediterranean — and still Mark had not said a word. He had decided to write to his father and tell him everything for he felt it would be easier to write. The only person in whom Mark could have confided was Deb — and Deb was not here.

CHAPTER
TWENTY-EIGHT

Titania's Dress

It was very quiet at Dunnian now. Humphrey was gone, Deb was still at Bournemouth, Celia was busy with her lessons. Mark spent a good deal of time with his mother on the terrace. She would sew quietly, sitting in old Aunt Celia's chair, and Mark would sit near her reading and smoking his pipe. Sometimes she would talk, but her talk was a little vague as if some part of her mind had moved on to a different plane. When she spoke of the future she spoke as if she would not be here — and yet Mark did not think she was aware of this, herself.

"It will be so nice for Humphrey to have you settled at Timperton," said Alice one day. "When Humphrey retires he may find it a little dull and lonely."

"But he'll have *you*," Mark pointed out.

"Yes, of course," agreed Alice, but she looked puzzled and doubtful.

"He doesn't want any one else when he has you."

"No," said Alice, smiling. She was silent for a little and then she said. "We haven't seen Tessa lately. You haven't quarrelled with Tessa, have you?"

"No, I haven't quarrelled with her," replied Mark. "She's gone away."

"Don't let her come between you and Humphrey," said Alice vaguely. "Humphrey will need you, Mark."

"How could she come between us?"

"She wants you all to herself," Alice replied. "She's like that, you know. At one time I thought she was very sweet but, lately, I've begun to see things differently. Sometimes things seem very clear and sometimes everything is misty. I can't explain it properly."

He was worried about Alice (if she did not improve soon he decided that she must be taken to see a specialist); he was worried about Becky as well. Becky gave him a fright. She fainted one day when she was going upstairs and Mark found her lying on the landing. For one awful moment he thought she was dead and his own heart almost stopped beating. It was one thing, Mark found, to be cool and collected when you were called in to see an ordinary patient, but it was quite another when you discovered one of your oldest and dearest friends lying in a twisted heap at the bottom of a flight of stairs.

Mark examined her carefully and found that no bones had been broken — which amazed him considerably — and they managed to carry her up to bed and revive her with smelling salts. "We had better send for Dr. Ferguson," Mark said in an undertone to one of the maids who had helped him to carry Becky up the stairs."

"Shall I go and telephone for him, sir?"

"Yes, please," said Mark.

"I'll not have any doctor but you," declared Becky, opening her eyes.

Mark was so unutterably relieved to hear this characteristic statement delivered in Becky's own firmly determined voice that he could not help laughing.

"I'll not," repeated Becky, looking at him defiantly. "I'll not have that old curmudgeon putting a finger on me. If I'm to be doctored it's you that'll have to do it."

"You don't sound as if you needed much doctoring," said Mark. "Let's have a look at you . . ."

"You can look at my tongue," Becky replied, pulling up the sheet and holding it under her chin.

"I want to examine you thoroughly."

"You can't. I'm perfectly all right. There's nothing wrong with me at all."

Mark was usually considered pretty good with recalcitrant patients, but he had met his match in Becky and he knew it. He felt her pulse and looked at her tongue — though what use that was he did not know — and inquired feebly whether she felt any pain.

"No pain at all," replied Becky promptly.

"You've been overdoing it," Mark told her. "It has been very hot and you've been running up and down stairs. A few days in bed will do you a lot of good and after that you'd better have a holiday."

"A holiday, indeed!" exclaimed Becky. "Where would I go? Would I go to my sister and do all the cooking or else to my niece and be landed with the baby? No, no, I'll maybe take a day in bed and you can give me a bottle — I suppose you can write out a bottle for me, can't you?"

Mark assured her that it was well within his power to prescribe a "bottle."

"You're sure?" she asked with some anxiety. "I'm not wanting to be poisoned or anything . . ."

"Oh, Becky, you're priceless!" declared Mark. "You're worth your weight in gold."

Becky smiled primly and replied, "Well, you should know about that since you carried me up the stair."

Becky was left reposing peacefully in bed, but that night, after dinner, when Mark went up to see his patient, he found she had disobeyed his orders. She had risen and dressed and was sitting in the old nursery sewing industriously.

"Becky, this is ridiculous!" exclaimed Mark. "I told you to stay in bed. If you don't do what I tell you we must get another doctor. You're a silly old woman, that's what you are."

"That's enough," replied Becky. "I may be a silly old woman but you're a very silly young man. There's some people can't tell gold from brass when it's under their very noses."

Mark sat down. He was feeling lonely and miserable and Becky's conversation was always entertaining — besides he had a feeling that Becky had something she wanted to tell him.

"In what way am I silly?" he asked.

"Oh, I'll not say you aren't well enough as a doctor — the bottle has done me a power of good already."

Mark smiled. It was just like Becky to make this absurd statement, to be convinced — because she happened to be feeling a little better — that one dose of his simple prescription of strychnine and glycerophosphates had worked a miracle.

"I'm quite a good doctor," said Mark, "but I can't tell the difference between gold and brass — that's what's the matter with me, is it?"

Becky hesitated for a moment and then she closed her lips.

"Do you remember," said Mark after a little silence. "Do you remember when you used to tell me stories — all sorts of interesting stories about Dunnian? I've never forgotten them, Becky."

"You were a nice wee boy."

"It seems a long time ago."

"Not to me. The years pass quickly when you get old. I've seen you all grow up but it seems like yesterday you were children in the house."

"It's a quiet house now."

"Too quiet," nodded Becky. "We should have Miss Deb back. Mrs. Dunne will be very lonely when you've gone to Timperton."

"I know," agreed Mark, "but Deb is enjoying herself — she's having a holiday."

"She'd come back to-morrow if you asked her."

"I wonder," said Mark.

"You needn't wonder," replied Becky tartly. "If you had left her alone and not tormented her she would never have gone away."

Mark was silent. He watched Becky's nimble fingers . . . her needle flashed as it went in and out of the soft fine fabric she was sewing.

"What's that you're making?" asked Mark at last.

She shook it out and held it up before his eyes, it was a dress of fine white gauze trimmed with silver, with a silver girdle round the waist.

"It looks like a fancy dress!" exclaimed Mark in surprise.

"It *was* a fancy dress, but I'm altering it — I'm making it into an evening frock for Celia. It's doing no good lying there in the cupboard."

"I don't remember seeing it before."

"That's not surprising," replied Becky dryly. "It's never been worn. It's the dress Miss Deb was going to wear in the play." She hesitated for a moment and then added in a lower tone, "It was not like you to turn her out of the play, Mr. Mark."

"Turn her out of the play!" cried Mark in amazement.

"That's what I said. It wasn't like you . . . it wasn't fair . . . it was a shabby thing to do."

"You've got it all wrong, Becky. We didn't turn her out — as you put it — she turned herself out. She funked it at the last moment; that's what happened. She couldn't learn her part."

"Her part was learnt. She said it to me over and over; she had it all off by heart — every word — and her dress was ready. She made it herself, every stitch."

"Then why —" began Mark in bewildered tones.

"She was looking forward to it," Becky told him. "She wasn't frightened of it. Why should she be frightened?"

"But, Becky, she told Tessa she was frightened —"

"No, Mr. Mark."

"Yes, honestly."

"I was here," said Becky, raising her eyes and looking Mark straight in the face with her level gaze. "I was here in this very room when Miss Skene came in. She sat on that table and she laid down the law. You wanted Miss Angela in the play — that was what she said — and there was no part for her unless Miss Deb would give up Titania. 'You don't mind, do you?' she said; those were her very words."

"Becky!"

"Of course Miss Deb minded. She's only a young thing for all her old-fashioned ways. 'We don't need you now,' said Miss Skene. Then Miss Deb said, 'Did Mark say that?' 'Yes, of course,' said Miss Skene."

"Oh, Becky, I can't believe —"

"You think I'm lying to you?" asked Becky, who never minced her words.

"No," said Mark unhappily.

"I wouldn't lie to you — even for your good," declared Becky, and with this somewhat enigmatic statement she took up the dress and began to sew.

"It's dreadful," said Mark at last. "It's so mean and petty. She let me go on thinking that Deb had let us down — how could she do that?"

"That's the worst bit of it," Becky agreed in a cheerful tone.

"Of course it is. It was bad enough to take the part away from her — I wanted Deb to play it; I thought it would be good for her —"

"So it would have been."

"— but it was far worse to let me think that Deb had let us down."

284

"Far worse," agreed Becky, more cheerfully still. "A person who could do that could do almost anything."

Mark got up and went away for he was so upset that he could not discuss it further. At first he clung to the idea that there must be some mistake, and he cast his mind back and tried to remember what Tessa had said to him about it. He remembered that he had been studying in the library and Tessa had come in and perched herself on the arm of the chair. "I'm afraid Debbie has got cold feet," she had said, looking down at him with a worried expression on her face. "Poor little Debbie," we can't make her go on with it, Mark." Mark remembered that he had risen and said he would speak to Deb, but Tessa had prevented him. "Don't do that," Tessa had said. "You'll only make her unhappy. She's shy and frightened — she can't help it, you know — and she's so afraid you'll be angry with her. I said I'd put it all right with you." "But, Tess, what are we to do? She *must* go on with it," Mark had said. Tessa had shaken her head at that: "No, Mark," she had said. "It would be unkind to make her do it when she dreads it so much — besides she would probably let us down on the night." Mark had been angry and disappointed in Deb — it was rotten of her to let them down like this — and Tessa had taken Deb's part and stood up for Deb. "She can't help it," Tessa had reiterated.

Oddly enough Mark remembered every word of the argument and of the discussion which had ensued as to who could be roped in at the last minute to take the vacant place. He, himself, had suggested Angela, and

285

Tessa had clapped her hands and exclaimed, "Of course — Angela — she's the very person!"

There was no mistake possible, no shadow of a mistake. It was almost past belief that any one could have been so deceitful, could have acted the abominable part with such conviction — but Tessa was a very good actress and Tessa had acted it. Why had she done it? Why had she wanted Deb out of the play? It seemed senseless to Mark. It was not as if Angela had played the part better; Angela was no actress and her memory was poor, she had been the weak link in the play . . . but *that* was all over now, *that* didn't matter; what mattered was the discovery of Tessa's nature. "A person who could do that could do almost anything" — yes, it was perfectly true.

It took Mark all night, turning and twisting in his bed, before he could face the thing squarely, but once he had managed it he felt a good deal better. The only thing to do was to take Tessa right out of his life and make up his mind to forget her. This seemed difficult but it was not quite so difficult as it seemed because the Tessa he had worshipped was not a real person but merely a figment of his imagination. The flaws he had found in her and for which he had found excuses were part of her nature. She was rotten to the core.

In one way at least Mark found instant relief: Tessa had accused him of deceiving her and this had worried him a good deal, but, whereas he had deceived her unwittingly, Tessa had deceived him with deliberate intent . . . he need distress himself about *that* no more, thought Mark with a wry smile.

CHAPTER
TWENTY-NINE

Mark's House

It was almost worth while going away from Dunnian to have the pleasure of coming back — so Deb thought, the morning after her arrival, as she leaned out of her bedroom window and looked at the trees and the hills and heard the gentle murmur of the Rydd Water. She had enjoyed Bournemouth — Grannie had been very kind and sweet — but Dunnian was her real home.

Deb dressed quickly and ran out into the sunshine, she drew in long breaths of the sparkling air . . . she was home again and everything was all right. Aunt Alice had been delighted to see her — so much delighted that Deb felt quite guilty at having stayed away so long — and Mark had been just like his old self, friendly and kind and smiling. There had been no mention of Oliver, no talk of "marriage," everything was comfortable again.

Old Johnson was weeding the herbaceous border in front of the house and Deb saw that he was smiling at her, so she went across the lawn and shook hands with him.

"It's easy to see you're glad to be home," Johnson said.

"I expect I looked silly," said Deb, blushing.

"You looked happy, Miss Debbie. I'm aye happy myself when I've been away to Hawick to see my brother and I get home again There's worse places than Dunnian."

"I haven't found any half as good."

"That's fine," said Johnson, nodding. "You're needed here. It's a quiet house these days and it'll be quieter than ever when Mr. Mark goes off to Timperton."

Johnson was an old man now but he still loved a chat — or a crack as he called it — he leaned on his hoe and they discussed all that had happened while Deb was away. Deb often wondered how Johnson obtained all his information; there was nothing that went on in the family that Johnson did not know.

"Miss Joyce ought to be home," Johnson said. "Och yes, I know she's to be married. It's a London business man, they're saying, so she'll be settled in London near Miss Edith — Mrs. Rewden, I mean. I've only been to London once in my life and I was glad to get away with a whole skin. Them taxis!" said Johnson, shaking his head gravely. "Them buses, with their screeching brakes! I was all but run down in yon wide street — Pawl Mawl, they call it."

"Were you really!" exclaimed Deb, with suitable dismay.

"All but run down," repeated Johnson. "And the queer way the folks talk! I couldn't make out what they were saying half the time! Aye, it's a queer place, London . . . They were saying that Mr. Mark has taken a wee house at Timperton," continued Johnson after a barely perceptible pause. "You'll be going over to see it, no doubt."

"Yes," agreed Deb. "We're going over this afternoon. I've promised to help him to settle in."

"And Miss Skene," said Johnson. "Miss Skene is away — and Mr. Skene as well."

"They've gone to London on business," said Deb, for this was what she had been told.

"H'm," said Johnson — and that was all — but he managed in this one syallable to express scorn and disbelief and suspicion. Johnson had no use at all for the Skenes.

They were still talking, discussing the dogs and the garden, when the breakfast gong was sounded and Deb had to go in.

Deb had been away so long that there were scores of household problems needing her attention, but she put them aside in the meantime for she wanted to go to Timperton with Mark. The linen cupboard was in a muddle — but it had been like that for weeks, so if it remained in a muddle for a few days longer it would do no harm. Mrs. Drummond — who was still ruling the kitchen — had several complaints to make, she wanted a new kitchen-maid, and new pans, and she wanted Miss Debbie to go through the store cupboard with her, but Deb was determined not to be drawn into a whirl of domestic duties — all that must wait until Mark was settled.

"It's awfully good of you," Mark said as they got into the little car together and drove off. "I thought I would be able to manage all right but I don't seem very good in the domestic line. The Misses Anderson have found me two maids but they aren't coming till next week, so I've got a woman to come in every day and do a bit of cleaning."

"I'm delighted to help you," Deb replied — and so she was. It seemed odd that Tessa had not stayed to help him, but perhaps it was not so very odd after all (thought Deb) for Tessa did not like doing troublesome things, she preferred to have them done for her by other people.

Mark drove quickly but carefully; he was intent on his business and they did not talk much. Deb glanced at him once or twice and wondered if he had spoken to Tessa, if he and Tessa were officially engaged. His face puzzled her a little for it was neither the blissfully happy face of a newly engaged lover, nor the slightly anxious face of a lover who has not yet put his fate to the test. Mark's face was cheerful and calm and friendly.

The house was charming — Deb fell in love with it at once — it was so bright and airy and the rooms were well shaped and exactly the right size. She liked the plain wood and the cream paper and the self-coloured carpets and the few good etchings which hung on the walls. It was a dear little house — but it had been badly kept. A thorough cleaning was what it needed. The dining-room and the sitting-room faced south, opening on to the garden, but the room which Mark had begun to call his consulting room faced north and was badly lit and inconvenient.

"I know it's a horrid room but what can I do?" said Mark. "Do you think if I had the walls repapered with very light paper it would cheer it up a bit?"

"No," replied Deb. "No, it won't do at all. You must use the dining-room. It's horrid for patients to be shown into a dark, gloomy room when they come to see you."

"Use the dining-room!"

"Yes, we'll change the furniture. This room will do quite well as a dining-room, won't it?"

"How clever of you, Deb!" exclaimed Mark. "I never thought of changing the rooms about — it's an absolute brain-wave. There will be far more space for my bookcase in the bigger room —"

They started to move the furniture at once, helped by the daily woman (Mrs. Craig by name) and the gardener. It was a difficult business, for the house was small, and at one moment the hall was so full of furniture — some coming and some going, as Mark put it — that Mark was obliged to climb over the top of the sideboard before he could open the dining-room door. Deb began to wonder, somewhat anxiously, whether the furniture would all fit in . . . but they managed it somehow and stood back to view the results of their labours. Mark's new consulting room was delightful; the new dining-room was not so good.

"Oh dear, I hope Tessa won't mind!" exclaimed Deb in sudden anxiety.

There was a little silence and then Mark said, "Tessa isn't coming to live here."

"Oh!" said Deb, trying to hide her surprise.

Mark took up a duster and began to rub the table. He said, "No. I meant to tell you. It was all a mistake."

"Oh!" said Deb again.

"She found she didn't — didn't love me enough," continued Mark in a gruff voice, polishing the table as if his life depended upon it. "That was all, really . . . so I shall be living here by myself . . . so the dining-room will be quite big enough, you see."

"Yes," said Deb. It was difficult to know what else to say. Mark's attitude did not invite sympathy.

Mark hesitated for a moment and then continued, "There's something else I want to tell you, Deb. It's about the play. Tessa said we didn't need you . . . well, it wasn't true."

It seemed so long ago and so much had happened to Deb since the play that she had almost forgotten the incident — almost but not quite. "Oh, you mean Titania!" said Deb. "It didn't matter, it was perfectly all right."

"It wasn't all right," said Mark gravely. "It was very much all wrong. Tessa told you that I said we didn't need you, but that wasn't true. I wanted you to be in the play, Deb."

"It was because Angela —"

"Listen," said Mark. "I want you to understand. Tessa told me that you had backed out of it at the last minute and let us down."

"Did she?" asked Deb.

"Yes, wasn't it dreadful?"

Somehow or other Deb did not feel very much surprised or shocked at this revelation of Tessa's duplicity. She thought in her own mind that it was just the sort of thing Tessa would do.

"I was horrified when I found out about it," said Mark. "Simply horrified."

He looked so distressed that Deb sought to comfort him. "Never mind," she said. "It's all over long ago. It was a small thing, Mark."

"It wasn't a small thing," he declared. "She said you had let us down and I was angry with you, Deb — that's the horrible part." He looked at her as he spoke and she saw real distress in his face. "I was angry with you, Deb," he repeated in a low voice.

"It's all over. It doesn't matter — now."

"Oh, Deb, it was so stupid of me. I should have known you better; I should have gone to you straight off and asked you about it. Instead of that I behaved like a bear with a sore head — what can you have thought of me!"

"I knew you were annoyed with me, but of course I didn't know why," said Deb slowly.

"You'll forgive me, won't you?"

"There's nothing to forgive," declared Deb with a brilliant smile, for all at once she felt very, very happy. "It's all over and done with long ago — don't think about it any more."

"Why did she do it?" asked Mark, disobeying the injunction. "Why on earth did she take all that trouble? Why did she want you out of the play. Angela was no use at all . . ."

Deb did not reply. Tessa's motive was fairly obvious to her, for she had watched Tessa at work and knew

293

Tessa's methods. Tessa was as clever as paint and she nearly always accomplished what she set out to do . . . so, if you wanted to discover her motive for an apparently senseless action, you had only to look at the results obtained. In this case, of course, the result of Tessa's action had been a breach between Deb and Mark. It was too simple, thought Deb, smiling.

Mrs. Craig brought a tray of tea and bread and butter into the sitting-room and Deb and Mark sat down together comfortably. Deb lay back in her chair, she was wan and dishevelled and there was a streak of dust across her forehead, but none of this detracted from her appearance in Mark's eyes — for it was in his service that she had got dirty and tired. He looked at her with deep affection and noted several interesting things about her: her slim figure was not so flat and boyish as it used to be (she had filled out a little while she was at Bournemouth) there were feminine curves in her figure now — very slight curves, of course, but quite perceptible to the eye of affection. Her slim legs were more shapely and this made her ankles seem finer and her feet smaller and more delicately arched.

"I shouldn't have let you wear yourself out," said Mark in sudden solicitude.

"I'm not worn out — just pleasantly tired."

"You're ever so much stronger than you used to be." Deb nodded. "Oh yes, my visit to Grannie did me a lot of good. I enjoyed it tremendously, you know."

"Tell me about it," Mark said. "You haven't told me anything . . ."

Deb was in good spirits in spite of her fatigue and she made a very amusing tale of her visit to Bournemouth. She told him all that she thought would interest him, about the place and about the people she had met. "You would love Henrietta," she declared. "She's the dearest little old lady, wise and witty and kind."

"Who else did you meet when you were there?" asked Mark with sudden urgency, for it had struck him that Deb might have met an attractive man and fallen in love with him. That would account for the new liveliness in Deb, the new assurance and poise.

"I've told you," said Deb, smiling. "I met scores of people."

"Mostly old people, I suppose."

"Old and young and middle-aged," she replied with a little gleam in her eyes. "Henrietta knows everybody, she's tremendously popular."

"Did you call her Henrietta?"

"Sometimes," admitted Deb. "Everybody calls her Henrietta — it suits her so well. She rather liked it when I was cheeky to her — we got on splendidly."

Mark sighed. He tried to think of a leading question. "You must have been sorry to come away —" he began.

"Oh, no!" cried Deb. "Oh, no! I was very glad to come home. Very glad indeed."

"Good," said Mark, nodding.

Deb chattered on, and, now that his fears were at rest, Mark found it delightful to sit back and listen to her . . . she had such a soft, low voice, such an infectious, rippling laugh. It was delightful to look at her, too, to see her sitting opposite to him in one of his own chairs, pouring out his tea.

"I wonder," said Mark at last in a thoughtful manner. "I wonder if Mother could possibly spare you for a bit — just until I get properly settled. It would be such a help to have you. I've got to start work the day after to-morrow and there's still a lot to do in the house."

Deb hesitated, but only for a moment. "I should like to help you," she said slowly.

"Mother has got Becky, hasn't she?"

"Yes, of course."

"Would you *like* to come?" Mark asked, for he had a feeling that there had been a slight reluctance on her part to accept the invitation.

"Yes," replied Deb. "If Aunt Alice says it's all right I'd like to come."

"Mother has got Becky," repeated Mark. "Mother will be perfectly all right with Becky — just for a few days."

They returned to Dunnian that night, locking up the little house behind them. Mark was full of his plan to have Deb to stay with him and his mother offered no objections.

"You need her more than I do," said Alice in that vague sort of voice which Deb found so pathetic. "Of course she must help you, Mark, you can't live in the house by yourself."

"You're sure you can spare her?"

"Just for a few days," nodded Alice. "Don't keep her too long. She's such a comfort to me, Mark. Of course if she was going to be married it would be different."

"What do you mean, Mother?"

296

"I should *have* to do without her, then," said Alice smiling at him.

"But Deb isn't going to be married, is she?" asked Mark in alarm.

"No, of course not," said Deb, smiling.

The plan was discussed and arranged — Deb took no part in the discussion, she let them arrange it as they pleased.

The next day was fine and sunny. Mark and Deb went back to Timperton together, taking their luggage with them in the car. Mrs. Craig was waiting for them on the doorstep and soon all three were hard at work putting the house in order.

"Which room are ye having, Miss Dunne?" asked Mrs. Craig, coming into the scullery where Deb was scouring pans. "If ye tell me which room I'll take the luggage up the stair."

"The smaller room," replied Deb, "and, by the way, I'm not Miss Dunne. Miss Halley is my name."

"I thocht ye would be his sister!"

"No, I'm his cousin. Don't forget to put that hot water bottle I gave you in his bed. You had better do it now in case the bed is damp."

"I'll see to it," replied Mrs. Craig.

Mrs. Craig left early and Deb and Mark got their own supper. There was cold ham and boiled eggs and a crisp lettuce from the garden, and bread and butter and honey. Deb made the salad dressing and the coffee.

"I hope you've had enough to eat," she said, looking at him anxiously.

Mark laughed. "If I never fare worse I shall be lucky. It was a lovely supper, Deb."

They washed the dishes together, laughing over the unaccustomed task.

"It's fun," said Mark, as he dried them carefully and put them away on the shelf. "It's tremendous fun washing dishes, isn't it? I like to see them all nice and clean and shining . . . all the cups hanging on their own little hooks."

Deb agreed. She stoked the fire so that the water should be hot for Mark's bath and followed him into the sitting-room. It was dark now, but warm and still; they sat at the open windows and looked out at the stars. They did not talk much for they were both weary . . . it was lovely to sit and rest after the day's work.

"Bed early," said Mark at last, rising and knocking out his pipe. "I've got to be up early to-morrow . . . I'll lock up now, I think."

Deb liked her little room and the bed was comfortable but she lay awake for a long time listening to Mark's footsteps going to and fro. She heard him in the bathroom, splashing in his bath, and then she heard him in his bedroom next door. He was moving about unpacking his things — the wardrobe door creaked and the drawers scraped as he opened and shut them. Deb was happy to be here, helping Mark, but she was a little unhappy, too. She wondered what Henrietta would say if she knew about it. Deb had tried not to be too like a doormat — but so far she had not tried dynamite.

CHAPTER
THIRTY

Mark Alone

Mark went off next morning looking very smart in his new tweed suit. When she had said good-bye to him at the gate Deb started work; the house was clean, now, but there was still plenty to do: curtains and cushion covers to be washed and hung out to dry, brasses to be polished. Mrs. Craig cooked the lunch — it was midday dinner, really — and soon after one o'clock Mark returned.

"How did you get on?" asked Deb, meeting him at the door. "Was everything all right? Were they nice patients?"

"I got on quite well," replied Mark shortly.

He said no more, and he seemed so withdrawn and preoccupied that Deb did not bother him with questions. She glanced at him anxiously several times as they ate their dinner together, and she saw that his brows were knitted in a frown. Mark was not worried, he was *angry* — whatever could it be? After they had finished their silent meal Mark rose and took out his pipe and began to fill it carefully.

"Mark, is something wrong?" asked Deb.

"Yes."

"What is it, Mark?"

"It's the most awful nonsense I ever heard in all my life," declared Mark emphatically. "I wish I'd never come to this damned place — they're nothing but a lot of gossiping old women, that's what they are."

Deb looked at him in dismay.

"It's — it's an insult, really," continued Mark, heatedly. "It's made me feel — feel that I don't want to stay here at all — if that's what they're like — narrow-minded, bigoted old women!"

"What is it all about?" asked Deb in bewildered tones.

"About you," he replied savagely. "Mrs. Craig has been talking — apparently it's not 'the correct thing' for me to have you here."

"Oh, that's what it is!" exclaimed Deb in great relief.

"Yes, that's what it is. Dr. Anderson spoke to me about it. He was quite nice, as a matter of fact. I explained to him that you were my sister in all but actual fact, that we had been brought up together and that you were one of the family. He understood, of course, but he said other people might not understand and that it would lead to a lot of talk — people had already started to talk, he said. Isn't it absurd?"

"Yes," said Deb, smiling.

"You seem amused!"

"Yes. You said, yourself, it was absurd."

"It's sickening," declared Mark, frowning more than ever. "Fancy those brutes *talking* about *us*. I wonder how Mrs. Craig guessed you weren't really my sister — nosey old thing! We were having such a happy time together, weren't we?"

"What will you do?" asked Deb.

Mark looked at her sharply. He was surprised at her attitude, surprised and a trifle hurt. He had expected her to be surprised or angry or embarrassed or distressed. He had expected her to say, "Oh, Mark, how silly of them. I've always been your sister, haven't I?" — or words to that effect; but, instead of that, Deb seemed rather amused. She was taking it very calmly, she did not seem to be worrying about it at all. "What will you do?" she had said in a casual sort of voice as if it did not matter very much what he did.

"Fortunately," said Mark in a solemn tone. "Fortunately the Misses Anderson have managed to arrange with the two maids to come to-morrow instead of next week. I must manage to-night as best I can."

"That's splendid, isn't it?" said Deb cheerfully. "I had better go and pack. Perhaps you would ring up Dunnian and arrange for Downie to come over and fetch me."

That evening, when Mark returned, there was no Deb to greet him at the door. The house was empty. He found the key under the mat — where Deb had left it for him — and opened the door and went in. He was alone in the house. It was rather an odd feeling to be quite alone — Mark had never been alone in a house before. The clock in the hall was ticking loudly, the stairs creaked as he went up to take off his shoes. He could hear a window blind flapping — a maddening sound — and he traced it to Deb's room and went in and shut the window. Deb's room! She had slept in it for one night and nothing remained in to to show that she had been here . . . but somehow the room seemed full of Deb. That was odd, wasn't it?

His supper was ready for him on the dining-room table — the same kind of supper as last night, ham and salad, honey and brown bread — all that Mark had to do was to heat the coffee and boil an egg and he accomplished this not very onerous task without any difficulty. Supper over — and over in record time — Mark removed the dishes to the pantry and proceeded to wash up. He had enjoyed the task last night but to-night it was no fun at all; in fact it was an unmitigated bore. One of the cups slipped through his fingers and fell with a crash on the floor and Mark was so angry with the beastly thing that he kicked the pieces under the sink and left them there.

It was a still, dark night and the stars were shining but Mark drew the curtains and lit the light — you couldn't sit and look at the stars all by yourself — he took up a book and began to read. Every now and then he looked up and his eyes strayed to "Deb's chair," the chair in which Deb had sat last night. It was an old-fashioned chair with an upholstered back, rather straight, and it had wooden arms ornamented with carving. Not a pretty chair, not even a very comfortable one but Mark decided that there was something rather nice about it. He went on reading, but the words did not make much sense . . . he found himself listening . . .

Curse those old busy-bodies, thought Mark. If it had not been for them Deb would be here now, sitting in her chair, talking to him. How utterly ridiculous it was! He wanted Deb — he really needed her — and Deb liked being here, but just because she was not really his sister he could not have her, she could not come. How small-minded people were! How dense and stupid and unreasonable!

Mark had worked himself up into such a state of fury that he lay in bed for a long time before he could get to sleep and when his alarm went off at seven o'clock he felt as if he had had no rest at all; however, it was no use grumbling. He rose at once, boiled an egg and made himself some tea and ate his breakfast at the kitchen table, drinking out of a cracked cup, which he found on the shelf in the kitchen. He did not make toast, nor heat up the porridge (it was too much trouble) and he did not wash the dishes. The maids would be here to-day — they could wash up.

At one o'clock when Mark returned, expecting to find the maids installed and his lunch ready, he found instead an empty house. He ate some bread and cheese and drank a glass of water. They did not arrive at tea-time, nor at supper-time either. The scullery sink was full of dirty dishes waiting to be washed and the larder was almost bare. Mark had not thought of ordering in any food from the shops — he was not used to housekeeping. There was a little milk in the larder and a crust of stale bread and a tin of beans. Mark took these not very delectable viands into the kitchen and ate them without much appetite. He was too angry to be hungry, and too much alarmed — supposing the maids did not come at all! What on earth was he to do!

At ten o'clock the garden gate creaked and the two maids walked in; they were a curious pair — or so Mark thought — blowsy-looking girls, dressed up in shabby finery and not particularly clean, but, for all that, Mark was delighted to see them. He opened the door and let them in, he showed them round. They were not very pleased when they saw the dirty dishes (in fact it was touch and go whether or not they would turn round and walk out) but Dr. Dunne seemed a nice gentleman so they decided to stay.

Mark went to bed in high glee for he thought his troubles were over, and so they were in some ways. His bed was made, his meals were prepared at the right hour and there was always plenty of hot water, but in spite of these creature comforts Mark was not happy. He was restless, he could not settle down to read, he could not sleep properly . . . and the odd thing was that although there were now two females in the house, swishing about with dusters and mops and conversing with one another from room to room in raucous voices, the house still felt empty.

Jean was not really a bad cook but she was careless and uninterested. She gave Mark mince and potatoes, followed by a stodgy rice pudding and somewhat wizened prunes . . . and the next day there was stewed steak and potatoes, sago pudding and rhubarb . . . then it was Irish stew and apple dumpling . . . then it was mince again. There was nothing to complain of, really, but still . . .

Mark put down his knife and fork and looked at his plate with positive loathing. I'm ill, he thought in alarm. The food isn't bad — I've eaten far worse in hospital and never given it a thought — it's me. He knew so

304

much about the frailties of the human frame and especially of the digestive organs; and, in the last few days he had seen so many people suffering from faulty digestion, that he was ripe for alarm. Yes, thought Mark, yes, that's what it is. I can't sleep properly, I feel restless, I loathe the sight of food . . .

CHAPTER
THIRTY-ONE

Dynamite

Two more days passed and Mark was no better. He felt tired and depressed, he was beginning to lose weight. I mustn't worry about myself, he decided. Worry is the very worst thing . . . and he worried all the more.

On the third day he returned from his afternoon round in a very dejected condition and, calling to Clara that he wanted his tea at once, he opened the door of the sitting-room and walked in . . . and there was Deb sitting in the arm-chair by the window with a pile of socks and a work-basket beside her on the floor.

"Deb!" exclaimed Mark in amazement.

"Hallo!" she said, smiling at him across the room. "Aunt Alice was worried about you so I thought I'd come over and see how you were getting on. It's just as well I did, for you haven't a whole pair of socks to your name . . . Look, Mark!" She held up a sock as she spoke and waggled a finger at him through the toe.

"It's *lovely* to see you," declared Mark enthusiastically.

"Did you miss me?"

"Miss you! Of course I did. I've been horribly lonely."

"Nobody could object to your having your cousin to tea, could they?"

"Nobody," replied Mark. "They'd better try. I shall know what to say to them." He dropped into a chair as he spoke and feasted his eyes upon her. What a dear she was! How kind and comfortable and companionable! How easy to look at! The sun was shining in at the window and finding lights in her smooth brown hair, her eyes were soft and sparkling.

"It's ridiculous that I can't have you here," said Mark in an aggrieved tone of voice. "I've been thinking about it a lot and the more I think about it the more ridiculous it seems. It's those old hags — they have nothing to do all day but poke their noses into other people's affairs. If it were not for them you would come over and stay with me now and then, couldn't you?"

"Yes," said Deb, but she said it doubtfully.

"I mean you like being here and I like having you — it's absurd, isn't it? You've always been my sister, haven't you?"

"No," said Deb.

"No!" echoed Mark in amazement. "What do you mean, Deb?" He looked at her as he spoke and saw that she had raised her head and was looking back at him with a level gaze. Her face was flushed, her eyes were very bright.

"No, Mark," said Deb steadily. "I haven't been your sister for a long time — not for years and years — I haven't wanted to be."

"Deb —"

"It's all right, Mark," she continued. "You needn't worry about it. It's just that I thought it better to tell you, that's all. We've always been able to tell each other things, haven't we?"

"But Deb —"

"I thought it *straighter* to tell you," said Deb, picking up another sock and examining it closely. "That's what I thought. It seemed — wrong somehow — to let you go on talking about sisters — it seemed — silly —"

"Oh, Deb, I never thought —"

"I know," she said, nodding. "I know you didn't. Why should you? It doesn't matter any way. It doesn't change anything, Mark."

"Oh yes, it does —" began Mark.

"No," said Deb firmly. "No, it doesn't change anything at all. We're friends, Mark; that's better than brother and sister because you choose your friends."

"Oh, Deb, what a fool I've been!"

"No, you haven't. You mustn't worry! I'm perfectly happy, you see. Perfectly happy and contented," said Deb raising her head again and smiling at him cheerfully.

"Deb, darling —"

"No, Mark, please. Please understand —"

"I've been the most awful fool —"

"No, you haven't —"

"Yes, I have," he cried. "Yes, I've been the biggest fool in creation. Deb darling — dearest Deb, can you ever forgive me for being such a fool? Of course I love you! Of course I want you! I've been wanting you every moment. I've been miserable without you, utterly miserable, and I never realised what was the matter with

308

me. Did you ever hear of a man being such a fool!" He knelt down beside her on the floor and put his arm round her very gently.

"No, Mark," said Deb. "Please don't . . . I didn't mean . . ." and she pushed him away. She had one of his socks over her hand, a grey woollen sock with a large hole in the heel of it — Mark took the hand, sock and all, and squeezed it tenderly.

"It isn't the slightest use saying 'no' to me," declared Mark. "Not the very slightest. It isn't any use trying to push me away, either. You may as well make up your mind to that."

"Oh, Mark, I shouldn't have told you!"

"No, you should have let me go on being miserable," agreed Mark. "Perhaps, in two or three years' time, I might have realised what was the matter with me — unless I had died in the meantime, of course."

"Don't be silly," said Deb, smiling through tears.

"I can't help being silly," replied Mark gravely. "I must have been born silly, I'm afraid. Fancy being madly desperately, crazily in love and treating yourself for indigestion! I can't think of anything sillier, can you?"

"Oh, Mark, aren't they feeding you properly?" asked Deb with sudden anxiety.

At this moment, before Mark could reply, there was a thump on the door; it sounded as though some heavy wooden object had been thrown against the panel. Deb looked up in alarm, but Mark knew what it portended, he sprang to his feet and stood with his hands in his pockets looking out of the window. "Yes, it's a beautiful afternoon," Mark said loudly.

In came Clara with the tea-tray; she shut the door behind her with her foot and dumped the tray on the table, breathing heavily the while.

"The milk's not come," she said in a hoarse voice. "Will ye wait on it or take yer teas noo?"

Mark was about to reply that they would wait, but Deb got in before him.

"Bring a lemon, please," said Deb sweetly. "Dr. Dunne likes his tea with a slice of lemon in it . . . and please change your apron, it's very dirty."

She saw that Mark was laughing silently, his shoulders were heaving with the stress of emotion but she managed to keep a straight face until Clara had retired. Then they both laughed together, uproariously, and they were still weak and hysterical when Clara returned, clad in a clean apron with a teapot in one hand and a lemon in the other. She put the lemon and the teapot on the table, side by side, and went away.

"I really don't know what we're laughing at," said Deb at last, mopping her eyes with her handkerchief.

"Don't you?" gasped Mark. "The answer is a lemon — that's all —" and he laughed again, louder than before.

After a little while they became more sensible. They drank their tea with slices of lemon in it and talked of all sorts of things; of the time when they were children together and of all the things they had done and said; Deb reminded Mark of their first walk in the woods when they had seen the ruined cottage and found the silver spoon. She still possessed the spoon; she had cleaned it and hidden it away in a drawer, wrapped in tissue paper. It was one of her greatest treasures and always would be.

"We loved each other, then," declared Mark. "We've always loved each other, Deb, only I never knew it. The maddest thing I ever did was to try to persuade you to marry Oliver — it was a crazy thing to do. The fact was I wanted you to be settled near Dunnian so that I could see you sometimes —"

"No, Mark," said Deb, interrupting this ingenious explanation with a decided air. "No, Mark, that wasn't the reason at all. Why should we invent things? You didn't love me then; you were fond of me, of course, but it was Tessa you loved. Don't let's pretend; let's face it, Mark. As long as you're sure you love me, now, that's all that matters."

"Dearest," said Mark earnestly. "Dear, dear Deb, I've loved you all the time."

"No, Mark."

"Yes, really. It was poppy-dust in my eyes that made me think I loved Tessa — just poppy-dust."

It was time now for Deb to go home. Downie was waiting for her with the car and Deb was too considerate to keep him waiting long. She picked up her hat off the chair and Mark helped her on with her coat.

"I'm afraid Clara will leave," said Mark apprehensively. "I could see she was annoyed . . ."

"Of course she'll leave," said Deb calmly, "and the cook can go too — those scones were a perfect disgrace.

It will be better to have one really experienced maid, we shall be much more comfortable."

Mark saw her off in the car and then he went upstairs; he took the bismuth mixture off the shelf and emptied it into the sink — then he stretched his arms above his head and laughed for sheer happiness. His supper was ready by this time and he ate it with relish, he ate it thinking of Deb. Dear Deb, how sweet she was, how pretty and kind! He had always loved Deb, he was sure of it. They suited each other perfectly. There was nothing in Deb to excuse or overlook, he knew her to the depths of her soul and she was pure gold all through. Every now and then during the evening Mark raised his head and looked at Deb's chair ... and smiled happily. He was still restless but it was a different kind of restlessness. He was restless because he was full of joy. Mark felt he wanted to sing and dance, he wanted to rush out into the garden and shout at the top of his voice ... but he managed to curb these peculiar impulses. He sat and looked at the fire thinking of Deb and smiling fatuously — then he thought of himself, and of what a fool he had been, and chuckled aloud. Mark was still chuckling when he went upstairs to bed.

But after he had been lying there for a little while an uncomfortable thought crossed his mind. He and Deb had talked of all sorts of things, they had straightened things out between them, and cleared up every vestige of misunderstanding, but he could not remember asking Deb to marry him; he had never once put the all-important question into plain words. Did Deb *really* understand? Did she realise that he wanted to marry her at once, as soon as possible, that he could not possibly live without her? Mark sat up in bed and tried to think; he went back and tried to remember all that had been said . . .

Yes, it was all right, thought Mark with a sigh of relief. Yes, it was perfectly all right; Deb had used the word "we," she had said: "We shall be much more comfortable." Mark lay down and went straight off to sleep.

CHAPTER
THIRTY-TWO

Christmas, 1932

Billy was on his way home to Dunnian on leave. It was four years since he had been home and during that time he had been in a gun-boat on the Yangtse River chasing Chinese pirates. It was an exciting life, in some ways a good life, and Billy had quite enjoyed it. He was now twenty-five years old but he felt a great deal older. Billy had not informed his family that they were to have the pleasure of seeing him for he thought it would be fun to walk in and surprise them, but when he reached Ryddelton Station and saw what the weather was like he began to wish he had informed them of his arrival. It was snowing hard, great white flakes were drifting down from a leaden sky and settling comfortably upon the white ground. Billy descended from the train with several bags and cases and stood upon the little platform looking round and shivering.

"Are ye being met?" asked the station master approaching him in a friendly manner.

"No, Mr. Grieve," replied Billy, grinning. "I never told them I was coming."

"Master Billy!" exclaimed Grieve in amazement. "Master Billy, I never knew you! It's a sight for sore eyes to see you after all these years. Come away into the lamp-room — I've a nice fire there."

"I think I'll be getting on my way," replied Billy. "I'll leave my luggage here and walk home. I want to surprise them, you see."

Mr. Grieve was doubtful as to the wisdom of this course. It was three miles to Dunnian by the footpath — and the storm was increasing. He advised delay and offered to ring up the house and ask for the car to be sent, but Billy was determined to carry out his plan and surprise his family. He chatted for a few minutes to Mr. Grieve and learned some of the local news, and especially the news of Dunnian. Mr. Grieve's daughter was head-housemaid at Dunnian so he knew all that there was to know.

"Aye, the Admiral is well enough," said Grieve. "He was sair forlatten when Mrs. Dunne went — she was as nice a lady as ever stepped, with a kind wurrd for every-buddy — but he's better the last wee while and taking mair interest. Miss Celia looks after him weel — she's as capable as she's bonny and that's saying a guid deal. It's a small household noo — just the two of them — but the family is expected hame for Christmas, Jean was saying."

"All of them!" exclaimed Billy. "It *will* be fun to see them all again!" His words sounded cheerful, but Billy did not feel quite as cheerful as he sounded, for one person would be missing from the gathering. Dunnian would feel very queer without Mother — very queer indeed.

Billy said good-bye to Mr. Grieve and started on his way. He had a moment of indecision as he walked out of the station yard and felt the bitterly cold wind in his face. It was only three o'clock in the afternoon but already the light was fading ... the station looked cosy, the firelight was flickering in the lamp-room, lighting up the little window with a rosy glow; ahead of him lay the moors, bleak and white and windswept. However, Billy had a stubborn nature, he had made up his mind to walk and he would stick to his purpose. The first part of his walk was along the road, which had been cleared by the snow-plough, so it was easy walking, but, when he reached the stile where the foot-path began, he saw that he might have more difficulty ... the snow was deep, it spread over fields and hedges and moors like a thick, white counterpane obliterating the landmarks. Billy knew the way well. He climbed the stile and mounted the hill ... when he reached the top he felt the full force of the wind. It was laden with powdery snow which stung his cheeks and crusted upon his eyelashes. He wrapped his coat about him, turned up his collar, and struggled on manfully. The snow was drifting here, sweeping across the moor, piling itself against the dry stone dykes. It was difficult to see where the path should be and every now and then Billy lost it and floundered into drifts which came well above his knees. There was something eerie about the moors, the sky was dark and ominous, the world was white and deserted by man and beast ...

This was the worst part of his journey for it was high and exposed. After a little, Billy reached the shelter of the Dunnian Woods and paused to take breath. He was warm after his battle with the storm and he felt a strange elation now that he was on Dunnian soil . . . the woods were all white, there was not a sound in the woods, not a sign of life. The crisp snow crunched beneath his feet as he plodded on . . . a few minutes more and he had reached Dunnian garden and the path up to the house.

Billy opened the hall door very quietly, he peeled off his coat and knocked the snow off his boots. Dunnian was just the same, warm and welcoming. How odd it was to be here! How it took Billy back to his childhood! The old clock was still ticking — tick tock, tick tock — it had been ticking all these years when Billy had been chugging up the Yangtse, when Billy had been celebrating in Shanghai — tick tock, tick tock — what an astounding thought! The floor was as shiny and polished as ever. Billy remembered that he and Celia used to take off their shoes and slide across it from end to end, and he remembered how angry Becky had been when she discovered the reason for the enormous holes in the soles of their socks! Becky had gone too, thought Billy with a sigh. He wouldn't see dear old Becky either . . .

He tiptoed across the hall and opened the drawing-room door as quietly as he could . . . his father and Celia were sitting at a table drawn up in front of the fire, having tea. Celia was just raising the tea-pot to pour out a cup of tea when she saw him — she put the teapot down with a bang.

"Billy!" exclaimed Celia incredulously.

Humphrey turned in his chair. "Billy!" he cried.

They said no more, but sat and gazed at him as if he were a visitor from Mars.

"Yes, it's me," said Billy, laughing delightedly. "I thought I'd give you a shock. I just got in yesterday and managed to get leave right away . . ."

The next moment they were all talking at once, all laughing, all asking questions. Celia was hugging him, Humphrey was thumping him on the back.

It was some little time before the excitement died down and Celia was able to collect her wits and give her brother some tea.

"You don't mean to say you walked from the station?" asked Humphrey.

"Your feet are soaking wet," said Celia in dismay.

"I'll change afterwards," Billy said. "I want my tea first . . . the same dear old cake," he added, helping himself to a large chunk as he spoke.

"The same dear old appetite," said Celia, looking at him fondly.

There were all sorts of things that Humphrey wanted to ask — but they could wait. He was not going to pester the boy with questions. He lay back in his chair and watched Billy with satisfaction and pride. Billy had grown into a splendid young fellow, fit and hardy and full of self-confidence.

"We'll all be together for Christmas," Celia was saying. "Mark and Deb are coming to-morrow, and Edith and Douglas and their little girls, and Joyce and Charles and their two little boys. It makes it ten times nicer having you here —"

"Will there be room?" asked Billy anxiously.

318

"Room!" echoed Celia in amazement. "There's your own room, of course."

"Good," said Billy smiling. It was lovely to know that his old room was still his own room and that it was waiting for him.

It was late when Billy went up to bed. He and his father had had a long talk, sitting at the library fire, toasting their toes and smoking. He realised that he had never appreciated his father before. Humphrey had been away so much and, when he was at home, there were so many people — all claiming his attention — that Billy had never got to know his father properly. To-night there had been nobody else and they had talked for hours, delving into each other's minds. Humphrey was sound (thought Billy) he was wise and kind and very clear-sighted. Billy had lived for so long with other men who, although friendly and pleasant, were really only strangers that he was almost surprised at his father's interest and solicitude. It was marvellous to have someone "like that," thought Billy as he got into bed, it was marvellous to have someone who was deeply, vitally interested in all one's doings, who was (so to speak) on one's own side of the wall. It gave one a warm, comfortable feeling, thought Billy, as he put his head on the pillow . . . and shut his eyes.

Billy had been away so long that he was able to look at each member of his family dispassionately, with unprejudiced eyes. He saw Edith as a slightly discontented young woman, very pretty of course and exceedingly smart but not particularly happy. If Edith did not look out those lines of discontent would write themselves permanently upon her face. Edith's two little girls were like their father, fair and quiet and uninteresting (Billy was fond of children but he could not make any headway with his nieces). Joyce was a very different case for she had all she wanted; her Charles was a good sort and her two little boys were full of vim and vigour. Joyce had become more human, more kindly, more interested in other people, she had improved a good deal as people sometimes do when they are innocently happy. Mark and Deb were devoted to each other — it was easy to see that. They did not parade their devotion, and they were pleasant and cheerful with everyone, but they were conscious of one another all the time. They had no children and, as they had now been married for about eight years, it did not look as if they were going to have any. Unless Billy, himself, got married and produced a son their branch of the Dunne family would peter out — it seemed a pity.

They were all very pleased to see Billy again and they all wanted to hear the story of his adventures. Billy was quite willing to oblige. His adventures had been pretty hectic in parts, pretty hair-raising, for the Chinese pirates had little regard for human life and some of their customs were curious, to say the least of it. He toned down his story for the benefit of the women, but, after dinner, when the women had gone and the port was circulating, he let his audience have it straight. It was amusing to watch the four faces, Billy found, and to see their different reactions to the more highly-coloured portions of his narrative. Humphrey saw the whole thing from a service point of view — his view was almost identical with that of the narrator — Mark took a doctor's standpoint and Charles saw it from the angle of a man of the world. Douglas Rewden was the only member of the audience who was shocked at Billy's revelations — his face of hurt disapproval goaded Billy to further efforts.

"What's happened to the Skenes?" asked Billy at last when he had talked himself hoarse.

"They're both married," said Mark shortly — and that was all. There was such an air of finality in Mark's reply that Billy did not inquire further. He would get all the information he wanted from Celia. As a matter of fact there were various matters upon which he wanted information, but the house was so full and Celia was so busy looking after the comfort of the guests that it was impossible to get her alone for a moment.

Billy's old room gave him a great deal of pleasure. He liked pottering about in it when he went up to bed. He had always liked "pottering" but, in the old days, there had been the danger of Becky suddenly appearing at the door and asking why he was not in bed and making inquiries as to whether he had washed. Now, he could potter to his heart's content ... it seemed rather odd, somehow. The room was not very large and the ceiling was low and camceiled. There were pictures of ships on the walls, coloured photogravures which Billy had cut out of illustrated papers, pasted on to boards and varnished with his own hands. There was a bookcase full of books of travel and adventure, and there was a glass case with birds' eggs in it. The window was almost square with wavy glass in the small square panes. Billy pulled up the blind and looked out upon a magic world of moonlight and snow, of silver light and velvet-dark shadows. The trees were bowed with glistening snow, the ground was white and untrodden. He remembered suddenly that he had had an arrangement of mirrors whereby he could see the garden when he was lying in bed. He had made the arrangement when he was laid up with chickenpox and was extremely bored with his isolation. Three mirrors were needed, two on the walls and one on the ceiling above the window — and there they were, hanging in their accustomed places. One of them was slightly crooked and another required a little wedge on the left side. Having made the necessary adjustments Billy got into bed ... yes, it worked. He could see the garden — a small piece of bright glistening-white lawn, and the trees beyond. He lay there enjoying it, and smiling to himself at his childishness.

Suddenly there was a little scratching noise on the door and Celia looked in. "You aren't asleep, are you?" she asked in a low voice.

"No, of course not —"

"Hush," she said, coming in and closing the door softly. "We'll have to be very quiet. Douglas is using the room next door as a dressing-room. He would think it awful —"

"He's an old woman, isn't he?" said Billy chuckling. "Doesn't smoke, doesn't drink ... but I notice he eats plenty. Here, wrap yourself up in the eiderdown. I want to talk to you."

She took the eiderdown and wrapped it round her and curled herself up on the end of his bed. To Billy she looked exactly the same as she had looked as a small child. Her eyes were as bright, her dark hair as shiny and curly. Often and often Celia had come into his room, when Becky believed her to be sound asleep in bed, and had sat for hours talking to him just as she was doing now. But, whereas in the old days Billy had accepted her merely as his very best friend, without regard for her appearance, he now perceived that she was extremely good-looking and attractive. He had always called her Monkey-face — for there was something in her bright glance that had reminded him of a little monkey. There was still the same eager, slightly mischievous look . . .

"What do you think of them?" Celia asked.

Billy told her his opinion of the family without fear or favour and Celia nodded and agreed with all he said.

"It's a pity people can't get what they want," said Celia thoughtfully. "Deb wants a baby awfully badly . . . it's hard, isn't it? Edith wants a son."

"They want an heir for Sharme, I suppose," said Billy. "If she goes on trying long enough she'll probably get one."

"You needn't be horrid about it."

"I didn't mean to be," returned Billy. "It's only that Edith always used to get all she wanted so easily. So I can't feel very sympathetic, somehow."

"Yes, I know what you mean," agreed Celia. "Things work out in a queer way; but I'm awfully sorry for Edith. I think she has paid enough." Celia hesitated and then added, "Mrs. Rewden is so nasty to her — she's a foul old witch."

"Celia!" exclaimed Billy, pretending to be shocked.

"Well, she is," declared Celia smiling. "I wish Edith could have a son — just to be even with her. It seems hard that Joyce should have two — and a much nicer husband into the bargain."

Billy asked about the Skenes and learned the reason for the slight embarrassment which had been caused by the mention of their name. Oliver was the culprit, of course. He had blotted his copy book by running away with a married woman. Her husband had divorced her so that she and Oliver could be married and they were coming to live at Ryddelton House shortly. Now that old Lady Skene was dead the place belonged to Oliver and required his care.

"The county is in a buzz," said Celia, chuckling. "It can't make up its dear little mind whether to call or not. I shall call. I always liked Oliver."

"I didn't," said Billy. "He was always chipping me in that supercilious way of his."

"He was very keen on Deb at one time. I wasn't supposed to know about it, of course, but there was such a kaffuffle that nobody except a born idiot could have failed to know . . . Tessa has made what is usually called 'a good marriage' — she would, of course."

"I thought she had her claws into Mark," said Billy, stifling a yawn.

"What about you?" asked Celia. "All this talk about marriage . . . but I notice you don't say much."

"Neither do you," replied Billy grinning.

"I haven't seen any one I like better than you," said Celia gravely.

"Cross your heart?"

"M'hm," nodded Celia.

"Same here, really," declared Billy. "Of course I've been in love once or twice but it wasn't devastating. Sometimes I think it would be nice to marry someone and have a home to go back to — if you know what I mean."

"Your home is here, Billy."

"Yes, as long as Dad is here —"

"Always," declared Celia. "Dunnian is mine after — after Dad. I suppose you thought it would go to Mark."

Billy was very much surprised and interested — so much so that he felt no more inclination to yawn — and he questioned Celia eagerly until he had heard about Aunt Celia's will and everything connected with it.

"So you see," said Celia at last. "You see Dunnian will always be your home — whether you're married or not — whether I'm married or not — Dunnian will be your home as long as I'm alive."

She unwrapped the eiderdown and prepared to take her departure. "Good-night, old thing," she said, blowing him a kiss.

"Good-night, Monkey-face," said Billy affectionately.

PART 4

War Measures in the House

CHAPTER
THIRTY-THREE

June, 1942

Celia rolled over in bed, stretched out her hand and turned on the wireless; she was just in time to hear Big Ben — and this was lucky because she liked to start the day with Big Ben. Whether the news was good or bad Big Ben was always the same. His voice was strong and sure and comforting, ringing out over London and, through the agency of the B.B.C., over most of the civilised world. Celia liked to think of all the other people who were listening to him: soldiers and sailors and women like herself with a prayer for their loved ones in their hearts. Celia thought of her brothers, they were both at sea — Mark had given up his practice at the very beginning of the war and had obtained a post as surgeon-commander in one of our big ships, Billy was in a cruiser in the Mediterranean — she prayed for them night and morning, using the beautiful words in the Book of Common Prayer, for these words seemed to express her hopes and feelings perfectly. In fact the prayer seemed to have been made for Celia, it fitted her so well.

"Oh Almighty God, whose way is in the sea and whose parts are in the great waters; Be present, we beseech thee, with our brethren in the manifold dangers of the deep; Protect them from all its perils; Prosper them in their course; and in safety bring them, with a grateful sense of thy mercies, to the haven where they would be . . ."

Celia listened to the news as she dressed; then she slipped into her overall and ran downstairs to see about breakfast. There were changed days at Dunnian now, for, instead of seven experienced servants, there were two little girls of fifteen and sixteen — and they only came in by the day for they were afraid of sleeping in the big house which felt so empty and quiet. Deb had come back to Dunnian when Mark went to sea, and she and Celia and Humphrey kept house together.

Celia's first job was to light the boiler fire to warm up the water for her father's bath. When she had begun this job it had caused her endless trouble — but she had got the hang of it now; the fire was going strong when Deb appeared on the scene.

"You wretch!" exclaimed Deb. "Why didn't you waken me?"

"I hate wakening people," replied Celia. "It always seems such a frightfully cruel thing to do . . . besides I can manage the fire beautifully now."

Deb began to bustle about the kitchen. She took the porridge pot out of the hay-box and put it on the electric stove. "Where are the flowers?" she asked. This was the generic name which Deb and Celia had bestowed upon the two girls who came in to help them.

"They haven't come yet," replied Celia. "At least I haven't seen them — they get later and later every day."

"Jasmine isn't bad," said Deb as she took a wooden spoon from the drawer and began to stir the porridge.

"Lily is awful," said Celia with a sigh. "Lily doesn't like scrubbing or peeling potatoes ... she doesn't like doing things she doesn't like, if you know what I mean ..."

"Badly brought up!"

"Queerly brought up," amended Celia in a thoughtful tone. "She can't go through life doing only the things she likes, can she?"

"She'll be luckier than most people if she can!"

"Have you wakened Dad?"

"He doesn't need wakening," said Humphrey, stalking into the kitchen attired in a large brown woollen dressing-gown with a red cord round his waist.

"Hallo, Admiral dear, how are you this morning?" said Celia, standing on tiptoe to kiss her father's cheek.

"All the better for seeing you," replied Humphrey, smiling.

Deb's greeting was more conventional but no less cordial. They were all three the best of friends.

"Your tea's just ready," said Celia. "Your shaving water is in that jug. Perhaps you would take it up with you when you go."

"I've decided to stop having tea in the morning."

"Why?" cried the two girls in chorus.

"Because I don't need it." Humphrey took his shaving water and went away.

"Celia, he must have his tea," said Deb.

"Yes, if we can make him," agreed Celia. She added, "You know the reason, don't you? It's because he's a

331

'useless mouth.' He said yesterday that people who couldn't help in the war effort ought to have less food. I said what about *us*, and he said we were young and the country needed us but he was no use to anybody."

"Oh Celia, that's why he's stopped eating meat!"

"That's why," nodded Celia. "It's ridiculous, of course, because he did his bit in the last war — and a very big bit too — but he doesn't see that. I'm sorry for Dad. I wish to goodness they would have him in the Home Guard or something."

Deb had put the frying pan on the stove. She had found a small packet of bacon and was disentangling the rashers and piling them into the pan.

"Here, I say! Go easy with the bacon," Celia adjured her. "That little lot has got to last us till Monday."

"We can have Spam to-morrow," Deb replied. "I like Spam. I know there are all sorts of jokes about it but, personally, I think it is extremely good. It has such a nice, hammy flavour."

"Do you remember how we used to have *whole hams*?" asked Celia in awed tones. "Whole hams sitting on the sideboard every morning — just as a side dish!"

"Don't! You're making my mouth water," said Deb laughing.

"This war is making me greedy," continued Celia gravely. "I never used to think about food very much — but now I yearn for all sorts of things I can't have. The first thing I want is a roast of beef — with lots of fat on it — and then I should like peaches and ice-cream."

"Will you shut up!" cried Deb, laughing more than before.

They were moving about the kitchen as they talked, so the conversation was disjointed and punctuated by the rattle of pans and the chink of crockery.

"Sometimes I feel quite glad Aunt Alice isn't here," said Deb.

"Oh, I don't know. I believe Mother would have taken all this in her stride; Becky would have minded far more — us doing things, I mean — Becky would have seven fits if she could see my hands when I've finished wrestling with the boiler flues . . . and Mrs. Drummond! Oh, Deb, *can* you imagine Mrs. Drummond coping with the flowers?"

Deb could not. She said with a little chuckle, "You know, Celia, when I began to come into the kitchen and scratch about I had an uncomfortable feeling that Mrs. Drummond was watching me. I half-expected her to pop out of the cupboard in one of her rages."

"She *was* here," declared Celia. "I felt the same thing. She *knew* when I let the potatoes burn and ruined the pan."

"You've done awfully well," said Deb quickly.

"Oh yeah!" returned Celia, smiling.

"But you have," urged Deb. "That fish soufflé last night —"

"It wasn't bad, was it? I just did exactly what the book said and, lo and behold, it happened. It seemed like a miracle when I opened the oven door and saw that the thing looked like a soufflé! All the same I feel a bit of a worm; that soufflé cost me hours of tense anxiety — look at the soufflés Mrs. Drummond made without turning a hair!"

"With an experienced kitchen maid to wait on her, hand and foot."

"Could you manage without me?" asked Celia after a little pause.

"Oh, Celia!"

"Well, I feel I ought to do *something*," said Celia, shaking her head. "Of course I've been exempted because of Dad and the house and everything, but I don't feel I'm pulling my weight."

"You're running the W.V.S. in Ryddelton —"

"I know," agreed Celia; "but that isn't much, really, Here am I, an unattached female, aged thirty-two, strong and fit and reasonably intelligent . . ."

Deb had been expecting this for some time. It was natural that Celia should want to do real war-work, but she was quite certain she could not carry on at Dunnian without her. Deb said slowly, "We could shut up the house, of course, that would be the only thing to do —"

"Would it?"

"Yes, I'm afraid so. The fact is I'm going to have a baby, so you see —"

"Deb!" cried Celia in amazement.

"Incredible, isn't it?"

"Deb, how perfectly marvellous!"

Suddenly Deb felt Celia's strong arms round her and Celia's kisses on her cheek . . . she was moved almost to tears.

"Darling!" cried Celia. "Darling pet, of course I shan't leave you — don't worry about it any more — I had no idea — it's heavenly, isn't it? It's what you

334

always wanted — a son for Mark! Does he know about it?"

"Not yet," said Deb huskily. "I would have told him in my letters but I don't know where he is and I thought it would just worry him."

"My dear, he'll be delighted — he'll be as pleased as Punch — Oh Deb, isn't it lovely!"

"I don't know that it is," replied Deb in sober tones. "I think it's rather idiotic, to tell you the truth."

"It's lovely —"

"After all these years," continued Deb. "After all these years when I was almost crazy because I wanted to have a baby so much — and then to start having one in the very middle of a war! It seems quite idiotic."

"No —"

"Yes, it does. I'm frightened, Celia. Supposing there's an invasion or something . . . Celia, I'm frightened!"

"For heaven's sake don't cry," said Celia, hugging her. "It's lovely — just fix your mind on that. I'll take care of you. I'll look after everything —"

"Oh, Celia, talk about worms!"

They were still hugging each other, somewhat hysterically, when the kitchen door opened very slowly and a head appeared round the corner of it . . . "Good heavens!" exclaimed a well-known voice.

"Mark, where *have* you come from!" cried Celia in astonishment.

Deb was dumb with surprise and delight, she ran to Mark and flung herself into his arms . . . this was the moment that the porridge chose to boil over; it rose like a volcano in eruption and poured down the sides of the pan and spread itself over the top of the stove, sizzling and spluttering.

"Damn!" cried Celia rushing at it. By the time she had rescued what remained of the porridge and wiped up the mess the excitement of Mark's return had died down a little.

"Didn't you get my cable?" asked Mark. "I cabled to you from Gib that I was on my way home . . . what can have happened to the cable, I wonder. And what on earth are you two doing in the kitchen?"

"We're trying to prepare the breakfast," Celia replied.

"Where's the cook?"

"My dear!" exclaimed Celia. "Are you Rip van Winkle by any chance? The cook is probably making boiling lead for Hitler — or the modern equivalent of boiling lead —"

"Do you mean you haven't got a cook?" asked Mark incredulously.

"We have two flowers," replied Celia patiently. "We have Lily and Jasmine; they exude sweet fragrance in the house, but they can't be trusted with food. Food is precious. If it's burnt you have to go without. As a matter of fact the porridge *is* burnt — but that was your fault — not mine."

"I like that cereal stuff you get in packets —" began Mark.

"That takes points."

"Takes points?" asked Mark in a bewildered voice.

"Coupons, you know. Tickets out of the pink books. We can't squander coupons on breakfast cereals, we need them for prunes and tinned meat and things like that."

"I'd rather have breakfast cereals than prunes —" began Mark.

"You wouldn't if prunes was the only kind of fruit you could get," retorted Celia.

Mark left that subject. He still did not understand the position. "I never knew you could cook," he said.

"Neither did I," replied Celia frankly. "But needs must when the devil drives —"

"She's a marvellous cook," declared Deb.

These were the first words Deb had uttered since Mark's arrival and Celia was exceedingly glad to hear them for she had been rather anxious about Deb. Shocks were not good — even pleasant shocks — and Mark's arrival had been so sudden and unexpected. Celia had been talking nonsense on purpose to restore the balance and to give Deb time to recover — now that Deb had recovered a change of air was indicated.

"Take him away," said Celia. "Take him into the library for pity's sake. We'll get no breakfast at all at this rate."

"But Celia —"

"Go away," cried Celia flapping her dish-cloth at them. "*Do* go away. I hate having surgeon-commanders under my feet when I'm busy."

Deb smiled. She and Celia understood each other very well. She let Mark lead her away from the scene of action and they went into the library — which was the only public room in use — and sat down very close together on the sofa.

"Darling," said Mark happily.

"Darling Mark," said Deb with a sigh of bliss.

They had not seen each other for three months and then only for a brief week-end in a crowded London hotel (it was nearly a year since Mark had been to Dunnian) so they had a good deal to talk about. Mark learned the news about the baby and was at once amazed and overjoyed and proud and apprehensive. He had ushered scores of babies into the world with very few mishaps but this baby was different — this baby was already causing Mark anxiety. Deb reiterated the fears which she had expressed to Celia and Mark comforted her.

"I'm too old now," Deb declared.

"No, darling," said Mark. "No, of course not. You aren't a bit too old. It will be perfectly all right — but you must take it easy, you know. You must rest and feed up. You're far too thin."

"Yes," agreed Deb, but she couldn't help smiling: "Rest and feed up," sounded so easy.

"You must get servants," said Mark.

"We can't. They're all doing war-work. I don't really mind it very much," said Deb, smiling at him. "I've got quite used to it now, and the odd thing is I've become even more fond of dear old Dunnian since I started doing the housework. I know it so much better — every corner of it. I know every piece of furniture, too, and I like polishing things and seeing them shining."

"It's too much for you," Mark said. "Dunnian is far too big —"

338

"Yes, that's true, of course. Too big and too disconnected — it isn't a labour-saving sort of house. When Dunnian was planned you could get as much help as you wanted. That's the whole trouble, really."

"What about shutting it up and moving into a small house?"

"We thought of that, but small houses aren't to be had, besides your father would be so unhappy if we had to leave Dunnian." There was another reason, too, but Deb did not mention it: she wanted Mark's son to be born in Dunnian House.

"The other rooms seem to be shut up," said Mark. "I looked in and they were all full of furniture."

"Yes. You see Sharme was taken over by the War Office and Edith and Douglas had a week to clear out — so they sent most of their furniture here. It was Celia's idea and rather a brain wave really. They were at their wits' end what to do with the stuff. There's furniture from Hastley Dean, too; all the drawing-room furniture and carpets and things. They've got ten evacuees in the drawing-room."

Mark listened to all this in amazement. He had had letters from home, of course, but somehow the letters had not given him the slightest idea of what was happening in the country. It was not so much the changes that amazed him, it was the attitude of Deb and Celia that he found so remarkable.

"Will they take Dunnian?" he asked.

"No. They looked at it, of course, but there isn't enough water. It would mean putting in a new pipe-line or something. We haven't got evacuees either, because it's too far from the school. There were soldiers billeted here for a bit but now they've found billets nearer Ryddelton."

"You never told me about it in your letters."

"Didn't I?" she asked. "Oh, well, it all happened gradually. I suppose I didn't realise it properly. It was no good bothering you —"

"You didn't tell me about it when I saw you in London."

"It was such a rush, wasn't it," said Deb. "We had lots of other things to talk about." She rose as she spoke and added, "I must go and help Celia to bring in the breakfast. I shan't be long."

Deb had scarcely gone when Humphrey walked in, looking very clean and tidy though perhaps a trifle shabbier than usual. His brown tweed suit was faded and darned at the elbows, his shoes were old but exquisitely polished.

"Mark!" he exclaimed in surprise and delight. "What good wind has brought you home! This is grand! How are you, my boy! You're looking the picture of health!"

"Is everything all right, Dad?" asked Mark, smiling at this reversal of the usual question.

"Everything's fine, my lad," replied Humphrey. "Those girls are bricks — you ought to be proud of your wife and your sister; they're keeping the home fires burning." He began to move about the room as he spoke, opening a drawer and taking out a cloth and spreading it on the table near the window. It was the table at which Mark used to study his medical books — how long ago it seemed!

Mark went to his aid, but Humphrey waved him away. "This is one of my jobs," he explained. "I'm good at it, too. You'll only muddle me if you interfere. Knives and forks . . ." continued Humphrey, opening another drawer. "And spoons, of course . . . and cruets . . ."

"Wouldn't it be easier in a smaller house, Dad?"

"Easier, perhaps," agreed Humphrey. "But I don't want to leave Dunnian, and that monster of iniquity isn't going to drive me out of my home if I can help it. For one thing I promised Aunt Celia that the place shouldn't be shut up and, for another, I prefer to be here to look after it. Dunnian might be burnt to the ground if someone wasn't here . . . it's full of other people's furniture, too."

"I don't know how you manage —"

"We manage all right," nodded Humphrey. "The girls run the house. I do all the shoes, of course, and any little odd jobs that I can. We have plenty of fresh vegetables from the garden and I've started keeping hens. I didn't like them at first but I'm getting quite fond of the creatures. If we left Dunnian we wouldn't have that, of course, and we should need more meat —"

Breakfast was a cheerful meal and Mark began to feel less concern for his family. Obviously they had enough to eat and, although they were all thinner, they seemed well and happy.

There were changes outside the house as well as inside (Mark found). A good deal of ground had been put into potatoes, and the remainder, which was laid out in vegetables, was looked after by Humphrey and old Johnson and a village lad. They were lucky to have

Johnson for although he was over eighty he was still able to do light work such as pruning and staking and tying up the peas. Old Johnson was the "head gardener" and Humphrey took orders from him cheerfully, for Johnson knew exactly what must be done and what could be left undone with impunity. The paths were weedy and the hedges needed thinning and the greenhouses looked as if they would be the better of a coat of paint but the place was by no means derelict.

"We've got to have every bit of ground under cultivation," old Johnson explained. "That's how I see it, Mr. Mark. It doesn't matter about the looks of the place — not till we've got Hitler where we want him."

There were several large brown patches on the lawn. Mark pointed them out to his father and asked what had caused them.

"A pity, isn't it?" said Humphrey. "We'll have to rake those up and sow them when we have time. It was fire-bombs — incendiaries — they made a tremendous blaze. We had a shower of them here. Two fell on the roof but they rolled off without doing any damage. Dunnian roof is as strong as armour plating. I was ready for them, of course," said Humphrey complacently. "We'd practised fire-fighting, the girls and I, and we had the stirrup pump ready in a twinkling — and buckets and everything —"

Mark had a feeling Humphrey was quite sorry that his preparations had been needless. "What on earth were they doing here?" he asked. "What induced them to drop incendiaries on Dunnian?"

"It was a single plane — lost itself, I suppose — but as a matter of fact there are very few places, even in the depths of the country, that have never seen a bomb. You know Walker's cottage away up the glen?"

"Yes, of course. Mrs. Walker used to give us a glass of milk when we were fishing there."

"They bombed the Walkers' cottage," said Humphrey. "Mrs. Walker ran out of the cottage when the bomb fell and the Hun came down and picked her off with a machine-gun."

"Dad!"

"My blood boils when I think of it," declared Humphrey. "My blood boils . . . if only I could get at them, Mark, if only I could do something! If only I were thirty years younger!" He was silent for a moment and then he continued. "It's a horrible world, Mark — the whole foundation of society is rocking, everything is in the melting pot. I wish Celia had someone to look after her when I'm gone."

"Deb and I —"

"Oh, I know," said Humphrey, "but it isn't the same. The other girls are married. They've got their husbands to look after them. I wish to goodness Aunt Celia hadn't made that ridiculous will. I wish Dunnian was to be yours — if you and Deb were to be here when I've gone I wouldn't mind so much . . ." He was silent for a moment and then he sighed and added, "Celia and Dunnian — who will look after them when I'm gone?"

"I wonder why Celia hasn't married."

"It isn't for want of asking," said Humphrey smiling. "Celia doesn't like any of them — says they're dull and stupid, says they're all turned out of the same mould."

"Andrew Raeworth —" began Mark.

"I know. Nice fellow, Andrew, and crazy about Celia, but she won't look at him."

"What does she say?"

"Says nothing — just smiles — doesn't even get angry when I tell her she'll be an old maid. One day when I pressed her she said she was 'waiting.'"

Mark laughed at his father's disgusted expression.

"You may laugh," said Humphrey. "It seems to me she's waiting for an angel straight from heaven."

"An angel wouldn't suit Celia at all," Mark declared.

CHAPTER
THIRTY-FOUR

Second Chance

Humphrey emerged from Dunnian House and set off towards the gate. He did this every morning at exactly ten-fifty and Deb sometimes set her watch as she saw the slight upright figure of her father-in-law walking smartly down the drive. It was part of Humphrey's "war-work" to meet the postman at the side gate and save him the extra time and trouble of delivering the letters at Dunnian House. Humphrey had had a pretty hard time in the last war but he found this war a good deal harder to bear. Inactivity was hard to bear. Sometimes he felt cross and impatient. Why couldn't he do something? It was horrible having to potter about in the garden when other men were fighting and dying all over the world. They wouldn't even have him in the Home Guard — he was too old. Seventy-two sounded old, of course, but Humphrey was as strong and fit as any man of sixty, and men of sixty were accepted by the Home Guard. He could shoot Germans as well as any one — and, by heaven, he would shoot Germans if they showed their faces here! Humphrey straightened his back and marched on, swinging his stick as he went. He noted that the trees and bushes wanted trimming, they were encroaching on the drive, and the gravel was full of weeds, but it was no good worrying about that; there were other, more important things to be done. Once the war was over and the men came back they would soon get the old place ship-shape.

At eleven-five precisely Humphrey reached the small side gate which led on to the main road and a few moments later the postman appeared. He got off his bicycle and greeted Humphrey with a naval salute, for he was an old sailor and had served in the last war.

"Good-morning, Finlay," said Humphrey.

"Good-morning, sir. Looks like rain."

"I don't think so, Finlay," replied Humphrey, looking at the sky which was cloudy and grey. "There's too much wind in the upper strata. If the clouds break it will be a very warm day."

"They don't look like breaking to me."

"I wouldn't bet on it," said Humphrey gravely.

They discussed the weather every morning and usually exchanged views on the progress of the war. Finlay's son was in the Navy, he was serving in the same ship as Billy Dunne — so the two fathers had a good deal in common.

Presently the letters changed hands and Finlay mounted his bicycle and rode away, but Humphrey did not return to the house at once. He leaned on the little gate and ruminated sadly on his age, on the stupidity of the government in not making use of fit and hearty men — and like matters.

He was roused from his reverie by the sound of footsteps on the road, and, looking up, he saw a man coming towards him . . . a youngish officer in uniform, marching along in the very middle of the road with his head well up and his arms swinging smartly. He looked as if he ought to be leading a regiment, but he was quite alone. The young man was singing as he marched, singing in a very pleasant baritone; he was singing something about Santiander and the Mexico Plains — the tune and the words were, alike, strange to Humphrey. His uniform, was strange, too; it was khaki but slightly different from the usual pattern, and he had a slightly foreign air . . . yet, as he came nearer, Humphrey had an odd feeling that he had seen the man before . . .

"Good-morning," said Humphrey.

The young man saw Humphrey and stopped. "Good-morning," he replied, smiling in a friendly manner.

Humphrey looked at him in approval. He was very nice to look at, well set-up, strong and virile, with a sun-tanned face and bright brown eyes. Seen at close quarters there was still that oddness about him: he was at the same time strange and familiar . . . Why, of course, he's an American, thought Humphrey suddenly. That accounts for the difference in the uniform!

"Are you chaps coming to this neighbourhood?" asked Humphrey with interest.

"No, sir," replied the young man. "I believe I'm right in saying I'm the only American citizen within two hundred miles of this place. I'm spending a few days at Ryddelton, that's all."

Humphrey took out his cigarette case and offered it. They both lit up.

"How d'you like being here?" Humphrey inquired.

"It's fine. I like it. The colouring gets me — the greenness of the grass. There's a funny kind of feeling about Scotland. It's strange and yet it's not strange. I thought I was coming to the war," he added with a smile which disclosed a row of extremely fine white teeth.

"It's peaceful enough here."

"It's the most peaceful place I ever struck — and the people are peaceful. There's peace in their eyes. I got you all wrong at first," he continued. "I thought you folk were a bit half-hearted about the war, but I soon found my mistake. You don't talk about it much — you've got past that — you've just settled down to win it."

"How did you find that out?" asked Humphrey.

"Various ways. I'll tell you one of them. I met a girl on the train — a smart girl and as pretty as a picture. She was going to London to meet her brother and have a good time. I felt a bit envious of her brother," he added with a smile.

"Well, what about her?" asked Humphrey with an answering grin. "What was there about this girl that made you open your eyes."

"I talked to her," he replied. "I said to her, "The war doesn't bother you much, does it?" She didn't answer — not in words — but she took off her gloves and showed me her hands. I'd expected to see white soft hands manicured with red enamel — she looked that sort of girl — and I got a bit of a shock when I looked at them. They were stained with chemicals and scarred with burns. 'You needn't look like that," she said, laughing. "I'm proud of them." She was working at munitions —

348

something special, it was, but she didn't tell me exactly — she was getting what she called 'danger money.' What do you make of that?"

"Pretty good," said Humphrey.

He sighed. "Well, sir, I don't know," he said doubtfully. "It's good and it's bad."

"What else have you found out about us?" asked Humphrey.

"The food question bothers me. We get our own food so it doesn't affect me personally, but it seems to me you folk aren't getting enough."

"Plenty to keep us fit," said Humphrey quickly.

"Well, it looks that way," admitted the American. "I haven't seen any signs of malnutrition, but they wouldn't like your rations where I come from. Two ounces of butter a week per person and eight ounces of sugar, and not a drop of cream ... I've seen our coloured cook put more butter in a cake than you get in a month."

There was a little silence.

"Are you a regular officer," asked Humphrey.

"West Point," replied the American, smiling. "It's the same as your Sandhurst."

"I know," said Humphrey, returning the smile. Humphrey was used to judging men (to summing them up quickly) and he had taken a fancy to this one. *He's all right*, Humphrey decided, and this was the highest possible praise.

"What part of America do you come from?" Humphrey asked. "I know parts of New England ..."

"Virginia," said the young man. He hesitated and then, seeing that this very nice-looking old gentleman seemed interested in him, he decided to elaborate his answer a bit. "I lived with my grandfather," he said. "It happened like this: my father died and my mother married again, so I was sent to 'Glenway,' my grandfather's place near Raleigh, Virginia. My grandfather brought me up. He died last fall and the place was sold . . . it was a bit of a shock for it had always been my home. It gives you a funny feeling to have no home."

"Yes," agreed Humphrey. He reflected that it would give him a very funny feeling if he had not an anchorage at Dunnian. "Was Glenway a family place?" asked Humphrey.

"It belonged to my grandmother's people. Grandfather belonged to Pennsylvania. He had land there but he sold it up when he married."

Humphrey nodded understandingly. It was interesting to get a glimpse of the boy's background, he would have liked to know more but he was afraid of being thought inquisitive. "What made you come to Ryddelton for your leave?" Humphrey asked.

"That's quite a story. My great-grandmother came from this part of the country and I thought I'd like to have a look at the place. I thought maybe the people in the house would let me look around."

"Your great-grandmother," said Humphrey thoughtfully.

"Yes. I never saw the old lady, she died before I was born, but grandfather used to talk about it a lot — about Ryddelton, I mean — and I came across a bundle of letters one day — it was after the old man died and I was clearing up — letters written to my great-grandmother by her sister. Seems an old story, but I like old stories," said the young man, smiling apologetically.

"You're Dale!" exclaimed Humphrey with sudden excitement.

The American looked at him in surprise.

"You are, aren't you?" urged Humphrey. "Good heavens, of course you are! I've been wondering all the time why you seemed familiar — it's because you're a Dunne — you're Mary Dunne's great-grandson!"

"Gee, if that doesn't beat everything! Courtney Dale is my name. I was called after my great-grandfather —"

"I knew it!" cried Humphrey, seizing his hand and shaking it cordially. "I knew it — we're cousins — I'm Humphrey Dunne."

"Cousins!"

"Yes, cousins —"

"Then this is Dunnian!"

"Yes, of course . . . My dear fellow!" cried Humphrey, patting him on the back, "I can't tell you how glad I am. It's simply splendid. Come in and see the place. We must find Celia and tell her all about it."

"This is wonderful —" began Courtney Dale in a dazed sort of voice. "I never thought there might be Dunnes living here — it's — it's — wonderful —"

"It's marvellous," agreed Humphrey, laughing excitedly. "I've always wondered what had become of Mary Dunne's family — why did you disappear into thin air? But never mind that now, you're here and that's all that matters. I knew, the moment I saw you, that you weren't a stranger. It's because you have a look of old Humphrey, that's why."

"Old Humphrey!"

"The old chap who built Dunnian House. I'll show you his picture —"

"You're like my grandfather," declared Courtney Dale, looking at Humphrey and smiling. "I guess that's why I liked you the very first moment I saw you at the gate . . ."

"You can always tell a Dunne," replied Humphrey. "It's the shape of the face — something about the forehead — but, come along, don't stand there in the road. Come and see Dunnian. You'll come and stay here, of course, for the rest of your leave. We shall be delighted to have you."

"It's very good of you but I'm quite comfortable at the hotel —"

"At the Black Bull!" said Humphrey, laughing incredulously. "No, no, my boy, you'll come to Dunnian. We can make you a great deal more comfortable here."

"I'm sure of that — but what about food?" said young Dale, hanging back. "It's very, very good of you and I appreciate it a lot but I know it's difficult having guests —"

"You aren't a guest," declared Humphrey, taking his arm. "There will be food for you, war or no war. We'll manage all right — Good Lord, do you think I'd let you stay at the Black Bull! Come along, come in — I'll send a man down to the village for your bag . . ."

Courtney Dale made no further objections. He was quite as pleased and excited as this new-found cousin, though not quite so voluble. It had been a most extraordinary experience and he was still a trifle dazed from the effects of it. There he was, walking along a strange road in an absolutely strange country and feeling — if the truth were told — just a trifle homesick for his own land ... and suddenly he had been hailed by an extremely pleasant and personable old gentleman, whom he had never seen before, and called by name and accepted as one of the family, welcomed into the bosom of the family as a sort of prodigal son. If that didn't beat everything, Courtney Dale did not know what would!

They walked up the avenue together talking and laughing; Humphrey was trying to explain the exact relationship which existed between them but he was too excited to do it very well.

"My grandfather and your grandmother were brothers — I mean brother and sister — no, it was your great-grandmother, of course — so you're my second cousin once removed. Is that right? Well, it's quite *near* enough any way. Wait until I show you the tree —"

"A genealogical tree?"

"Yes. I must put you in. You can give me the details of your branch. I've always wanted to complete your branch of the family."

Dale was looking about him with interest. "The Dunnes have always lived here, haven't they?" he asked.

"Yes, there have been Dunnes here for centuries — long before Dunnian House was built. You must see the Peel. Celia will show it to you."

"Celia was the name of the old lady who wrote the letters," began Courtney Dale. "The letters to my great-grandmother —"

"Of course," nodded Humphrey. "My daughter, Celia, was called after her; just as you were called after your great-grandfather. It's odd —" began Humphrey, and then he stopped. Perhaps, later, when he knew young Dale better he would tell him about Aunt Celia's romance ... or perhaps he would never tell him. Humphrey was not quite sure.

As they came round a bend in the avenue they halted and Courtney Dale saw Dunnian for the first time. He looked at the old house in silence, for he felt a strange surge of emotion in beholding it. He had expected a good deal, and it was not quite as he had expected, not quite so big and imposing, but for all that it satisfied him. Dunnian was beautiful and symmetrical, it was part of the landscape; it seemed to belong to the ground, to spring from the ground as naturally as a tree.

"So that's Dunnian," said Courtney at last with a little sigh.

"That's Dunnian," agreed Humphrey.

"It's a lovely house," said Courtney slowly. "There's something about it — I don't quite know what it is — something very satisfying."

"Yes," said Humphrey encouragingly.

"I know," declared Courtney. "I've got it now. It's a home, that's what it is. That's what's so very special about it. Dunnian looks like a place for people to live in and be happy."

Humphrey smiled — no praise could have pleased him better.

They were still standing there when Celia came out of the front door. She hesitated for a moment and then began to walk towards them down the drive. Celia was wearing a cherry-coloured linen frock and her head was bare; she was carrying a basket on her arm.

And this, thought Courtney, as he went forward to meet his fate, this is one of the happy people who live at Dunnian House.

Suddenly the sun came out from behind the clouds and all the birds in the garden began to sing.

ISIS publish a wide range of books in large print, from fiction to biography. Any suggestions for books you would like to see in large print or audio are always welcome. Please send to the Editorial department at:

ISIS Publishing Ltd.
7 Centremead
Osney Mead
Oxford OX2 0ES
(01865) 250 333

A full list of titles is available free of charge from:
Ulverscroft large print books

(UK)
The Green
Bradgate Road, Anstey
Leicester LE7 7FU
Tel: (0116) 236 4325

(Australia)
P.O Box 953
Crows Nest
NSW 1585
Tel: (02) 9436 2622

(USA)
1881 Ridge Road
P.O Box 1230, West Seneca,
N.Y. 14224-1230
Tel: (716) 674 4270

(Canada)
P.O Box 80038
Burlington
Ontario L7L 6B1
Tel: (905) 637 8734

(New Zealand)
P.O Box 456
Feilding
Tel: (06) 323 6828

Details of **ISIS** complete and unabridged audio books are also available from these offices. Alternatively, contact your local library for details of their collection of **ISIS** large print and unabridged audio books.